I0657411

CYBORG DREAMS

THE BURIED PAST
(VOLUME 2)

CYBORG DREAMS
THE BURIED PAST

H.A. BURNS

ABSOLUTELY AMAZING eBOOKS

ABSOLUTELY AMAZING eBOOKS

Published by Whiz Bang LLC, 926 Truman Avenue, Key West, Florida 33040, USA.

Cyborg Dreams: The Buried Past (Volume 2) copyright © 2018 by H.A. Burns. Electronic compilation / paperback edition copyright © 2018 by Whiz Bang LLC.

All rights reserved. No part of this book may be reproduced, scanned, or transmitted in any form or by any means, electronic or mechanical, including photocopying, recording, or any information storage and retrieval system, without permission in writing from the publisher. Please do not participate in or encourage piracy of copyrighted materials in violation of the author's rights. Purchase only authorized ebook editions.

This is a work of fiction. Names, characters, places, and incidents either are the product of the author's imagination or are used fictitiously, and any resemblance to actual persons, living or dead, businesses, companies, events, or locales is entirely coincidental. While the author has made every effort to provide accurate information at the time of publication, neither the publisher nor the author assumes any responsibility for errors, or for changes that occur after publication. Further, the publisher does not have any control over and does not assume any responsibility for author or third-party websites or their contents. How the ebook displays on a given reader is beyond the publisher's control.

For information contact:
Publisher@AbsolutelyAmazingEbooks.com

ISBN-13: 978-1945772948 (Absolutely Amazing Ebooks)

ISBN-10: 1945772948

To Julie Cooperrider for her unfailing kindness and generosity without which I would never have been able to write.

CYBORG DREAMS

THE BURIED PAST
(VOLUME 2)

Prologue:

Cliff usually let his dreams take him wherever they wanted. Today he dreamt he had rockets for legs that were jetting him up into a lavender sunset. Blue fire roared from his metal appendages. Pulsed beams shot from his hands and created circular clouds radiating for miles, getting bigger and bigger as they dissipated.

He laughed as a giant eagle landed on his left shoulder, hanging on for the fiery rocket ride. He spun in circles to see if the bird would get dizzy and fall off. It clutched on effortlessly, peering calmly down with piercing, beady eyes.

Cliff stopped spinning, the bird flew out in front of him; it was leading him forward. He followed it until it landed on a juniper brush jutting out from a red rocky mountain cliff.

He recognized the cliff when he looked down to see a teenage girl hanging on the edge and screaming. He turned and fired a pulsed blast back at the bird for taking him there to see her, but the eagle had already disappeared.

The whole scene changed as his anger welled up. The rocks around his feet started to levitate and the cliff broke apart as he screamed. The horizon in every direction was soon filled with floating rocks and broken mountainside. There was rumbling and tumbling until it exploded into rusty dust.

What was left after it cleared was Cliff standing in a dark office of a hospital, the details coming more into focus. He stood behind his brother, Daniel, who was sleeping at his desk at work at the UCLA neurology department. Daniel faded in and out of focus. Cliff noticed an odd object on his brother's desk – it was a small microchip.

He held the microchip up for inspection and a woman's face appeared behind it. She smiled and held out her hand to take his. As their hands touched, he rocketed forward into bright, shimmering light. The light broke into a world of glimmering, spiral skyscrapers surrounded by ships in the air. Tiers of the skyscrapers were layered with trees. It was amazing, it was beautiful ... it was the future.

When Cliff awoke from the dream, he couldn't help but feel sudden claustrophobia at the dark grey walls surrounding him. Panic struck as he blinked into the dim florescent bulbs of a laboratory, burrowed deep within a cave. In comparison to his dream, the reality in which he awoke was a nightmare.

Chapter 1

Home Sweet Home

Beth Jahren's feet sank into soft mud, hitting the hidden riverbed before she even knew there was a river bed to hit. The mud began sucking her into a trench within the cave she had been exploring with her husband, Martin. In the sketchy light given off by her kerosene lantern, the rock and muck below were one and now her boots and muck were one as well. She fell back onto her butt with her feet flying into the air, boots no longer attached. The ends of her socks dangled off her toes.

"Well, there goes another pair of boots, honey," she said, slinging mud behind her in the direction her husband had last been seen inspecting the cavern walls.

"Huh? What did you lose this time? Hummm ... You should see these petroglyphs. I speculate we are in close proximity to what we are seeking," he said, not even peeling his eyes away to gaze in her direction.

The cave was pitch black except for the shifty light brought in by the reconnoitering couple. Beth could barely see her husband behind her. He stood near the back wall of the small alcove deep within the Colorado mountains. He flicked his wavy brown hair out of his glasses as he inspected the walls in unwavering intrigue – lamp at his nose and hair often dangerously close to being lit on fire. He was a tall, stout, and proudly

1

German biochemist who was on a mission. He had a one-track mind: to find the remains of the individuals who lived in these caverns years ago and to harness the remnants of a lethal virus that wiped them all out. At least, that's what he hoped.

"I think I found that river we've been hearing. It's mostly mud right now though," Beth explained while trying to salvage her shoes and becoming more and more entrenched. "I think a little further up we might reach water."

Her long, dirty-blonde hair was tied in two loose braids hanging down the back of her green polyester jumpsuit that was now mostly red-brown as it was covered in iron infused sludge. She squinted her bright, ocean-blue eyes out into the distance as far as she could see with the limited light from the flickering lamp. The alcove they were in had stalagmites, snowy quartz cubes, and wet, dripping walls. Every flash of light revealed minerals gleaming different shades of reds, creams and browns.

"Good, good, hummm ... Yes. I see, here! There, yes, hummm..." Martin mumbled, completely engrossed in thought and humming enough for it to be a song.

"You know, honey, you aren't making any sense," Beth replied, looking back towards her husband who had his nose about an inch from the cavern face. His sharp mind was obviously scattered by the variety of etched and painted objects and symbols on the wall.

"A river you say? Hummmm ... I think this petroglyph is telling us to follow a river to 'The Death of a Thousand Deaths.' How interesting. Hummm ...

What does that even mean? Hummm ... A thousand deaths of a death ... Quatsch!" He still had a thick Bavarian accent although he had lived in the USA for the last 15 years. The accent didn't help in him making sense to Beth right now. She was staring in his direction in complete bewilderment, mouthing in horror the term 'death of a thousand deaths.'

He finally broke away from the wall and gazed in the direction where his wife was struggling in the mud. "Honey, I think you are making the situation worse."

"How can I make a thousand deaths worse? That isn't a nice thing to say, Martin!"

"No. The situation in which you are completely covered in mud and have no boots. The suction is pulling all your belongings under. Tugging like that isn't helping you. Might I suggest you use your walking stick to poke a hole near the shoes and allow air to move. Then you will be easily able to scoop them out. I would also suggest you attempt this from a hard surface so that you are not pushing yourself in further. I am sure you can find a rock to sit on to attain the proper leverage. Where is your walking stick?"

"Remember, I lost it back at the entrance when I got it wedged and it broke in half." She began looking for a rock and tried to ignore the condescending tone from her husband – he was only trying to be helpful, probably.

They met at John Hopkins University in Maryland while taking organic chemistry together their second year and they'd been inseparable ever since. He kept her grounded and focused. She taught him how to get out of the books and experiment with real life and not just life in the laboratory. In fact, if it were up to him, they'd probably live in a laboratory.

"Oh, that's right. Well, here, use my walking stick," he said as he carefully maneuvered to where she was encumbered. He made an obvious show of how to determine proper footing with his stick the entire way over to Beth, to drive in the message. She purposefully ignored him so that she didn't strangle him or shove his head into the mud when he eventually arrived by her side.

"So, what is this "death of a thousand deaths" you mentioned?" She was finally pulling herself out of the muck and onto a large rock that he'd pointed out for her. The rock had been right next to her the whole time. But, he wasn't smiling smugly or anything when he pointed it out; no way he would do that! She didn't look at him – just in case – or she might just smack him with his own walking stick.

He sat on another rock next to hers and helped her get her boots free, although he spent more time cleaning his glasses from the sludge tossed up in the struggle.

"I believe it is in reference to what we are searching for..." he began.

"Death of a thousand deaths?" she interrupted.

"Yes, yes that's, well, my interpretation anyway ... Probably the virus that wiped out the ... I suspect Navajo tribe? Yes, it is doubtless the Navajo carved out these tunnels."

"We're making progress then!"

"Yes, yes ... Maybe." he continued, still working on getting her shoes out of the mud, now wrestling the right one with his wife. "Truly, it could be anything from a burial site for the dead to the location of a bat cave of blood sucking creatures ... I know how much you love bats."

She stopped wrestling at the mention of bats. Bat guano was good for a wide variety of applications and she was thinking about a venture one of her colleagues had discussed for a new mascara line. He seized the break in her struggle as an opportunity to poke and pull according to his plan, wrenching free her right boot at last. He tried – unsuccessfully – not to smile too smugly, evoking the ire of his wife.

"The markings on the cave were inscribed at separate times, and most likely by several civilizations. Who knows where this all started ... why and what they did ... the symbols are unclear and the message is mixed. As far as I can tell, and mind you I am no expert, some of the messages are just about large game to the east, one is about following a lake to a river..."

"We found the river bed!" she said, scooping up a handful of the sludge that was bringing her back to childhood memories of mud-pies and fire-flies out in east Pennsylvania. "So, that means we're close, right?"

"I am an expert in viruses, not petroglyphs, honey. It is tough to say. The large stone work symbol over there..." he pointed and held his lantern towards an odd granite stone that stood out amidst the limestone and quartz. Beth couldn't see any symbols from this distance but she nodded anyway to get him to continue.

"It indicates a great amount of deaths that lead to deaths. I postulate if we follow the river we will find out more," he was trying to sound matter-of-fact but she could hear the anticipation in his voice that meant he was onto something big.

"That's sick!" she exclaimed as she wrenched her last boot free, inadvertently flinging muck into both of their faces. "Sorry, honey. I promise to try not to be such a spaz."

"Yes. Well, it certainly baffles me how you have managed to survive this long without me. Let's stay near the cave wall, away from the mud. You can use the stick to check the ground from here on out, agreed?"

"Agreed. This mud isn't so bad. It is probably full of microorganisms and minerals that aid in detoxification and cellular regrowth. We could bottle it up and I bet I could sell it to snooty women for facials back east. That's if lab testing shows it's viable, which I'm sure it'll be. Want to collect some and test it out?" She put a little bit on the tip of his nose and on hers.

"That's my wife – always making the best out of any situation. Gets entrenched in the mud so resolves to give herself a facial while postulating a marketing plan," he said, chuckling to himself and unpacking a few glass jars from his backpack to collect mud samples.

Beth got her boots back on, the mud jars full and back in the backpack, and her footing worked out. Then they were able to continue their long quest in the dark. They stuck close to the cavern wall, following the sound of the running water up ahead until they got to another alcove, this one the largest they had encountered yet. The opening in the ceiling height alone had to be hundred feet from the sound of their boots and breath echoing around them and emptying out into the fathomless distance.

What was more exciting was that up ahead they could see light reflecting off of a massive, bright mound. It was stark in comparison to the void of darkness inside the cave that seemed to swallow all light and sound at its infinite edges. As they approached they could see the giant, dingy, yellow mound was composed of layers of matted straw wrapping smaller bundles. Each layer was a few feet thick, stacked neatly in an ascending pyramid reaching at least ten feet high.

Martin brought his lamp up to the end of one of the wrapped bundles within the layers. He pulled back the straw cloth to reveal the remains of a black, shriveled foot.

"Get out your gloves, honey!" Beth exclaimed. He was so forgetful when it came to safety sometimes. "Who knows what could be in those remains!"

"You do realize these remains have been here a very long time. The likelihood of a live virus or bacteria that is dangerous is absolutely minuscule."

"I just have a bad feeling, okay? I know it is probably just 'superstitions bred into me from societies' ignorant obsession with the plague,'" she said this while holding her fingers up in quotations. She was quoting him and they both knew it. She continued, "but you never know what we could find down here. Any risk is too much in my opinion. It wouldn't hurt to wear gloves and take a few extra precautions. For me, honey, okay?"

He said nothing as he pulled out a pair of gloves, a glass vial, some small bags, and a razor. He was excited to have finally found exactly what he was hoping to find – dead bodies. It had been weeks of cave diving in southern Colorado with no evidence of plague before they found this cave, where they had spent the last few days exploring without finding anything until now. One breach of protocol for a brief second and his wife went on a nagging spree. He shoved the gloves on grumpily.

Dead bodies made Beth squeamish, and she was particularly nauseated today. So, she eyeballed the petroglyphs on the wall near the mound to keep from hurling her lunch. She had no idea what any of them said – she just liked to trace her finger along the indentions in the rock. When she proposed the idea of searching for ancient viruses to harness for his oncolytic research, she was simply trying to get her husband's mind off of his mother's recent passing. She never expected they would find anything.

"At least it isn't a bat cave full of ravenous blood suckers ready to pounce that they were writing about," she said while squinting at a symbol of several x's surrounded by swirling lines radiating out into straight lines. "Though, bat guano would also make some good products for snooty ladies too, you know, that we could sell. I know someone who'd be interested..."

"Would you like to help me?" he asked, yanking at a body to remove it from the mound. It was solidly wedged and not moving much as he pulled.

"Urgh! You know I don't have the stomach for dead body stuff," she said, putting down her bags and replacing the thick hide gloves she'd been wearing with the disposable latex ones they'd brought just in case they found something. The whole time she was changing gloves, her husband was impatiently glaring at her. So, she delicately placed them on her hands one finger at a time – just to annoy him further. She then slid her arm deep into the straw-clothed pile to get a good hold on the body.

"Ready?" he asked, the annoyance echoing in his voice if not shouting out of his wide eyes gleaming in the flickering light.

"Ready," she said and then tugged at the body to pull it from the mound right as a large, hairy spider ran straight up her forearm with its eight fuzzy, freaky legs. She screamed, let go with a backwards jerk, and then launched the spider as far away as she possibly could.

"Ah! I told you I had a bad feeling! There IS something alive in here!" she screamed.

"It was simply a tarantula, they aren't dangerous," Martin replied, holding back mirth at her irrational antics.

"Do you think there are more? I'm not touching that thing if I end up covered in spiders!"

"Too late," Martin said as he plucked another spider off of her shoulder.

"Aaaaahhhh!" she screamed, jumping up and dancing around in a circle scanning for more spiders on her body.

Martin had fallen backwards with Beth when the body came out of the mound in a quick rush and he was now rolling on the ground laughing. He obviously found it highly amusing that she was dancing and spinning. His laughing increased when she started hopping around like a little kid throwing a fit.

"I can feel them, they are everywhere!! Martin, they are everywhere, get them off!" She stomped her feet and her two braids flopped wildly. She couldn't have cared less what he thought. She hated spiders with a passion that involved blood-boiling, skin-crawling dread at their touch.

"I think you scared them all. Please, you're making my ribs hurt," he said, trying not to gaze at his normally beautiful and refined, PhD in microbiology, wife. Right now, she appeared absolutely ridiculous covered in muck and throwing a tantrum over tarantulas.

When she finally calmed down, she took his walking stick and started poking at him in the ribs, "I'll make your ribs hurt!"

He easily avoided the jabs, yanked her down onto him on the ground with the stick and gave her a big kiss, saying, "Come on, we need to get back to work before more spiders come to get you." Her gregarious smile after the kiss turned to a frown and an expression of determination quickly.

"Let's get booking!" she said.

"From the appearance of this piled heap of bodies, I think we have found what we have come for ... this skin is treated with ... tar, I suspect, from the smell" he said as they examined the body and collected various tissue and bone samples in the low light. "Not much assiduousness was taken to swathe these in this straw-like sheeting. This is a positive sign of a virulent outbreak, the most advantageous kind I need for synthesizing an amalgamate."

"Let's hope so. I know you'll be the one to find a cure, Martin, I just know it. You're the most brilliant man I've ever met." She put the small collection of samples her husband was cutting away into containers and then carefully into her backpack. She was still trying not to look in the direction of the dead body. Man, the sight was sickening!

"There, I think that is enough. Unless, of course, you want to try another body?" he asked.

"No thanks! I think we should put this one back exactly how we found it for now too, out of respect for the dead."

"Respect? They are dead; they don't care about respect," he said as he begrudgingly helped his wife shove the body back into its place in the stack. She knew how he felt, but she was stubborn. Even though she knew her logic was irrational, it was hard to break superstition. Especially when she had an eerie feeling in the dark.

"What do you say we find out where the river ends? It sounds like it could be a waterfall. I could use a shower. I still feel like spiders are all over me, crawling ... Uuuugh! And, I think the mud is leaching my skin bare."

"Bare skin you say? Skinny dipping in a waterfall sounds like a great way to end this successful venture. Brilliant idea," he replied with a wide, mischievous grin.

The waterfall turned out to be inside the cave, only about fifty more feet from where the straw mound of bodies was found. The two climbed down to the bottom to find a secure place to put their belongings before jumping into the water. They were happy to find a small opening to the cave as well. It was the first break to the outside world they had seen in hours of spelunking through tunnels, alcoves, and crevices. The cave opening was just a few feet from the waterfall. It had a small ledge and a grand view of the rocky mountain valley below. It was already dark out, but the moon was full and bright on a clear, brisk, starry night.

"You don't get views like this in Maryland!" she exclaimed, taking in a deep breath of the clean air wafting in on a summer breeze. Then she began pulling off all her clothes and belongings – troublesome boots first.

"Not covered in mud anyway," he replied while staring at his disrobing wife. Then he gave her a wink. He could not care less about the view of the rocky valley and was more interested in her curves.

"Come on, let's jump in," she said, giving him a gentle kiss while removing and then setting aside his glasses. He was already kicking off his shoes and had detached his backpack.

The sizable pool beneath the waterfall was cool, but not too cold with the desert valley summer heat emanating from outside. So, the shivering was minimal as they warily slid into the unknown depths.

The water had been purified from years of filtering through the rocks of the mountainside. The moon was low and large, and the stars were numerous enough to accumulate into a blanket of sparkles over the water. Jutting outcrops of quartz also picked up the light, making the room glow in light pinkish jagged streaks along the cavern walls.

"Isn't this the most beautiful thing you've ever seen, Martin?" she said, pulling her hair out of the braids to clean out the sludge and marveling at the twinkles and glittering glistening on the walls and water.

"Yes," he said as he cleaned some muck off her cheek, and continued with, "though you did appropriate my spectacles. So, I am half-blind at present."

"I have a great feeling about this place. What if we bought some land out here and stayed?" she asked, filled with excitement at the idea that just came into her head. She bit her lip, "that's bananas, isn't it?"

"Well, the inheritance from my mother could subsidize rudimentary land; but, we would need to endeavor to create something habitable. And, by some means, build a facility for my continued research," he replied.

"You're considering it?!?" she exclaimed, completely surprised he would regard the idea as serious. Then, her mind began racing at the possibilities. "You don't think it's too far out?"

"My mother was all I had. I spent my life seeking a cure to save her and now she is ... she is..." he swallowed hard. It was still difficult for him to accept his mother's death. He had worked so hard, for so many years to save her. In the end, he had a solution but was unable to administer the serum due to concerns by the hospital staff. Concerns that generated paperwork and wasted precious time. Time she didn't have. Institutional bureaucracy prevented from saving his own mother's life. He fought the anger and swallowed hard again. "There is nothing left for me back east, except you Beth," he explained. "You are my everything now."

"You know you couldn't save your mother. The cancer spread too fast and came on too quickly this time. Your research is going to save millions more, though. I just know it," she said, coming over to Martin, to hold him. She pushed back his wavy hair from his face, staring deeply into his eyes and kissed him. "You are everything to me too," she said and laid her head on his chest.

"What about your family? Won't you miss them if we move all the way out here to Colorado?" he asked, squeezing her warm body close in the chilly water.

"What? My narcissistic mother and manic-depressive sister who thinks that because I married an atheist German I am somehow Eva Braun?" she replied. "I still love them, but man – they drive me bonkers! I could use a little distance, I think."

"Your mother is a narcissist?" he asked, perplexed. She'd always been so nice to him just to make her xenophobic jabs behind his back less believable – so she never mentioned them. Her mother was the most manipulative person she'd ever met, she could use a break from it all, really.

"Oh, she's the definition!"

"Your sister thinks I'm Hitler?"

"Hey, we're married now: the bones are falling out of the closet," she laughed. She'd been avoiding telling him these things because she didn't want him to dislike her family. But, knowing the truth now might help convince him to stay here in Colorado.

"Well, you know how much I like skeletons," he said right as a shooting star flashed across the night sky, lighting the whole valley.

Beth closed her eyes and made a wish on the shooting star, then said, "These caves are perfect for laboratories. The temperature and humidity are naturally controlled. These Navajo tunnels and alcoves have been around for God knows how long so they must be reasonably stable. We can make a research facility in no time and then you'll have free reigns on your work." Her eyes were shining in the starlight, and she was getting more excited with every word. "Free reigns, imagine what you could accomplish!"

She looked up to see her husband deep in thought with a quizzical brow, then added, "I can sell the mud to pay for the upgrades to the tunnels and to make a nice house down in the valley."

"You're rather confident regarding that mud," he gave her a curious expression and held her at arm's length, probably wondering what had gotten into his wife.

"Well, I will have to run a few tests on it, but yeah. I think the stuff could sell. I have a good feeling about it. There is a ton of it back there, untouched. I'm sure the land has other resources too. Not to mention this," she held up a handful of water and let it slip through her fingers as she continued with, "natural spring water we are desecrating. We could sell that too."

"We're not desecrating it yet," he said as he brought her closer for a kiss.

"We'll have to get rid of the spiders," she said, pushing him back.

"Yes, of course," he was trying to bring her closer again but she was swimming away.

"And the dead bodies. I mean, we can't keep those around." She continued moving further away.

"Of course, no dead bodies." He was chasing her in the pool.

"Maybe we should find those bats," she said playfully as she jumped out of the water, "bat guano is good money too."

"I'm not so sure there are any bats, honey," he said as he climbed out and began carefully searching for his glasses so he could have a better chance at catching his wife, who continued to elude him in a blur.

"Too bad. We could use the extra income right now, with a growing family," she smiled, looking down at her stomach and rubbing it with her two hands.

"You're...?!?" he said, putting his hand on her belly, overcome with emotion.

"Yes," she nodded. "I think this is a much better place to raise a family too, don't you think? Away from east coast politics and my insane family."

"I don't know what to say ... I am overwhelmed!" he had both hands in his hair now, on top of his head and he was grinning from ear to ear. "We've been trying for years. I didn't think it would happen!"

"Maybe it is all the fresh air we've been getting lately, running around in caves."

"Right, fresh air in caves ... Ha! I don't know what to say!"

"Just say 'Yes.' To this place, and a new life."

"Yes!" he laughed, picking up his wife and spinning her around in the moonlight.

Then she covered him in kisses and said, "Welcome home then, honey. I have a great feeling about this place!"

Chapter 2

Let's Take a Walk

Tsintah Hunt had seen quite a few strange people in her life, but this family was the most peculiar. Nothing like the people of her native tribe. Their large Craftsman house was full of experimental test set-ups. Microscopes, vials, and all sorts of machines were strewn all over. Weirdest of all was that half the kitchen was taken up with a system of pulleys and levers directing the flow of coffee through the house. It was set according to a giant German cuckoo clock in the entryway that ran many of the other tests as well.

Part of Tsintah's job was to make sure the two young sons of doctor Beth and Martin Jahren didn't get any of the coffee passing through the kitchen and the hallways. For some reason, the Jahrens found that particularly important: no coffee for the kids.

Primarily, she was paid to feed the children regularly and make sure they didn't get into too much trouble that would distract the doctors from their unremitting investigation into god only knew what. For her part, Tsintah felt getting the kids outside of the chaos in this mad scientist lair was her biggest daily challenge. That made taking the boys on a walk her most important endeavor of each day.

The eldest son, Daniel, was a bit easier to wrangle than his younger brother Cliff. At ten, Daniel knew he needed to let off some steam. He welcomed daily walks in the wilderness. So, he was easy to coax outdoors most days. The only exception was when one of his tests was not working out well – then there was no breaking him away. Cliff, seven, almost always had several experiments going at once. So, it was harder to get him to drop them all at their various stages.

Tsintah began her search for the boys in the large house by calling their names. She had no idea where the kids' parents were either; there were so many passages, nooks, crannies and hidden doorways in the house. The doctors were constantly disappearing. When they were around, they would suddenly pop out of nowhere with a cup of coffee in hand.

A loud bang reverberated in the house. It sounded like it came from one of the front rooms. Tsintah headed in that direction.

"Daniel, it is time to take a break," she said when she found him in his favorite location, the den converted into a library. He had his face buried in a rather large book with several others open around him on a grand mahogany desk. There wasn't an inch of wall space in the room that didn't have a book, and more books arrived weekly. The doctors felt the education of their children meant extensive reading on anything and everything, and that is exactly what the books in the room represented. A novel by Jane Austin sat on an encyclopedia of invertebrate, an atlas on a tome of poetry by Poe.

"Miss Tinny, is it already that time of day? Okay. I'm almost at a good place. Need help with Cliff I bet, huh?" Daniel replied while still moving his finger along the page, continuing to read as he talked. He wrote a note in his journal and then picked up another book. He compared it to the first one, wrote another note and then finally put his pen down before standing up to stretch. He was a dark haired, lean and amiable boy that took heavily after his father.

"Yes, I can't find him and that noise sounded like trouble," she said staring down at Daniel's notes in his journal. It appeared as if he was reading another native American language, one unfamiliar to Tsintah. "What was that you were writing?"

"Oh, I found some information on Aztec languages that I'm exploring. It's fascinating. The symbols are each a whole sentence. I'm trying my own method of translation ... using the dots here, see..." he said, flipping between pages of different books to show off what he was learning and then pointing to the dots above some strange symbols.

"Were you looking for me?" said a meek voice from behind where the two bent over the books.

"Cliff, sweetie! Yes, it's time for our daily walk. Are you ready to go? What's that on your face?" Tsintah asked, walking over to the pint-sized, chubby-cheeked Cliff standing in the doorway. Black smudge shrouded his face and blonde hair, and his eyebrows were scorched.

"Were you dismantling fireworks again to see if you can get your trains to go faster?" Daniel asked.

Cliff nodded, he was still in a daze. "There was a spark on the track … I must not have cleaned up well…"

"Awe, poor thing. You're lucky to still have your eyebrows!" Tsintah said, brushing back his eyebrows with a small comb after wiping his face clean with a cloth. She always wore a blue-jean, bejeweled fanny around her waist that was packed full of useful things – like combs and washcloths. If she could fit more stuff in it, she would. "Come on, let's get some fresh air."

"Yeah, the fresh air should clear the smoke out of your lungs, little brother," Daniel said as he tussled Cliff's hair. "I'm ready. Where are we heading today, Miss Tinny?"

"Can we go by the lake?" Cliff asked, "I had a dream about the lake last night."

"Oh, Cliff, it wasn't a nightmare again, was it?" Tsintah inquired as she hurried the boys out of the house before they became sidetracked.

Distractions were everywhere. There was another dose of coffee moving down the conveyer belt that they had to duck under when leaving the den. On the kitchen table there was a mock-up of the entire rocky mountain range. It had simulations of volcanic eruptions on a timer, and it was going off.

Even more distracting was the cat. It was riding around on the train set, holding on for dear life. Cliff must have managed to get the train moving at close to 40 mph! Somehow the cat had become attached by the claws to one of the railcars.

"No, not exactly a nightmare…" Cliff said, detaching the cat from the train and putting her down on the floor. Her black and white hackles were up and her bright green eyes were as wide as could be, whites showing and everything. She stayed there, petrified for a few moments before realizing she wasn't riding the train anymore and then she fled under the china cabinet.

"We should take out the trash before we leave," Daniel announced, pressing a button next to the cuckoo clock that started a conveyer moving. Levers and handles activated in the kitchen, one of which got stuck on the lid of the trash can and couldn't quite lift it up.

"I can fix this," he declared, running over and moving a lever at the sink that kept clicking, "It's not getting enough torque, the bag must be over full."

Oh no, something to fix! It was the worst kind of distraction for these boys! Tsintah thought.

"Let's just do it the old-fashioned way today," she said, pulling the bag out of the trashcan and hurrying out the door. She pushed Cliff ahead of her. She knew if she let them get diverted with fixing the garbage disposal system then she might never get them out of the house today.

The trash system usually went out the front window and right to the barrels outside. So, she had to lift a conveyer belt and move a pulley system aside just to attempt to open the lid of the barrel.

"'Work smarter, not harder,' Mom always says," remarked Cliff under his breath to Daniel, who had just come outside from the kitchen where he had been fixing the lever system. Cliff was smiling as Tsintah struggled to get the trash put away. She tried to ignore his comment and smug little grin.

She was not very tall, and the trash barrel was larger than her. Clamoring and stumbling, she felt she might fall into the rancid waste bin of steaming goo trying to push back the heavy conveyer system above. Thankfully, Daniel took the bag and placed it into the barrel while she held up the contraption they called a lid. Daniel even gave Cliff a stern scowl, then shook his head at him for not helping her.

"All of this technology, it is making you boys lazy," she said, pinching one of Cliff's chubby cheeks. "Hard work gets your blood moving and keeps you healthy. I know a good path out to the lake from here. Let's head out."

Tsintah put a hand on each boy's back and led them out of the yard towards the sparsely wooded desert beyond. Finally, she had them out of the house! Success! she thought, breathing in the clean air while taking satisfaction in her triumph.

They took a red dirt path made from wild horses that were common in the region. The summer heat had turned the path into a fine dust but the horse prints were still visible.

"So, what was this dream you had Cliff?" Daniel asked, breaking the silence on the trail, "and stop shuffling your feet."

Cliff had been peering off into the distance, eyes unfocused, mouth slightly ajar and feet barely picking up enough to move forward but just enough to kick rocks annoyingly in every direction. "Well, I can't remember much ... I remember the lake, and a girl with a big smile..."

"A girl?" asked Daniel. He had snuck a Rubik cube in his pocket and was working on how many moves it took to solve it without looking. He dropped the cube when he heard the word 'girl' come out of his brother's mouth, and lost count of his moves.

"Yes, she was very friendly but then she stole something of mine. I can't remember what," Cliff said and immediately went back into contemplation, followed by shuffling feet and rock kicking. "It was my GI Joe set I think," he said at last.

"Stop shuffling your feet! Did you even tie your shoes today? You're dragging your laces through the dirt!" exclaimed Daniel.

"Here, let me help you," Tsintah said bending down to fix Cliff's shoes. The laces were undone from all the shuffling and covered in dirt. "You should be more careful, you could trip over these things."

"I think I will get Mom to buy me some of those Velcro shoes I saw on TV and then I won't have to tie these bogus things again," said Cliff.

"Velcro?" Daniel asked, bending down to help with the right shoe. The laces had tangled and collected debris, including some thorns. Tsintah didn't even have to warn him, he was already carefully pulling out the thorns before tying the laces.

"Yes, it is a new material they are using to replace shoelaces. No more tying would be great!" Cliff declared.

"I'll have to check that out. You still shouldn't shuffle your feet, Cliff. It is annoying." Daniel said.

"I feel tired," Cliff moaned, "How much further to the lake, Miss Tinny?"

"Another mile or so. We just started; are you okay? Would you like a Fruit Roll-Up? It will give you a little more energy," she offered, and pulled out a snack for Cliff from her handy bejeweled fanny-pack.

The treat seemed to satisfy him for a little while. He was a little bit chubby, especially in the lower half and calves, and was always hungry. He needed to walk much more than his lean older brother. Both boys took after their German father heavily and would likely be just as broad and tall one day. But, the younger brother had his mother's dark blue eyes and dirty blonde hair. Daniel had his father's wavy brown hair but he had the strangest hazel eyes; they changed from every shade of brown, including almost golden in the sun, all the way to a deep hunter green. Tsintah couldn't help but stare at them sometimes, they were so mesmerizing in their uniqueness. Everyone in her tribe had dark brown, straight hair with equally dark eyes and nowhere near as pale of skin. Skin that is turning red, oh no! she realized

"Oh, I forgot! I need to put sunscreen on you boys," she swiftly announced, dishing out the liquid from her trusty bag. She began slathering Cliff's face first. Their mother would throw a fit if she brought them back red and they had already been out for 15 minutes in the desert.

Daniel put the Rubik cube back into his pocket to get his sunscreen slathering. He wasn't much shorter than her even though she was a grown woman, whereas he had just turned ten this past August.

"Are you getting smaller?" he asked her with a smile and a patronizing pat on her head.

"Very funny..." she began.

"Hey, see what I found!" Cliff held up a lizard's tail an inch in front of her eyes. He then ran off giggling. The shock of the sudden lizard tail appearance caused her to squirt sunscreen into Daniel's face.

"I'm so sorry, Daniel!"

He flung-off the excess sunscreen into the dirt while squeezing his eyes shut and groaning at the stinging liquid. She took a tissue for him out of her pack and asked: "What happened to the rest of the lizard?"

"He likes to collect the tails. Sometimes he feeds them to the cat," Daniel explained. Tsintah must have appeared as horrified as she felt at the suggestion of feeding cats lizard tails because Daniel continued with, "The lizard's tails grow back. It is alright, the lizards are fine. Good source of protein for the cat too."

That somehow didn't ease the gut-reactive revulsion to the idea of ripping off reptile appendages for fun. She was still staring warily over at Cliff, brow furrowed.

Daniel had cleared the excess sunscreen out of his eyes. He peered over at the concerned nanny wondering how to console her. "You know, fish would be better for the cat. We have never been fishing. Is there fishing allowed at the lake?"

"Yes, though we can't fish today because I didn't bring any equipment. I can bring a couple of poles and show you two next time we're there though." Tsintah said, motioning Cliff to come back from the lizard chase he was on over by a pile of rocks.

They continued walking, enjoying the early autumn breeze carrying the scent of sage and threadleaf. Daniel and Tsintah followed a few feet behind Cliff, who was zig zagging on a sugar high up ahead along the path. He was still managing to shuffle his feet along the dirt though, kicking up a dusty red haze in front of them.

"We have to have a pole to catch fish? Don't your people catch them with your hands?" Daniel asked, sincerely.

"Pardon?"

"I'm sorry, I just assumed..."

"That I am a backwards, backwoods ... barbarian catching fish with my hands?" she interrupted, fervently.

"I'm sorry, Miss Tinny. I've never been fishing. I've only read about it."

"Yes. Well, you have a lot to learn, including about fishing." she tried not to be angry. These boys had very little social exposure because their parents homeschooled them. The doctors felt the local school was inadequate.

Maybe she could bring them to the reservation sometime to get acquainted with others? Oh, not a good idea! she realized almost as soon as she had the thought. Her family and most of the tribe wasn't very happy with the Jahrens after they bought the old mine and most of the surrounding hillside.

The 'improvements' to land over the last decade without any consult just made the situation even worse. The Jahrens thought that buying the land meant they could do whatever they wanted with it. Some of the tribe members were furious, and likely would cast blame on the kids. Poor kids, they were doomed to be ostracized simply because of their parents' mistakes, she thought.

"I'm grateful to have you to teach me, Miss Tinny." Daniel was such a sweet boy. She gave him a hug and they continued walking in silence, enjoying the crisp air and warm sun rays.

Upon arriving at the lake, they were surprised to find they were not the only ones. A few families had come to take refuge by the water – it was a caravan of campers. The threesome passed along the waterfront and said 'hi' to the picnicking families sprawled-out on blankets in the grass, apparently enjoying lunch.

The Mesa Heights area was utterly secluded, being not on any main Transamerica path or near a national monument. Consequently, visitors were scarce. The population of the town was barely over 100, with most of the residents getting close to 100 themselves – here to retire. That also meant even local residents were rare at the lake. The Navajo reservation to the southwest was the largest town for miles. So, for the boys, it was typically Native Americans they would see in the area, not Caucasians in campers.

"We should, perhaps, go ... they keep staring at you Miss Tinny," remarked Cliff, noticing that some people must not have ever seen a full-blooded native by the ogling she was being given.

As they headed back into the woods, an upside-down head popped out right in front of them, stopping all three in their tracks.

"Hello!" said the fluffy, curly, blonde-haired head. The head happened to be attached to a young girl dangling from a branch by the knees. She wore a blue jean jumper and white t-shirt with a little purple pony on it. She had on rainbow socks inside white Velcro tennis shoes that Cliff walked around to inspect. She did a little flip to get out of the tree she was hanging from and stood smiling. With one hand on her hip, her glancing eyes taking in all three with excitement, she held out her other hand for anyone to shake.

"Hi," said Daniel first, taking up the outreached hand.

"I'm Amy, Amy Shipley. Nice to meet you!" she said, shaking his hand vigorously.

"I'm Daniel, Daniel Jahren and this is my brother, Cliff. This is our nanny, Miss Tinny."

"You have a nanny? Do you live here? We're all just passing through but the Johnsons over there are having problems with their transmission. So, we might be staying a while. What's there to do around here anyway? Caves? Canyons? Ancient cities? I think I saw a cave up there that I'm gonna to try to explore tomorrow..." Amy just kept talking and talking and Daniel had no idea what to do but stand there and nod.

Cliff took Tsintah's hand and pulled her away, leaving Daniel to fend for himself. "It's the girl from my dream," he whispered when they were at a respectable distance. She took a step back in shock. Cliff never made things up and having someone appear out of a dream was not normal.

"Are you sure?" she whispered back.

"Yes. Dimples, smile, big blue eyes ... Is she going to steal my GI Joe set Miss Tinny? I won't let her!" he declared and crossed his arms over his chest in defiance.

"No, that isn't how dreams usually work. They're never literal. It's all symbolic. And most of the time, they don't come true ... I..." she didn't know what to say. Was Cliff a dream-walker? This wasn't the first time he seemed to have a predictive dream, but it was the first time someone showed up out of his dreams.

"What do you mean? I thought dreams were supposed to come true. On TV they are constantly say things like 'dream,' 'keep on dreaming,' or 'I have a dream!' What do you mean they don't come true?" He was stomping his feet, trampling the grass and throwing a mini-temper tantrum.

She held his arm and faced him towards her, then said, "What I mean is that most dreams are simply your spirit speaking to your mind in symbols to help you connect more deeply with your inner desires. Does that make sense?" That stopped his stomping enough to make him think. He scratched his head and squinted his eyes up at her. She wasn't sure what part of what she had said confused him.

"No, what spirit?" Cliff said after a bit of contemplation.

"Your spirit, your soul." She was shocked at the question. "You've heard of that, right?"

Cliff shook his head, eager for an explanation.

"It's the thing inside that makes you ... well You." Tsintah tried to put the right words together but the shock was tying her tongue. These kids had no religious education except for books, and Cliff preferred only books that helped him with his inventions and experiments. Unlike his brother Daniel, who explored all aspects of life.

What did their parents even believe? Were they Christian like most of the other white people she had met? Tsintah realized she had never asked.

They rarely watched TV and usually only to turn on the nightly news. Cliff did have the TV on sometimes when working on his train set, he liked to watch cartoons. She understood then that Cliff had probably never heard of a spirit or a soul his entire life, and he was 7!

"I don't like her," Cliff declared, still cross in attitude and in arms and staring at the little girl fifteen feet away.

Daniel and Amy were getting along great. He was showing her his Rubik cube and she was showing him her Chihuahua that had been tied to the tree she'd been climbing. They were sitting under the shade of an old cedar, smiling and giggling.

"It looks like your brother may have a new friend," Tsintah said, "You should be happy for him. You two never get to meet people."

"He better not let her near my G.I Joe set!" Cliff yelled, loud enough for the two under the tree to hear. They completely ignored him.

"Oh, stop it, Cliff! I told you that dreams aren't literal," she explained. "She isn't going to steal anything. Little girls are sugar and spice and everything nice, don't you know that?"

"You said that dreams don't come true; but, there she is, explain that!"

Tsintah thought for a minute, not sure what to say. It was rare when someone had predictive dreams like Cliff. She would need to consult her sister, who knew far more about dream-walkers than she did. But, for now she should let him know what she remembered about dreaming. She just thought of something she heard about once. "Sometimes, when important people come into your life you can have a dream that foreshadows them. It's never happened to me but it has to other people I know. The spirit world doesn't operate in the same time and space that we do."

"So, you are saying that I have a 'spirit' and that it is from another dimension?"

Wow, that was a good take on it, especially for a seven-year-old, she thought.

"Yes," she affirmed. "This young woman must be important. And, she's not going to steal anything from you; that's not how it works."

"How does it work?"

"Well, what did you feel when you thought of your GI Joe set?"

"What did I feel? What kind of bogus question is that?"

"Searching your feelings, they will reveal the truth your spirit is trying to tell you." That much she knew for certain. Everything in a dream has more to do with how you feel about the images and happenings than anything else.

"Search my feelings?" Cliff asked, kicking rocks. "Like using 'The Force' from Star Wars?"

The kid knew about Star Wars but not about spirits and souls! TV was not the best way to raise children, that Tsintah knew for certain.

Cliff picked up a rock to throw it at the girl. "I feel like I don't like her!"

Tsintah managed to stop his arm in time for the rock to land just a foot from Daniel and Amy's feet. "I think it's time to head back," Tsintah announced loud enough for everyone to hear. This conversation was getting too deep and she wasn't sure their parents wanted her talking about such things. "We'll talk about this more later, okay?" she whispered to Cliff.

~ ~ ~

"Nice to meet you!" Amy said to the three, waving goodbye. Daniel waved at Amy as he was walking backwards, being dragged by the arm by his nanny. He then turned around and started skipping along the path home, excited to have made a new friend.

"So, I found out about the caravan of people here. They might be here for a while. I may, possibly, be able to help with the transmission problem the Johnsons are having. I will see if we have a book on that at home," Daniel said, smiling from ear to ear and stretching his crisscrossed hands out in front of him like he always did when he proposed a new project to work on.

"I don't like her Daniel. I don't think you should go back and see her again," Cliff said. He was still sulking while ambling along the path kicking rocks and shuffling his feet.

"Stop shuffling your feet! Your shoe laces are going to come undone again," Daniel said, purposefully ignoring his brother's request to not see the girl again.

Cliff stopped shuffling his feet but then started marching fast towards home. That compelled Daniel to want to keep up, so he started marching beside him. Then they started going faster and faster until they were running.

Miss Tinny didn't even try to keep up with them, she knew how competitive they could get. Daniel tried not to embarrass his little brother too much, so ran just fast enough to be slightly ahead of him. Cliff was tiring out but determined to get past Daniel. Cliff was becoming redder and redder, and more out of breath ... until finally he tripped on his own feet – or his laces had become unstrung again. All Daniel saw was him doing a diving face plant from the corner of his eye.

"Are you okay?" Daniel attempted to help his brother up. Cliff merely pushed him away. He searched for Miss Tinny, with her bag of Band-Aids and ointments, but she had been lost long ago at the start of their run. She was far behind on the trail now.

"No. I think something is wrong. My legs feel ... weak," Cliff said as he tried to get up and was having trouble standing. His legs were buckling from under him whenever he tried to put weight on them.

"Let me help you," Daniel pleaded.

"No! This is your fault, you made me run. You like that girl!" Cliff yelled.

"My fault! I didn't make you run, and so what if I like a girl!" Daniel yelled back.

"I had a dream that she is going to steal my GI Joe set! Miss Tinny says it means something about my spirit but I just don't like that girl, okay?"

"Come on now, that girl doesn't matter. She will be gone in just a few days. I am here, and I am your brother. Let me help you," Daniel asked.

"I don't know what is wrong with me. I feel so weak and I can't stand it!" Cliff said in frustration. He picked up a handful of rocks and threw them at a tree.

They sat there for a few breaths, Daniel felt like maybe Cliff just needed to calm down.

"Don't worry, Mom and Dad will know what to do," Daniel said, reassuringly placing his hand on Cliff's shoulder. "Let's just get home."

Cliff sat sulking for a minute before he nodded, indicating with a pouty lip and chin up that he would accept help at last, but wasn't happy about it. Daniel lifted him up, putting his arm around his shoulders.

"Do you think they will let me have some of their coffee? I mean, it always seems to give them energy," asked Cliff.

"That stuff smells gross. You really want to try it?" Daniel asked, looking back along the trail for signs of their nanny. "Hey, if we get there before Miss Tinny, we can swipe you some without asking, okay?"

"Deal!" said Cliff, grinning at the idea of getting past his nanny to get to the coffee she was sworn to protect.

Chapter 3

Food for Thought, and the Cat

Unfortunately for Cliff's and Daniel's aspirations of sneaking some coffee, their father was standing in the kitchen and staring at the cuckoo clock when they stumbled through the front door.

"What happened?" Martin immediately took hold of Cliff from an exhausted and out of breath Daniel.

"We were running and he fell," Daniel answered. "He said he was weak. We haven't had lunch. Maybe he is just hungry?"

"Hungry? Where is Miss Tinny?" Martin lifted Cliff onto the kitchen counter in one smooth motion.

"She is coming..." Cliff started to say but just then the nanny walked through the door, answering the question in the flesh.

"Tsintah, what happened?" Martin demanded, his attention still on Cliff, who was looking forlornly at the coffee.

"Hi, Dr. Jahren," Tsintah said calmly standing just inside the doorway. "Cliff's been dragging his feet all day, and he'd been more tired than usual."

"I see," Martin said, feeling his youngest son's forehead and then looking at his palms. No fever, no sweaty palms. He did have a slight sunburn and was a bit flushed, nothing alarming.

"He got upset because Daniel was talking to a little girl we met at the lake today. He tried to race his older brother home. I let them go ahead. From the markings in the dirt on the path that they left, it looked like they might have gotten into a fight."

"We didn't get into a fight! I noticed he'd been shuffling his feet all day too but he ran fine before he face-planted into the dirt. I helped him home ... I hope there's nothing wrong with his legs. Maybe he's just hungry?" Daniel jumped up to sit on the counter next to his brother and nudged him. "I'm hungry too."

"You better get your mom, Daniel. She is in the third study, you know the code. Schnell!!" said Martin.

Daniel jumped down and headed out right away. He knew that when his father started using German, things were going to get intense.

"Tsintah, we will no longer need your services today. Thank you for the detailed explanation of events and we will see you tomorrow." He was already pushing her out the door, he didn't need any of the locals butting into family affairs. If there was something seriously wrong with his son, it was none of their business.

"Thank you, sir, let me know if there is anything I can do," she tried to say as she was being walked out backwards.

"Father, we haven't even had lunch yet!" Cliff whined.

"Oh, stop whining! You aren't hungry. How does this feel?" he said, poking and prodding at Cliff's legs. He lifted Cliff's arms up and made him hold them out as he tested the strength of each arm, pushing down slightly.

"Fine. I feel fine, just weak. Ow!" Cliff yelled when he dinged him below the knee cap with a ladle. Cliff's reflexes were not good – it took too long for his leg to kick up and it barely moved. "And I AM hungry. I'm always hungry!"

"What happened?" Beth said, gliding into the kitchen and giving her youngest son a little kiss on the forehead.

"He fell..." Daniel started to say.

"He is suffering from muscular atrophy..." Martin started at the same time.

"I'm just hungry..." Cliff began, simultaneous to the other two.

Beth peered around the room at the three guys talking at once, then held up her hand to shush them all. Cliff's stomach growled in the brief silence loud enough for everyone to hear.

"See!" said Cliff, grabbing his belly with both hands.

"Martin, make the poor boy a sandwich!" she said, and gave Cliff a big hug.

Twenty minutes later (and a few turkey, bacon, lettuce and tomato sandwiches between the foursome) and they were all feeling better.

"So, who's up for a trip to Denver?" Beth asked when they were all done, carrying plates into the kitchen. To Martin's surprise, she decided to help him with the dishes.

"When?" Daniel asked, gazing up from the journal he was writing in on what should have been a dining room table. He had the journal propped between the

Olympic Peninsula and the Cascade Mountains in the Rocky Mountain display that took up most of the room.

"Denver! Can we go see the new Star Wars movie?" Cliff asked, starting a drum roll with his hands in excitement on the kitchen counter where he was still seated.

"Yes, Cliff. And, we'll visit our friend Dr. Jorgensen while we're there," Beth suggested.

"The rheumatologist we encountered at that conference in Orlando four years ago? I would hardly call him a friend," Martin replied, handing her a freshly washed dish to put away. "Though he is the single individual we are acquainted with who would have a more thorough comprehension of the predicament than us."

"We could run preliminary tests ourselves ... But yes, David Jorgensen is a specialist and I want my son to have the best care available." Beth was looking through the cabinets trying to figure out which one the plates were typically stored. Daniel took the plate from his mom and put it in the cabinet behind the three-foot coffee-making contraption.

"How about I start some tests now, and you give David a call to arrange a time?" Martin could not argue with her sound logic but needed to check a few things himself first before relying on another's expertise.

"Sounds like a good plan, honey," Beth said. She dried her hands with the dishtowel and went straight for her rolodex next to the phone to search for the doctor's number.

"Cliff, we're going to the basement," Martin said, picking him up and flinging him over the back of his shoulders. Cliff hung on like a gorilla baby, crossing his legs around his father's waist.

"The basement? Can I come Father? You never let us in the basement," Daniel pleaded.

"No, Daniel. It is prudent not to conglomerate in that space. I am confident you have an abundance of studying to do: some CLEPs, or GED, ACT perhaps SAT's pre-exams? You must have adequate preparation for college entrance." Martin said, sternly for severity's sake. "Unless you need me to assign new work..."

"No thanks, Father. I've got plenty to keep me busy," Daniel quickly interjected, heading grudgingly towards the den.

"I've never been in the basement. What's in there?" Cliff asked almost right into Martin's ear. Cliff had laid his head on his shoulders and his mouth was less than an inch away. He tried to ignore the moist, turkey-sandwich smelling breath on his neck as he walked.

"You will see," Martin replied. He pushed open a side wall in the back of the house that opened into a tunnel lit with candelabras-like lanterns strung together with large green cables going straight into the mountainside about 100 feet from the house.

The basement was no basement. It took a few minutes of walking in a dimly lit, damp tunnel and then going through a substantial metal door to reach "the basement." The door needed a combo to open because it was made from an old bank safe. Once open, they arrived in Martin's personal work space – a laboratory built into the side of the mountain.

He sat Cliff down on one of the lab chairs, saying "Don't move, I need to prepare some solutions." He headed over to a large yellow cabinet full of chemicals.

It was an expansive and heavily cluttered room. Not particularly well lit either. There were desk lights on each table, but they were mostly off to save power. Everything was wired to cords bundled up together and leading out to the back of the room where there was a large generator. Between books on the floor, and vials, beakers and test equipment on every shelf, there was hardly any space to move around. But, most days it was just Martin so there was no need for more room.

"What kind of microscope is that? I have never seen one like that before," Cliff asked, staring straight ahead at a massive microscope connected to several metal boxes and a vacuum chamber. The magnification portion of the scope was completely surrounded by a rectangular glass enclosure.

"Oh that, it is an experimental electron microscope. Don't move and don't touch anything," Martin said, coming back over to place a container of rubbing alcohol on the desk. He swiped Cliff's hand away from the microscope and then spun him around in the chair.

"Wow, Dad. How many computers do you need? Is that a Commodore 64?" Cliff inquired, he was now spinning himself around on the chair and checking out the 'basement' in 360.

"I need as many as it takes," Martin yelled over to his son from where he was mixing chemicals under a fume hood that was very loudly clearing the air.

"What are those?" Cliff pointed over to a set of enormous refrigerators full of blue vials, and beakers of red liquid sitting next to a four-level shelf full of small jars with the tiny organs of various creatures.

"Those are refrigerators," Martin replied over the noise of the fume hood and then walked back to where Cliff was sitting. He pulled some needles out of a drawer and placed them on the counter. He started rummaging through a few more drawers until he found some cotton balls.

"Duhh, what's IN the refrigerators?" asked Cliff, slightly annoyed.

"My work," Martin replied, "This may hurt a bit," he wiped down Cliff's right arm with alcohol-soaked cotton balls and then drew some blood.

Cliff gave a slight wince when the needle went into his arm. "So, what are you working on?"

"Oncolytic virotherapy," Martin replied, curtly. "You know that, or have you forgotten?"

"Oh yeah. I thought it would be, you know, cooler or something."

"Not glamorous enough for you, son? Trust me, it astounds under the microscope."

"Really, can I see?"

"No."

'C'mon!"

"No." Martin said as he removed the needle. He then put the three vials of blood he had taken into a spinning centrifuge. He put a small cotton ball onto Cliff's arm and said, "Hold this down for a few minutes."

"C'mon Dad!"

"No."

Cliff opened his mouth again, but Martin put up his finger and squinted his eyes, which only made Cliff emulate him and giggle. So, Martin smacked Cliff's finger back and then spun him around on the chair again.

"Have you had weakness in your legs before today Cliff? How long have your calves been that swollen?" Martin asked.

"I don't know, Dad." Cliff stopped the spinning to let him examine his legs a bit more.

"Try to think."

"Hummmm ... I had trouble climbing a hill a couple of weeks ago. Been extra hungry lately. So, a couple of weeks, maybe? Nothing as bad as today though. Do you know what is wrong, Dad?"

"Precisely, no ... we shall find out more from the tests running. In Denver, our friend will perform more thorough examinations that should lead to a conclusive answer."

"Am I gonna die?" Cliff was making a sad face, pushing out his lower lip and opening his eyes wide in mock shock and dismay.

Martin tried not to make eye contact with his son, the situation was severe and he knew Cliff wasn't prepared to know the details. It was wise to wait until all the results were in, no need to say anything that will make anyone worry. "We will all die, one day. But you, my son, are going to live a very long life," he assured Cliff, pulling playfully on his son's protruding lower lip.

"You aren't giving him SAL-142 are you Martin?!!?" Beth exclaimed. She had just come into the room and all she heard was the last thing he had said.

"No, but that isn't a bad idea!" he declared, jumping up out of his chair and towards one of the refrigerators that held his latest salix alba concoction.

Beth stopped him, taking him by the arm and pulling him aside to whisper, "That is highly experimental, don't you think? Especially with your family history of cancer? It could be dangerous."

"Yes, of course. We should hold off to find out what Dr. Jorgensen says first, honey. Of course. Oh, what about BNR-73? I suggest we initiate immunization with that one if we proceed with SAL-142." Martin whispered back, getting more excited. Beth motioned him to shush, he was apparently whispering too loudly. He adjusted his glasses in irritation.

"No, Martin. I think this is a dangerous road to even think about starting down. It is one thing if we experiment on ourselves, it is another if we start inoculating our children. They don't even understand the risks." The irritation in Beth's voice added an unmitigated volume that made her prior shushing seem quite hypocritical.

"What risks?" Cliff asked, startling the two by unexpectedly standing right between them. Standing. He hadn't stood since falling down earlier. Beth and Martin were flabbergasted at both the standing and where he was standing. "You're experimenting on yourselves? How?"

"So, you are feeling better already? Walking okay now?" Martin inquired, no longer feigning to whisper, holding onto Cliff's arm in case he needed support. He glanced over at Beth, who was still speechless.

"What risks? What experiments? Do you have something to make me better?" Cliff was quite invigorated. "Will I get super powers like spider-man? Can you make me grow a tail like a lizard?"

"We do have a lizard amalga ..." Martin began to say before getting a nudge from his wife.

Beth shook her head, gave Martin a look of consternation and said: "No, son. We are going to Denver to a specialist. We have an appointment on Friday, so we need to go upstairs and start packing right away."

"That quickly! I assume you managed to contact David directly?" Martin didn't expect for the doctor to create an opening in his schedule so rapidly, he was touted as one of the finest in the country and he expected it might take weeks for him to find time to see his son.

"Yes, and I already discussed some of the symptoms. He has a good idea of what it is ... we'll find out more soon," her voice was breaking and she was blinking away tears. That was a very bad sign.

"We can fix anything, together," Martin took her hand and brought her in for a hug. He gave her a kiss on the cheek and she relaxed into his arms until he yelled "Don't touch that!" right into her ear, unintentionally. He meant it for Cliff who was about to lift up the glass rectangular enclosure next to the microscope.

"Ouch!" Beth exclaimed, "I think I am going to go deaf!" She rubbed a finger on the inside of her ear to dull the pain.

"Sorry, Father. Sorry, Mom. Is that a wasp under there? Its huge!"

"Yes, it is a tarantula hawk wasp. We are utilizing them to expunge the tunnels of all the tarantulas. Their venom is proving advantageous in some of my experiments and your mother is analyzing their gland structure under the microscope," Martin answered. "You must not touch anything here. The wasp carcass needs to remain in vacuum for the electron diffraction to function and you destroyed the seal."

"Honey, maybe I should take him back upstairs?" Beth said. "I think seven-year-old's and a lab full of deadly viruses is not a wise combination."

"What deadly viruses?" Cliff was about to open one of the refrigerators before his mother ran over and stopped him.

"Yes, I have enough serum for the tests I need to execute. I'll be above ground in a few hours with the anticipated results," Martin said. He had already begun working on re-sealing the rectangular enclosure. He turned on a loud vacuum pump; the sound of which, combined with the centrifuge and fume exhaust running, made the room too unbearably noisy to pursue further conversation.

~ ~ ~

"Mom, why do you want to kill the tarantulas?" Cliff asked, holding Beth's hand as she led him up to the main house through the mountain tunnel.

"Because they are hairy, evil, 8 legged things from nightmares that make your skin crawl and stare at you with strange, creepy eyes of dreadfulness!"

"So, you have nightmares about spiders?"

"Yes, they're the most horrible creatures, pure evil."

"I like Spider-Man, and spiders. I wouldn't mind being bitten by a radioactive spider and becoming a super hero. I don't have nightmares about spiders. I have nightmares about little girls stealing my GI Joes – now that is pure evil!" Cliff insisted, nodding as he talked.

"Little girls stealing you GI Joes?" Beth laughed; she couldn't help it. Spiders were far worse than little girls, but maybe not to little boys.

"Yes, and I met one today, she was horrible."

"You met a little girl? Where?" This was the first she had heard of it. They had focused on telling her about Cliff's fall and subsequent muscle weakness and not any of the events leading up to it.

"At the lake. Daniel talked to her. She told him that her caravan was stuck there for a few days. So, she could come steal my toys any day. You won't let her mom, will you?" Cliff begged, stopping her walking by yanking on her arm.

"Of course not! No little girl is going to steal your toys, I promise. Why would you think that?"

"She did in my nightmare," Cliff said, sulking and refusing to move further through the tunnel.

"It's only a dream. They mean nothing. It is merely your brain firing off images processed throughout the day. You probably saw something on TV with a little girl. Then, you played with your toys. When you went to sleep, your brain simply put it all together. Dreams have no meaning, they are purely jumbled non-sense."

"Miss Tinny says it is my 'spirit' trying to tell me something and I should look into my feelings," Cliff said, peeking up curiously at her. He clearly wanted to see how she would react, and it was important that she set some facts straight about the matter.

"Miss Tinny has very different beliefs than we do, and that's okay. Lots of people have different beliefs because of their culture or religion. From a scientific standpoint, dreams have not been proven to have any significance. They are just random thoughts being stimulated by events firing off in your brilliant imagination. Do you understand?"

She waited for him to acknowledge what she said, and he nodded. He still looked troubled.

"Little girls are nothing to be scared of, and they seldomly steal. I'll make sure no little girl even comes into this house if you like." Beth did not know how else to re-assure her son and she was going to have a word or two with Tsintah.

"Okay, Mom, thank you," Cliff said, sighing a breath of relief at last. She tried not to laugh, he was that bothered by a little girl?

"I do have one more question for you, honey," she began, taking his hand between both of hers, kneeing down so she was at his level to look him directly in the eyes, "What did you do to the cat?"

"I didn't do it, the cat jumped on the train," Cliff insisted. "I swear, it wasn't my fault!"

"Well, Dr. Whiskers hasn't gotten out from under the china hutch all day. Can you coax her out? Maybe give her a treat?"

"Oooh, I can give her this!" he exclaimed, digging a lizard's tail he must have collected on the trail earlier from his back pocket and suspending it in front of her face.

"Oh my! Sure. I'm sure she would love that," she said, trying to smile through the natural grimace response to seeing a dead piece of animal flesh wiggling so close to her nose. "You know, you seem to have a lot more energy, and you are walking fine now ... did your dad give you something down there? Did you get into anything? Be honest. I promise, you won't be in trouble."

Cliff appeared guilty: if the blushing and eye aversion didn't give it away, the fidgeting feet and hands sure did. Finally, he said, "I took a sip of dad's coffee on the desk while you two were talking. I'm sorry! It tasted nasty!!! I don't know why you like it so much. I won't drink it again, ever, I promise! Really, I promise!"

"Honey, thank you for being honest. You know coffee is off limits. We have a strict rule about that for a reason." Beth said. Well, that explained the sudden jolt of energy! But the sudden walking? What in the world in that tarry concoction of Martin's could have done that? she thought. She slid open the wall at the back of the house and led Cliff through. "Whatever made you want to break the rule today?"

"I was feeling so tired and you always look like coffee gives you energy. Dad sat it down right next to me, you two weren't looking ... I just thought it might help. Are you going to punish me?"

"Not today, though I may have a word or two for your father. We will find a better medicine for you when we go to Denver. No more, okay?"

"Yes, mom. Can I go feed the cat now?"

"Of course, honey," she said as she kissed him on the forehead and patted him on the back. "I'm just glad you're feeling better."

Cliff ran off gleefully towards the kitchen, dangling lizard tail in tow, saying "Here, kitty kitty ... I have a treat for you!"

Beth went into the master bedroom to start packing for the trip. They would need to leave first thing in the morning and she had a full family worth of bags and things to get ready.

"Mom, can I stay? Please? I want to see if I can help fix the transmission problems the campers at the lake are having," Daniel walked into the room and wasted no time making a request to his busy mother who was loading up suitcases.

"No honey, we all have to go," she replied off hand while trying to count the number of shirts she had pulled from the closet. "One, two, three ... Yes, that should be enough. How can you help with a transmission problem? You haven't studied auto mechanics yet, have you?"

"I know. I can't find anything on cars, trucks or RV's in the house. Maybe we should order some?" Daniel was so kind hearted, always wanting to help others and fix problems. A trait Beth wanted to encourage.

"We might be able to find something in Denver for you to study. There are a few great bo stores we can go to."

Daniel stood in the room, watching his mother pack. She had thought the bookstore idea would have him elated, but he appeared contemplative. He started to help her pack by folding some of the stacks of clothes she had shoved into a suitcase. Beth loved planning, but hated organizing. Daniel was so detail oriented, like his father. It was nice to have the help.

"I still want to stay ... I promised Amy I would come back to see her tomorrow ..." he said at last after moping for a few minutes.

"Amy? Is that the little girl you and Cliff met today?" she said while going into the bathroom to get toiletries.

"Yes, she was very nice. I told her about the eastern cliffs and she wants to climb them. She says she has climbed the Grand Canyon and every great canyon west of the Mississippi."

"I see. She sounds like a very impressive young lady." She could tell that Daniel really liked this girl, he had never spoken like this about anyone before.

"Yes, she is." He said, pointedly gazing down at the clothes he was folding extra carefully. "She might leave before we get back." He looked up with those sad eyes a mother never wants to see and can hardly resist.

"I can't just leave you here by yourself!" she exclaimed – it was getting harder to say no.

"I won't be alone. Miss Tinny can check on me. I promise, I'll be good." The hope in his voice was heartbreaking.

"I don't know. We would need to see if she is even available..." She hadn't finished her sentence before she was interrupted with Daniel yelling "I'll call her now!" and running off. She had planned to call Tsintah to watch the house while they were away anyway, but she wasn't expecting to ask her to watch her eldest son too.

Two minutes later she heard him hollering from the kitchen, "Mom! She says she can stay here! She wants to talk to you! MOM!" The words got increasing louder as he was running from the kitchen to the bedroom to tell her the good news.

"No running through the halls! You might trip!" Beth put down the shirt she was folding, wondering how she had been convinced to leave Daniel at home alone. She followed him through the hallway, being towed by the arm the entire time, then picked up the phone sitting on the kitchen counter.

"Hi, Tsintah. Daniel let you know we're heading out of town?" she wound the twisted phone cord connected to the wall absent-mindedly around her index finger and paced back and forth. Daniel followed her around, trying to listen-in on the conversation.

"Yes. I have no problem staying there and watching the cat and Daniel. I can tell he is very excited. I'm sorry you are having to go to Denver though. I hope it is nothing too serious," Her voice replied over the phone, the speaker making her sound older and distorted, with a bit of a crackle.

"Thank you. I hope so too. We're leaving first thing in the morning. We'll likely be back Saturday evening.

I'll give you double pay for all three days for the inconvenience. I appreciate your help."

"Oh, it's not a problem at all! I'm happy to spend time with Daniel, he's such a bright and sweet boy."

"Thank you again, Tsintah. I'll see you in the morning, 6 am. Thank you."

"Yay!!" Daniel yelled and hugged her when she hung up the phone.

Beth tried to untwist the cord that she had nervously twisted even more than before. Somehow during the brief conversation, she'd managed to get it wrapped around her leg, arm and even in her long blonde hair.

"Now you need to be careful with this girl, Amy. If you go climbing you need to bring your own gear and do the standard check from the checklist in the gear bag. Most importantly, you're not allowed to go anywhere without Tsintah, are we clear?" She used as mommy stern of a voice as she could manage.

Daniel was nodding in-between hugging.

"Miss Tinny can climb a cliff like a mountain goat, she loves them!" Daniel exclaimed.

"She loves mountain goats?"

"No, cliffs ... climbing. Maybe she loves goats too, I don't know. Oh, don't forget the book on transmissions when you go to Denver; I want to help my new friend if they haven't gotten it fixed by the time you get back."

There were few people in the area and it was good for her kids to make friends at any opportunity. Not having companions their own age was probably very hard on them and she felt like a horrible parent because of it. She had hoped more people would move to the town with kids, but in the last 10 years it was still mostly retirees.

"You aren't coming with us?" Cliff asked. He had Dr. Whiskers in his arms, and she had the lizard tail sticking out of her mouth. Beth held back a reactionary gag at the sight.

"Mom said I can stay and go climbing with Amy. Miss Tinny is coming to watch me."

"You're going to miss Return of the Jedi, are you sure you want to stay?" Cliff said, he seemed a bit in disbelief.

"You can tell me all about it and I can wait and see it when it comes out on VHS like we have seen all the rest." Daniel replied, unfazed.

"You aren't going to let that girl come over to our house while we're gone, are you?"

"Don't worry Cliff, I won't let her anywhere near your GI Joes," Daniel said, petting the cat, who was chewing on the lizard tail and appearing quite content, purring in Cliff's arms, eyes almost sparkling green.

Beth stared at her two boys and wondered how one could think so poorly of girls, and the other was so excited to meet one. With how much exposure to other people her kids were getting living here, she was surprised they even knew what a little girl looked like. I certainly must find a way to get more people to move to this town! she thought as she went to finish packing for the trip.

Chapter 4

Little Girls and Games

Amy Shipley spent her life on the road going across the United States of America from one national park to the next and everywhere in between. It was all she knew, besides her family. Her father was retired Army, a full-bird Colonel. Her mother was 20 years younger and loved adventure. Her younger brother, Doug, was three and barely talking, still in diapers and a snotty pain-in-the-butt that kept her mom busy all day cleaning up mess after mess. Her family had three Chihuahuas, but her favorite was Mimi. The other two generally just liked her mother. Mimi was Amy's best friend and went with her everywhere.

Amy loved meeting new people, especially boys. Unfortunately, where they were stuck now no one seemed to pass through. She'd been bored to death the last few days waiting for anyone to show up.

Her parents had relegated her to the lake area yesterday because her dad decided he wanted to fish and play cribbage with the Dukes instead of go hiking like she wanted. She'd gotten her rock skipping game down to an art before she started climbing trees to look for a better view of the valley.

Then she saw him: Daniel Jahren. He was the most interesting boy she'd ever come across. He'd showed her how to solve a Rubik's cube in ten moves, and she'd never even seen one solved before. Plus, he knew the entire area and said he could show her how to get to the top of the mountain near the lake.

She was so excited to see him again that she got up early and was out walking the tree line. She paced back and forth in the wet grass with only the sound of birds and the lapping of the water at the lake to distract her from her thoughts. Her fluffy purple socks were soaked with morning dew. Urgh, I've been up and about for an hour now. Where is he?? she thought.

The Ryans were hosting breakfast. The aroma of pancakes and sausage wafting through the air made her mouth water. But she didn't want to miss seeing Daniel come through the tree line first because she was afraid the Johnson twins would get to him and steal him away from her. Last night they had asked her like a million questions about him, his brother and his nanny. None of them had ever seen a Native American as a nanny before and she had looked so beautiful and mysterious.

Daniel's chubby little brother Cliff didn't seem to like Amy, he even threw a rock at her dog! She hoped he wouldn't be coming back today. He was probably a total brat, just like her own pants-craping younger sibling.

Mimi was getting dizzy following Amy around, pacing at the forest edge, and started to bark and whine. Her smooth and fluffy brown hair was standing up straight and her cream-colored paws were turning dark reddish-brown from the dirt. Amy picked her up and kept pacing, brushing off the grime from Mimi's tiny feet and cradling her to keep her warm.

"Did you chase him away being such a ditz, Amy?" Sarah Johnson asked. Her twin, Rebecca, mirrored the look of snide condescension she was directing at Amy. They dressed alike, talked alike and sometimes even walked alike, probably just to annoy and confuse everyone. The only way she could tell them apart was that Sarah had a one-inch, dark brown birthmark on her neck in the shape of a melting crescent moon and Rebecca was slightly taller and leaner. The dark auburn hair, large hazel eyes and perfectly porcelain skin accentuated their pink lips and rosy cheeks. They reminded her of well-crafted dolls. Their only flaw was a pig-like nose, and a snooty attitude to match.

"No, you're the airhead that chases everyone away, Sarah. Daniel said he'd be back today. He swore," Amy grimaced, staring into the tree line. Great, she was going to miss breakfast and the Johnson twins were ready to pounce on Daniel the minute he walked out! "Either of you want to get me a sausage?" Her request was met with disdain. "For Mimi?" Her stomach was rumbling, and Mimi gave a little bark of concern.

"Go get breakfast yourself! You're obviously hungry and poor Mimi deserves better," Rebecca said, petting Mimi who was licking what was likely the syrup from pancakes off of her fingers.

"Did you make Daniel pinky swear he would be back?" Sarah asked.

"No, I..."

"Lame!" Rebecca cut her off and snickered.

"I ... I'm going to go get something to eat," Amy said, the empty pit of her stomach growling louder and feeling heavier with each insult from the Johnson girls.

She dashed away towards the Ryans' old 1967 Volkswagen RV to get breakfast before they packed away the last morsels of delectable goodness. They made the best pancakes and today they had put wild berries in them, and even put the berries in their homemade syrup. They were every bit as delicious as they had smelled! she thought as she tore into a large pile of pancakes drenched in syrup and topped with fresh berries and cream. The thin sausages that came with the pancakes weren't the best, a bit freezer burnt. Mimi didn't mind finishing them off though.

Amy still kept her eyes glancing towards the tree line, but she had a gut-sinking feeling it would be unavoidable that the Johnson girls were going to snag Daniel today. She would have to fight them for his attention.

Before she was done eating, Amy's worst fears came true. Daniel stepped through the tree line, with his neat native nanny, and the Johnson girls swiftly surrounded him.

What were they saying? Dang it!

She shoved the remaining berries and pancakes into her mouth as fast as she could, getting blueberry juice all over her face and sending little bits to the ground that the dog happily seized with her tongue.

"Thank you, Miss Jude!" Amy said with a full mouth to old Jude Ryan, who was hunched over and hosing down a large pile of dishes. Amy went to hand her the empty plate but she was in such a rush that she didn't quite make Jude's gnarly, feeble hand for the transfer. The plate dropped into the mud puddle on the ground created from the dish washing overspray.

"Dang it!" she muttered. She decided to pick the plate up and put it and both her hands into the hose water to clean off the debris. But she ended up splashing poor Mimi. "Dang it!" she said again, a little louder. Now she had to dry off the dog and her hands.

"You might want to clean your face, dear." Miss Jude Ryan said, "You've got berry juice all over."

"Dang it! Dang it!" She kept muttering to herself the whole time she was cleaning off the mess she had made in her rush. Every second she was wasting was agonizing because she was not getting over to where Daniel and his nanny were talking, and she wanted to hear everything!

"Thank you, Miss Jude!" she yelled, running off with Mimi all wrapped up in a towel.

"Dead Man's Pass is too steep for children. I'd advise taking the fork at Siphon Draw to the left and head to a smaller embankment for today. We can try something different tomorrow if all goes well," Amy heard the native nanny say as she approached with Mimi.

"Amy, are you really going rock climbing? Isn't that dangerous? What did your Mom say when you asked her?" Sarah said with what sounded too close to a patronizing tone disguised as concern. She was standing far too close to Daniel for Amy's comfort too.

"I think you should stay here, we can play games. We know all sorts. Have you ever played 'Red light, Green light' or 'Bones'?" Rebecca asked, standing so close that she was practically sandwiching poor Daniel between her and her sister.

"I think we should play 'Red Rover' and go get Jack Williams to help. It'll be fun!" Sarah was jumping up and down slightly as she spoke, and she kept touching Daniel's arm, which Amy found very annoying.

"Hi Amy," Daniel finally said. Amy was beaming and gave Daniel a big, tight hug that made his eyes look like they were going to pop out of his head. He was wearing khaki pants and a grey cotton shirt with a small pocket in the front. He looked cute, clean and perfectly well dressed. A little too clean and perfect for the outdoors, really. He brought a large duffle bag and a backpack, and best of all, his nanny! She was smiling at Amy with those mystifying dark eyes and had her knee-length-long, black hair back in one compact braid. All she brought was that bejeweled fanny pack, the same one she had been wearing yesterday.

"Hi Daniel," Amy replied. "Mimi says hi too." She held the pooch up to Daniel for kisses but Mimi just barked – yapping and snapping wildly. She hurriedly pulled the dog back. "Sorry, she doesn't know you very well yet."

"That's okay," Daniel said. "I brought all my gear for climbing Dead Man's Pass like we talked about yesterday. Miss Tinny doesn't think it is a good idea though. So, we might have to start with something a bit easier today until we can prove to her we are both exceptional climbers. You don't mind, do you?"

"I didn't know we needed gear, why do we need gear?" Amy wondered. She hadn't realized that the cliff at the edge of the mountain was that steep. She might have over exaggerated yesterday about her climbing skills. Technically, she had never been climbing. How hard could it be though? She could figure it out.

Daniel opened his mouth to talk but was quickly interrupted by Rebecca, "You didn't tell your mom about climbing then! I'm going to tell her! I bet she won't let you go!"

"Rebecca, come on!" Amy exclaimed, she knew that her hopes of running off on an exploration of the mountains with a new friend were now dashed completely. Technically, she wasn't even allowed to leave the lake area today. If her mom knew anything about her going off climbing she would be in big trouble. She'd have to settle for hanging out with the twins for sure now, and with sharing her new friend. "Daniel, maybe there is something we can do here instead, for today. Have you ever played 'Red Rover'?"

Daniel looked just as disappointed as Amy felt, and he was frowning at Rebecca and Sarah who were peering over (quite self-satisfied) at Amy. "What is 'Red Rover'? Is it a board game? A puzzle?"

"No dummy, it's a playground game. You've seriously never heard of it?" Sarah laughed derisively.

"I've never played a playground game," Daniel admitted and was meet with snickering from the twins.

"We're going to have to teach you everything, aren't we?" Sarah said.

"Don't be mean to Daniel, Sarah," Amy scolded. Sarah's acidic attitude had driven off more than a few new people and everyone knew it. Amy didn't want her ruining this for her, so she snuck a hand behind Sarah's back and gave her hair a nice yank to ensure she got the message. Then she smiled and pretended like nothing happened.

"I'll go get Jack," Rebecca shouted, already running towards the Williams' large, white and tan Winnebago.

"Who's Jack?" asked Daniel.

"He's the Williams' son. He's about your age, 11?" Amy replied. She didn't like Jack, he once pushed her down into an ant pile. Later, when she was crying to her Mom while she was washing the ants out of her hair, her mother told her that little boys sometimes do mean things to girls they like. It never made sense to her that a boy could be mean to a girl that he liked. So, she generally avoided him if she could, she didn't want more ant bites! "Do we have to invite him?"

"We'll need more people if we're going to play, silly." Sarah remarked. "Do you want to join us Miss Tinny?" Sarah's tone was slightly politer, but she was still being obnoxious in Amy's opinion.

"I can, but I'd prefer if we played a less violent game than 'Red Rover,' something like 'Red light, Green light' might be good," Tsintah recommended. "Or 'Blind Man's Bluff'?"

"Oh, yeah, 'Blind Man's Bluff' would be fun! Who wants to be 'it' first?" Sarah exclaimed. "I know, we can play 'Rock, Paper, Scissors' to see who goes first. Whoever loses is 'it.' Ready?" she held her right hand in a fist over her left palm, leaning forward towards Amy.

Amy put Mimi down in the grass and faced off against Sarah. "1, 2, 3 ... go!"

"Rock beats scissors! You're 'it'!" Sarah shouted.

"Gosh dang it!" Amy declared, stomping her foot and causing Mimi to bark and run around in a circle.

"Rock beats scissors?" Daniel inquired, apparently confused. He must not know any games! Amy thought, but she was nice enough to keep that to herself, unlike Sarah.

"Haven't you ever played 'Rock, Paper, Scissors' before? Do you live under a rock? Geeze!" Sarah said, exasperated by Daniel's ignorance. Amy slipped her hand behind Sarah's back again and pulled her hair. This time Sarah put her hand behind Amy's back and pulled her hair too, making Amy grit her teeth and stomp on Sarah's foot. Then she smiled even bigger than before. Daniel seemed not to notice any of it, thankfully.

"I live in a house," Daniel replied, still just as confused and appearing a bit hurt with his shoulders slouched and chin down, kicking at the ground and not looking up at the two little girls. Tsintah put her hand on his back, comforting, while glaring disapprovingly at Sarah.

"I will explain that one later, Daniel. For now, we need to learn the rules of 'Blind Man's Bluff.' It's pretty easy..." Tsintah began but was interrupted by Amy.

"Ooh, let me tell him!" She begged, and with an approving nod from the nanny, she continued, "I will be blindfolded, as I am 'it', for now, and you and everyone else will have to stay here in this grassy area ... Umm ... we need something to mark it off ..." She took hold of his duffle bag and placed it 10 feet away. "Okay, between here and that tree," she was pointing at the large cottonwood tree, "and from the tree line there to that park bench is the game zone. You can stand anywhere in this area. They're going to blindfold me, spin me around until I'm dizzy and then everyone has to pick a spot to stand while I count to 10 slowly. I'll have to find everyone, and when I do I have to identify that person without taking off my blindfold. If I guess right, then that person is 'it' and we start again. Got it?"

He nodded and smiled a cute little grin at Amy that made butterflies dance in her belly. Mimi started barking and running around her feet.

"I need to go tie Mimi to the tree so she doesn't run off, I'll be right back," she said, heading over to the giant cottonwood that made up the north end of their established play area.

"If you guess wrong?" he yelled as she left. "How will you know those two apart? I can't even tell them apart with my eyes open," he was pointing at Sarah and Rebecca, who had come back with Jack. The girls were giggling and Jack was sizing Daniel up.

"So, you're Dan?" Jack asked with his chest flared and nose up in the air. "I'm Jack Williams, the only sane one around here." He held out his hand for a shake.

"My name is Daniel, not Dan. The insane don't know they are insane, you know," he said with a half grin and then added, "or maybe you don't know." He gave him a very strong handshake that left Jack knowing he wasn't to be messed with and made the twins giggle some more.

"Ha, very funny," Jack pulled his hand back and rubbed it. He wasn't used to being challenged and obviously wasn't sure what to make of it. Jack was slightly taller, but leaner than Daniel so they were probably evenly matched for strength. Neither boy looked ready to find out just yet.

"Daniel does bring up a good point, one of you will have to wear or do something different somehow so that we can tell you apart," Amy insisted, coming back and standing right next to Daniel who was facing off the twins and Jack. "It really isn't fair to the rest of us."

"Life's not fair," Rebecca said, sticking her tongue out. "Get over it, you'll just have to figure it out."

Geeze, she was just as irritating as her sister! Would Amy have to step on her foot too in order to get her to act nicer to their guest?

"How about I just sit this one out." Sarah offered. "Miss Tinny, do you want to meet my mother? She would love to meet you! She's been trying to make turquoise jewelry like the necklace you're wearing. You don't make jewelry, do you? Did you make that?" Sarah took the nanny by the arm and led her towards the end of the RV park to their blue and white GMC Motorhome before anyone had a chance to stop her, including Tsintah.

"Okay, that's settled then. Let's play!" Rebecca announced, pulling out a flowered scarf to use as a blindfold and grinning wildly.

After an hour, they switched from 'Blind-Man's-Bluff' to 'Bones' and then went to hand games, like 'Patty Cake.' Amy even got to teach Daniel the rules of 'Rock, Paper, Scissors.' By the time Tsintah and Sarah returned a few hours later they were all sitting in a circle clapping their hands together singing "Rockin' Robin" with Mimi snoozing in the middle. "Tweet!

Tweet! Tweet!" they shouted in unison when Sarah and Tsintah arrived.

"Miss Tinny! I have never had so much fun in my life!" Daniel jumped up to take Tsintah by the hand. "You have to play with us!"

"It's time for lunch. Did you want to eat what we packed, or do you want to visit with the Johnsons, they offered bologna sandwiches and grape juice," Tsintah used a neutral but polite tone in her voice. She then frowned with a slight shake of her head to Daniel when the Johnson girls weren't looking.

Amy couldn't help but chuckle. That sounded awful! "We're having fish tacos today. My dad's been fishing all morning and I'm sure they'll be delicious and fresh. My mom makes the best lemonade too ... oh, please come!"

"We've got the 49ers game on, if you want to come eat lunch at our Winnebago," Jack offered. His father had a 6-inch black and white tv with three channels. It was the envy of the whole caravan, even though it took them an hour to set-up the giant antenna it was hooked up to every time they stopped.

Everyone was staring at Daniel, begging their case and waiting for a decision on lunch. He was turning red, scratching his head and darting his eyes between them all. Finally, Amy just took him by the hand and directed him over towards her parent's aluminum Airstream, leaving the other three kids behind in dejection. You snooze you lose! she thought.

He smiled over at her and let out a long sigh of relief. It was nice holding his hand. He had learned all of the games today so rapidly and never had to be told the rules again, nor did he break any ... unlike Rebecca and Jack. She'd caught them both peeking out of their blindfolds during 'Blind-Man's-Bluff.' He was so smart! And so charming glancing over at her through his wavy brown hair that he kept tossing out of his face.

"Thank you, Amy," he said. "I've had so much fun today. I didn't want to hurt anyone's feelings, everyone's been so nice to me."

"Nice? Jack is a cruel nitwit and Rebecca is a stuck-up twerp!" Amy blurted out, realizing she sounded kind-of snooty herself as she said it. Her mom always said, "If you can't say anything nice, don't say anything at all" and she had just bad-mouthed her own friends the first chance she got. Not nice! She blushed and held her head down in shame. "Sorry, I guess that they aren't so bad. They're my friends and I shouldn't have said that."

"Do you have a lot of friends?"

"Sorta. I mean, I guess I do. I meet new people all the time and in all places; from national parks to Walmart parking lots. Some stay with the caravan for a week simply because they have the same destinations in mind. Others stay for years for the company." As they walked through the park, Amy explained to Daniel more about the different families and how the caravan of RV's that her family traveled with had formed organically over the years.

There were currently six families traveling together. A week ago, it had been nine but three didn't want to stay and wait for the Johnsons' RV to get fixed when they found out it would likely be another week before all the parts would arrive for the transmission repair.

"If you stay for the bonfire tonight, you'll get to see the best in everyone. Especially with you here, they'll want to show off their talents."

The Arabies played guitar, harmonica and sang. The Johnsons father played guitar too, and had a small drum set that they let anyone bang away on. The Dukes were good storytellers: they were a couple in their forties that made money publishing articles and books for a living. They liked to test their stories out on the group, some were a bit too dark for Amy's tastes and gave her nightmares. The Ryans were in their late 60s, retired, and mostly told stories about their grandkids from letters they received along the way at the established Post Office boxes. Amy and her Mom liked to recite poetry and dance.

"Sarah and Rebecca have their flaws but every now and then they will sew-up little jackets for Mimi and the other dogs and we put on a dog fashion show."

"A dog fashion show? How fascinating ... It's nice to have friends," he was looking down at her hand holding his as they walked. "I almost forgot! I brought you this." He pulled out a stone that was in his front pocket. It was shinny and black, shaped like a triangle, with chopped, razor-sharp edges.

"What is it?" She asked, taking the stone and rubbing the smooth top, trying not to cut her fingers on the sharp parts.

"It is an obsidian arrowhead. I shined it up for you yesterday myself. It's an ancient Native American tool and it came from this mountainside. See the red?" he took it back and moved it so that the sunlight caught the different colored elements set in the dark stone. "It has flecks of iron in it like all the rocks around here. That's what makes them red, the iron oxide." He placed it gently in her palm and closed her hand over it, then put his hand over hers. "I thought it would be great for you to remember me by," he peeked up into her eyes for a brief second but then quickly looked down at his hand.

Amy was overwhelmed, this was the neatest thing she had ever seen! Tears welled up in her eyes. She decided she wanted to give him something too but couldn't think of anything she had that was anywhere near as cool. An idea popped into her head and before she even knew what she was doing, she had given him a full-on kiss. Right on the lips!

They both looked at each other in amazement. Amy had never kissed a boy before. She kissed her dolls, her mom, even Mimi ... but never a boy! From the look he was giving her, he had never kissed a girl either.

"What was that?" Daniel finally asked after a long wide-eyes pause. The fingers of his left hand drifted to his lips.

Amy smiled, took his hand, and said, "Something to remember me by."

Chapter 5

Cliff on a Cliff

It had been six and a half years since Amy Shipley graced Mesa Heights with her presence. Daniel had been going to school at Mesa College in Grande Junction for most of those years. He was home for the summer and at his old desk in the den. The heavily worn-in chair and warm sunlight coming in from the window were almost as comforting as Dr. Whiskers laying curled up on his lap. He petted her absent-mindedly while going through a box of letters from Amy.

Amy's parents had decided to settle in New Mexico so that they could send her younger brother, Doug, to school. Doug had turned out to be too much for their parents to handle home-schooling and he needed special education. At least with her family settled down he could get regular letters from her. Lately she had been sending him poems. The latest had his whole family chuckling for the first time in a long time. It was titled "Fat Cat Fall-ee:"

> I wants a treat but you're takin' a bath
> I wants it now, or I'm gonna' be mad
> I'm on a ledge, I'm having a cow
> I wants a treat, I wants it now!
> Meow, Meow, Meow, Now!

Dang it, I slipped, now I'm all drenched
An icky feeling, and I'm entrenched
I have to get out, so I pounce
I hurl my huge belly, bounce
Pounce, Pounce, Pounce, Bounce!

Down I go again, Oh, this isn't right!
I'm stuck in the tub, try as I might
Sliding under, claws can't grasp
A desperate, wet, hairy mass
Splash, Splash, Splash, Fat-Ass!

What willful negligence, what disrespect
I'm in dreadful hot water, up to my neck
Laughing, mean human, mocking me
You won't be laughing, if I pee
Hehe, hehe, hehe, flee!!!

It was about Amy's kitty Pumpkin's misadventure with the bathtub, and how he was now too fat to get himself out of the tub but tried and tried non-the-less. She said he weighed 25 lbs. and still ate everything he could find but no longer begged her for treats when she was taking a bath after the 'incident' that inspired the poem.

"You're not re-reading that poem again, are you Dude?" Cliff remarked, bounding side to side into the room on crutches that he had rigged with springs and a shoulder strap that went around his back for support. Cliff's condition had deteriorated. He had been diagnosed with a severe form of muscular dystrophy and his parents had given up on Dr. David Jorgensen's help long ago. They were relied solely on their own methods now.

"No," Daniel protested, folding-up the most recent letter from Amy and slipping it away casually, trying not to notice Cliff's tone or the fact that he was on crutches today.

If Cliff was on his crutches, it meant he wasn't having a good day, because most days he could get around without them. The apparatus made it to where Cliff could be hands-free some of the time while walking. But that wasn't the only reason he wore it, he was also starting to lose muscle strength in his arms and he didn't want to admit it.

"Are you in love? Is she your girlfriend? Daniel and Amy sitting in a tree, k-i-s-s-i-n-g!" Cliff sang. He smacked the desk leg with his crutch at every letter of 'kissing' for emphasis. The cat jumped up and out of the room, not wanting to be any part of the conflict.

Cliff had gotten a bit chubbier from all the steroid treatments he had been given, and his hormones were out-of-whack so his cheeks were splotchy, filled with acne and stubbled with hair despite him being only 13. Daniel had grown almost a foot and a half in height, but Cliff was barely 4 inches taller than he had been at seven years old. Clearly, he acted as immature as he looked.

"No, she is just a friend. At least I have a friend," he said and immediately regretted it when he saw Cliff's face turn dark.

Both boys were so much younger than any of their classmates, so it had been hard to make any friends. Cliff had been at Mesa College for the last year and he had it worse than Daniel. Not only did no one want to be his friend, but there was a group of jocks that went out of their way to make his life miserable, and once pushed him down a flight of stairs. The girls were worse, though well meaning. About once a week one would ask him if he was lost and needed to find his mommy.

"I don't need friends; most people are idiots anyway. Just a waste of time, just like those letters. You could be doing so much more with your time than wasting it on writing letters about fat cats in bathtubs to some dumb girl you hardly even know."

"I've known Amy for over six years now. She's my best friend." Not only was Amy Daniel's only real friend, but she called him her best friend too, signing every letter with BFF (Best Friends Forever), which made him feel extra special.

"Yeah, in letters. Would you even recognize her if you saw her?"

"I would. She'll be here today, so you'll see." More exciting than the letters, and humorous poems, was that Amy was coming back to Colorado. Her parents missed being on the road and she had managed to convince them to take a detour through his town on their way from Zion National Park in Utah to Garden of the Gods in Colorado Springs. Daniel couldn't wait!

"Today? Wait, what? You've got to be joking?"

"Yes. Today. No, I'm not joking. I'm meeting her out at the lake this afternoon." Daniel took the grey metal box he kept Amy's letters in and put it on the top shelf of the cherry-wood bookshelf that was next to the desk. The den now had several bookshelves all along the walls to help organize the many books. There were less books in the room as well, because the boys now utilized the campus library for their studies. Daniel kept the box up there because he knew it would be hard for Cliff to reach. He'd also put a combination lock on the box after opening it once and finding scribbled snide remarks on a few of the letters.

After a minute of silence, Cliff unexpectedly asked, "Can I come?"

"No. We're going to hike up to climb Dead Man's Pass and you're in no condition today to make the trip." He also didn't want him there, but he didn't want to hurt his little brother's feelings.

"You know I can always drink some of that foul coffee Mom and Father put God-knows-what in ... let me come!" Cliff pleaded. Their parents refused to tell them what was in the drink, and still didn't want them to have it saying 'it isn't good for growing boys' and left it at that. But, Cliff was right – there was definitely something in that mixture that made him have movement back in his legs, temporarily. The two of them had managed to sneak a few cups and experiment. The biggest problem (besides the taste) is if Cliff didn't keep drinking it he would end up a crazed and half-dead mess within 24 hours afterwards. He'd also be in crutches for a week, which is a steep price to pay for one day of movement.

"I thought you didn't like Amy, and you're willing to drink that concoction to see her, what gives?" Daniel was not liking the idea of sharing his time with Amy with Cliff.

"So, you get to have a friend and I don't? Are you ashamed of me? Do you not want me seen by your friend?"

"Of course I'm not ashamed of you!"

"Or is it that you are going to go make-out with her and don't want me around?"

"If it means that much to you, you can come. Don't worry, we aren't going to make-out. We're just friends," Daniel said to placate his little brother, knowing that Cliff was behaving strangely but still wanting to make him happy. "You'd better go gulp down a pot of that stuff now though, I was just about to leave out the door to head down to the lake. And, more importantly, you better not let Mom, Father or Miss Tinny catch you!"

Cliff bounded out of the room leaving Daniel to wonder how he was going to manage getting all three of them through Dead Man's Pass. He would need to load up more gear. He started packing the extra equipment and realized he would also need some more food. So, he headed into the kitchen in time to see Miss Tinny getting duped by Cliff.

He was snagging the coffee behind her back while he distracted her by knocking down a pile of boxes near the door with one of his crutches. "Dr. Whiskers strikes again," he said, laughing and then taking sips in between words continuing with, "That cat sure is clumsy!" He knocked a glass down from the sink. "She's probably going senile. What is she, almost 14 now?"

"The cat isn't senile, what are you up to Cliff? Daniel, you look like you are up to something too, what's going on?" Miss Tinny was good at sensing when something was not quite right. She had her arms crossed and was glaring up at the two boys. She hadn't grown an inch, so both boys towered above her. She stood her ground though and her presence and demeanor was plenty intimidating enough to make up for the height.

"We're going to meet Amy at the lake this afternoon," Cliff answered for both of them.

"That's right, we're just in here getting food for a picnic that we're planning with her," Daniel had to be careful of what he said and knew if he mentioned the pass they intended to hike then Miss Tinny would not approve.

"Well that is exciting! Amy, of all people, coming into town! Cliff, do you mean to hike and picnic as well? Today doesn't look like one of your good days," she said with concern in her voice and eyes on his crutches.

"I'm fine, I was just testing out some new springs I installed, see," he unstrapped the contraption and set it to the side to prove his point. He lifted his hands up, but then leaned back against the counter to hide the fact that he was still a bit unsteady. It took a minute or two before the coffee kicked-in and it hadn't quite kicked-in yet.

"Should I come with you? I just put a casserole in the oven, but I can pull it out and start it later," Tsintah suggested.

"No, that's okay. I can watch Cliff, he'll be fine. I'm sure Dad is looking forward to that casserole," Daniel didn't want her to come up with any excuse to come along or start to think too much on it so he decided they should undoubtedly leave as soon as possible.

"Okay. Tell Amy I said 'Hi.' She was such a sweet young lady. It's so nice that she has kept in contact with you all these years. Are you sure you don't want me to come along?"

"No, we made plans already for today. Maybe tomorrow before she leaves." If she came along he would never get to show Amy the best view of the valley. He had even hidden the climbing gear in his backpack instead of the normal duffle bag so that Miss Tinny didn't suspect anything. "I'll get my bag. Cliff, don't forget to grab the peanut butter and jelly sandwiches!"

They managed to get out of the door without the nanny or parents intervening. Miss Tinny was very protective, even though she really wasn't their nanny anymore. She was more of a housekeeper and cook, lately. Their parents didn't have time for much of anything except research and had just kept her full time so that no one starved and the house didn't fall apart. She was like a second mom to the boys, or a first mom as their mom was kind of like a second dad.

Their mother was quite the entrepreneur in addition to her research. She had always made plenty of money from capitalizing on the patented drugs their father had developed, and the natural resources from the land they owned. But, a few years ago, she had started a manufacturing facility and research center in town to work on a larger variety of drugs in hopes of curing Cliff. The center only hired around 50 people, bringing them in from all corners of the world. But, it had boosted the economy up enough to have a McDonald's and a Walgreens, employing even more people. The local population was now up to almost six hundred people. Managing the business and having to participate in town hall meetings in a growing city meant that they never saw their mother.

Daniel and Cliff spent a lot of time with each other, especially now that they went to school together too. However, they hardly ever went out or did anything fun anymore. In fact, they hadn't gone to the lake since Cliff started getting sick.

It was pleasant walking out in the invigorating, June air. The familiar sage smelled wonderful and the trail was nice and dry because it hadn't rained in over a month. There were lizards basking on rocks and ravens cawing in the branches. They even heard a rattlesnake rattling in a bush. Daniel made a sport of counting the number of jack rabbits that were startled and went bounding into the woods – ten so far.

Cliff was keeping quiet, which was superb, and managing to keep up with Daniel's fast pace. The only thing that would make this day better would be seeing Amy. Would he recognize her? She had sent him pictures, but it had been years.

When he got to the lake, he knew her right away. She still had the same fluffy, curly blonde hair and bunny-like gait, and big dimples framing a big smile. When she saw him, she came running and had her arms wrapped around his back in a flash that left his head spinning. He felt like he was in a dream, he couldn't believe Amy was standing right there!

"Hi Amy, remember me?" Cliff asked, holding out his hand. He figured she must not have heard him because she was just staring at Daniel, smiling. Daniel and Amy were just standing there, staring, smiling like fools. "Umm, Amy? Hello! Hello!"

"Oh, I'm so sorry! Hey, Cliff!" Amy gave Cliff a hug, and continued with, "Of course I remember you! Duh! What's happenin'?"

Daniel felt like the world stopped and there was only Amy. She must have felt the same. She had grown into a beautiful young woman; her baby-fat cheeks were gone and she had curves under her skimpy tank top and cut-off jeans that he was trying not to notice too conspicuously. "Are you ready to climb up the mountain? Do you need to change into something that...?" He was trying to think of something to say that didn't make him sound like a pervert.

"What, you don't like my outfit?" she said, spinning around. "I cut these myself and added these jewels, she was pointing to her butt cheeks and the heart rhinestones on each of the back pockets.

"Sparkle butt, classy," Cliff laughed derisively and was met with a frown from Amy that made Daniel want to hit Cliff, hard. He didn't know why, but all he wanted was to see her smile.

"Where's your nanny?" she asked, staring at Cliff. That was probably one of the worst things she could have said. He was sensitive about how short he was, and she was practically calling him a little kid.

"Miss Tinny is busy, she said 'hi' though," Daniel reached out and took Cliff by the arm, half to re-assure him and half to hold him back.

"We're too old for a nanny, don't you think?" Cliff glared down at Daniel's hand on his arm and shrugged him off. "Daniel didn't want her to come because she wouldn't want us to climb the mountain. I think it's a dumb idea too."

"Oh, she's such a sweetheart," said Amy. "Maybe she can visit us tomorrow morning before we leave?"

"I'll ask, I'm sure she wouldn't mind. Come on, let's go. The sooner we get to the top, the sooner we can enjoy the view. There is nothing like it in the whole valley," Daniel could barely hold back the urge to start running towards the trail. He'd been talking up the view to Amy for years and they were so close to going now!

"Can I bring Mimi? She loves escapades," Amy begged, then started singing 'On an Escapade' by Janet Jackson. "Ooh, I need to get my Discman! I'll be right back."

A few minutes later, after having to deal with Cliff shaking his head and saying "Really?" every time Daniel made eye contact with him, Amy was back with Mimi and a dark grey, square CD player that she had clipped to her right pocket.

"Like, you so have to listen to this," she said to Daniel, putting her headphones on him as they walked the trail. It was 'On an Escapade' playing. "I think, like, it should be our theme song for the afternoon. What do you think? It's so rad."

"Theme song?" Cliff questioned, "We have a theme song?" The two just walked ahead and ignored him. He was being grumpy, and Daniel was still wondering why he had even wanted to come along. He followed along behind them, muttering and shuffling his feet all the way to the cliff face.

"Okay, we're at the point where we need to gear up," Daniel said as he dropped his backpack and started pulling out rigging, blocks and pulleys.

"Wow, you're like totally serious. Okay, I trust you," Amy smiled, watching amused as Daniel set her up. He tried not to blush while pulling the rigging over her scantily clad body.

"We might have to put Mimi and your Discman in my backpack. They'll be okay, we'll be at the top in no time. Hopefully she doesn't eat all the food in there."

"Oh, you brought food! Like, you are so prepared!" Amy giggled.

Cliff giggled, mocking Amy. Daniel shot him a scowl that shut him up.

"Cliff, did you need me to strap you up too, or do you remember how to do it yourself?"

"Of course I can do it myself! I'm not an idiot," Cliff glanced at Amy and snickered.

Daniel didn't like how Cliff looked at Amy when he said idiot. He had to fight a strong urge to hit him again.

They managed to make it up the mountain without too bad of an incident. Cliff slipped once, but Daniel succeeded in stopping him well before he went too far – thanks to the harness. It took a lot longer than he expected, over an hour. Amy was in pretty good shape, she had strong climbing legs and made the ascent look easy. It was Cliff that was slowing them down and having the most trouble. But, he made it up despite his difficulty.

"Oh my god, like this view is so like, super rad!" Amy exclaimed when she reached the top. "Mimi has to see this! Poor thing must be so scared." She opened Daniel's bag and pulled out the pintsized dog that had been yapping half the time they were climbing.

"Wait until you see the view from the cliff over there," Daniel said, pointing to the far side. He was busy helping his out-of-breath younger brother out of his gear.

The cliff had a grand view of the valley below. The cliff face was petrified sand, with little pools of water in areas where the sand had swirled and juniper brushes spread out sporadically. Amy sat down cross-legged, only a foot from the edge. Daniel put his backpack down and sat beside her.

"I'm ready to eat something. Daniel, can you hand me one of those peanut butter and jelly sandwiches?" Cliff asked, he was planted in front of Amy and blocking her view. "And a cranberry juice?"

While Daniel was busy opening the backpack, Cliff tried to sit. He almost landed on top of both her and Daniel.

"Oh, that sounds good. And while you're in there, get my CD player, we could use some Janet Jackson up here," Amy requested and moved over a few inches to let Cliff sit in between them so he wasn't right on top of them.

Daniel pulled out the CD player first, handing it across Cliff and over to Amy. He then started digging around for the sandwiches. They ended up being squashed fairly thoroughly with little paw prints. They were still edible though.

Amy laid back to eat her sandwich, and Daniel moved his backpack behind Cliff and laid back as well so he could be next to her and so Cliff couldn't get in between them again. They enjoyed staring up at the clouds passing by while eating the afternoon meal.

"Delicious!" she said and went to put the plastic bags they had used away in his backpack. "What's this?" she asked, pulling out a piece of paper.

"Oh, a poem I wrote for you in a letter I was going to send, want to read it?" Daniel had been excited to send her the next letter and brought the poem thinking it would make a perfect spot up on the mountain to see her reaction. "I had a dream about you and it inspired me."

"You dream about me?" she said, coyly, smiling and unfolding the paper. She had to set Mimi down to read it.

"Let me see that!" Cliff demanded, snatching the letter from Amy. "Daniel never said he had a dream about you. I'm the one who has dreams about you."

"What, you have dreams about Amy?" Daniel asked, perturbed at both the idea and him snatching the letter before Amy could read it. Then he remembered the first time they met and Cliff's ludicrous GI Joe dream and said, "Oh yeah, never mind."

"Never mind what?" she asked.

"Right before we first met you, Cliff dreamt about you and then thought you were a thief." Daniel said.

"No, I didn't!" Cliff was keeping the letter out of reach of both Amy and Daniel, who were trying to snag it back.

"How could you have a dream about me before you met me?"

"Exactly, I think he was just jealous because I had made a friend." Daniel explained.

"Miss Tinny said it was because you were important, but I don't think you are that important," Cliff remarked.

Amy looked at both boys and raised an eyebrow. "I'm flattered, but can you give me that back, I wasn't done reading it..." but as she reached for the letter the wind blew it out of Cliff's hands.

Mimi barked and went running for the paper, stumbling right over the edge of the cliff.

"No! Oh, No!" Amy was panic stricken.

There was a steep drop about 4 feet and the dog had landed on a tiny ledge with a thud and a sharp squeal that was heart wrenching. The three teenagers looked down to find the poor dog was still alive, miraculously.

"We have to get her!" Amy declared, climbing down before anyone could stop her.

"Wait, it's too dangerous!" Daniel was too late to get to her. She was already on the flimsy ledge and she had no gear on and no ropes attached. She'd just picked up the dog when the ledge fell out from beneath her feet. He reached for her hand and caught her in the nick of time.

"Help!" she screamed, clutching onto Mimi with one hand and desperately holding onto Daniel with the other. She would need both hands if she were to lift herself up. Daniel was barely holding onto her and unable to pull her up by one arm. "Help, please help!"

"I've got her," Cliff announced. "Get the dog." He took hold of Amy's arm so that Daniel could let go and maneuver for the pooch.

Daniel reached down and snagged her collar to jerk her up, freeing her from her frantic owner. She had been whining from the pain of her injuries. But, when she got into his arms, she started growling and biting and he almost lost his grip. He fell backwards trying to calm the crazed and wounded Chihuahua.

The terror in the little dog's eyes was nothing in comparison to what was about to happen; because the next thing he heard was a scream that would haunt him for the rest of his life.

Chapter 6

Blood is Thicker Than A lot of Things

Daniel sat straight up in his chair, he had fallen asleep studying again. He was dreaming of her: screaming, falling, reaching out to clutch a hand that wasn't there to take. The pain was as real as the day it happened.

His heart ached. He needed to see her again.

She was at the UCLA department of neurosurgery, the same place he got his PhD. The same place in which he now worked but in a different wing of their hospital. She had been in a coma for over ten years, and no one expected her to wake, her brain activity was less than 30%.

He could never give up, he had devoted his career to neuroscience and had left for LA as soon as he had gotten his residency at the best hospital he could find. He procured her a spot at the brain injury research center so he could be as close to her as possible.

They had surgically removed the injured and dead tissue a long time ago from the initial trauma, but she still wasn't waking. He was currently studying different electro-stimulus, or neuromodulation, approaches but didn't want to risk anymore damage and most of the work being done was high risk.

He heard a knock on his door, "Dr. Jahren? You're needed in the west wing. Charlie Abram may be speaking." The voice and knock came from one of his post-doctorate students who had been working the night shift.

"Thank you, I'll be right there," he was still in a half-awake daze as he pulled his white coat on over his scrubs. He was about to leave when the office phone rang. The caller ID said it was his parents in Colorado.

"Hello?" Daniel answered softly, voice still not fully awake.

"Hi, honey, it's your mom. We need you to come home. Your brother has gotten worse, we need your help," the voice on the other end of the line was strained. It sounded like she'd been crying.

"What happened?" Daniel couldn't help the tone of anger and annoyance creeping into his voice. He knew what probably happened, what he feared Cliff had finally done.

"I will tell you more when you get here. How soon can you make it?" The desperation in her voice was barely masked.

"I'll be on the first flight I can book."

"Okay, honey, see you soon," she hung up before he could ask her anything else. He almost didn't want to ask anyway. What had Cliff done now?

Daniel knew it had to be serious if his mother was calling, she never called. He talked to Tsintah, his old nanny, more than he talked to her. He rarely talked to his father or his brother either, they were consumed with treating Cliff's muscular dystrophy, despite his rapid decrease in functionality and their constant failures. They resented that Daniel didn't help and never understood why he devoted his life's work to helping people he didn't even know over his own family.

But, he loved Amy. He had fallen in love with her at 10 years old and didn't realize it until he thought he lost her forever after the accident. He would find a way to wake her up; at least, that is what he had been telling himself for over a decade. So many years. It was getting harder and harder to admit he might never bring her back.

In the meantime, he enjoyed helping the patients that he could, and training the next generation of doctors on the most advanced neurological developments on the planet.

Each patient was unique, and as he helped them he felt he was one step closer to seeing Amy open her eyes and smile. For instance, the patient who was waiting for him, Charlie, had a traumatic brain injury that was inoperable and resulted from a chronic subdural hematoma that had gone unnoticed for weeks. Daniel was trying direct current pulses to activate some of the dead brain tissue. Specifically, he was hooking up electrodes to the left temporal lobe and shocking Charlie regularly in order to help him regain his speech and left side of the body functionality.

Before he could call the travel agency and book his emergency ticket, he had to follow up with Charlie and ... he needed to see Amy. More importantly, he had to coordinate treatment for the both of them, and several other patients, while he was gone. He pulled out his BlackBerry, scrolled through his contacts. He would be calling in favors all night. It was a lot of trouble. If Cliff isn't dying, I'm going to kill him! he thought, and then immediately felt pangs of guilt and shame. What if he was dying? He forcibly put the thought out of his mind but added urgency to his efforts in making arrangements.

~ ~ ~

The taxi pulled up to the stone and cedar, single-story house he had called home for so many years. The cool air of the night, chirping of crickets, and howls of a distant coyote pack were all there was to greet him when he stepped out of the cab and onto the moonlit gravel entryway. The sights, smell of iron laden dust, and sounds brought back memories of a time of innocence he had suppressed for so long. How many years had it been? Eight?

Coughing down the rush of emotion entering his throat, he thanked and paid the cab driver. He forced himself to take a step towards his old home. An ever-increasing sense of foreboding crept into the pit of his stomach with every step towards the dark doorway shrouded with shadows in the dead of the night. By the time he reached his hand out to knock on the door, his heart had already begun to skip beats. It didn't help that the door opened silently before his hand even touched it, without anyone on the other side. The anxiety and confusion were only somewhat alleviated when he noticed a video camera above the door. His heart was still thudding in his chest, but he managed to smile and wave at the camera before pulling his luggage into the darkness within.

Less than a second after he closed the door behind him, the lights in the hallways came on. The kitchen and living room that had been full of gadgets and gizmos he and his brother tinkered with as children were now bare and cleared of any sign of the unique minds that dwelled in the house's hidden lower regions. A soft light came on automatically as he entered the kitchen and he noticed a note on the counter.

"You know the code, porcelain," Daniel read aloud and flipped the paper around looking for more information. Porcelain?

He looked around the room, taking in all the changes and yawning from the jetlag. Where were his parents? he wondered. It was just like his family to greet him with riddles instead of hugs.

He was about to head towards the den when his BlackBerry buzzed with a page that read 'LAB7.' Oh, so they were in lab 7. Was porcelain the lab door code somehow? Usually the code was alphanumeric. It was then that he noticed there were dishes in the sink. There were never dishes in the sink. It was one of his father's pet peeves. One of the dishes was a porcelain tea cup. His parents didn't drink tea, they drank only their 'special' coffee. On the bottom of the cup there were tiny letters 'R33L28R4.' Now that was about right for a door code. Why the added security?

He pulled on the third book (Hansel and Gretel) in the hallway bookshelf next to the old cuckoo clock that his father had brought from his hometown in Bavaria. The clock and bookshelf were some of the few things that remained in the now almost barren house. Although it was barren, it was neatly decorated in minimalist cream tones that made it look like the cover of a magazine. An elevator door opened up where the bookshelf had been and he pressed the B3 button to descend into the mountain. There used to only be a staircase and tunnel behind the bookshelf, they had installed another nice upgrade.

Laboratory 7 was their most secure lab, located furthest into the mountain than any other lab, at least it was when he was here last. Who knows what they had installed since. It took him ten minutes of walking through the tunnel to get to the steel door. Again, his head was filled with foreboding accentuated with a heartbeat that was pounding hard in his chest as he turned the dial of the combination lock on the door. Right twice to 33, left to 28 and then right again, stopping on 4.

His mother's dark grey-blue eyes were bloodshot and filled with tears as she flung her arms around his neck as soon as he entered the room. "I'm so glad you are here, honey. You're our only hope," she said softly in his ear between choking on tears.

He had never seen his mother cry. She was the most stubborn, outrageously positive person he had ever met in his entire life. She made the best of every situation and fought every obstacle in her life with a smile and a laugh. It was staggering.

He held her tighter as the tears threatened to burst from his eyes, he couldn't stand to see her this way. When he pulled himself together he gripped her shoulders with both hands, pushing her far enough away to look her dead in the eyes and say, "What can I do? What has he done?"

"The reaction has spread, it has gotten to his thighs, it's killing him!" she screeched, causing a round of screeching in the room. Monkeys screeching, and loud. It was only then that Daniel took a look at his surroundings.

There were cages of monkeys, rats and mice lined against the wall to the right, and to his left was a chemical mixing room and clean room. Straight ahead, behind his mother, was a figure lying on a bed and surrounded by plastic sheeting separating him from the rest of the room. His father sat in full bio-hazard gear beside him, his head down and shoulders slumped.

"I'll suit up," he said, not taking his eyes off his father and brother. "What are we dealing with, virus or bacteria?"

"It is a new virus, Tribus, that Cliff formulated himself. He'd been working with carbon nanotubes and managed to create a virus that turns cells into mini carbon factories; initiating and spreading monolayers through surrounding tissues," she was saying all of this while walking over to one of the monkey cages that had a large polycarbonate wall. It was quarantined from the rest of the primates. "It proved very effective for Artie here, we had to put him in a special cage after he ripped open the last two. His muscle density has tripled and his strength has more than quadrupled since he had injections of Tribus in each major muscle group."

"What is that black streaking along his legs?" Daniel asked, noticing vein-like black marks along Artie's muscles visible even through the fur.

"Some of the carbon escapes and goes into the veins and surrounding skin, embedding itself like a tattoo," she replied. "It's a purely aesthetic side effect, and nothing compared to the gains in muscle strength. Cliff was so excited, he..."

"What happened?" Daniel demanded.

She swallowed hard. "He injected himself yesterday, in both calves. I told him not to, but he didn't listen. I wanted him to test directly on human tissue samples first, but he couldn't wait. Just like his father, never planning for when things go wrong. Did you know they wouldn't even quarantine any of this at first, I had to insist!"

"I can believe it. Do we know if the virus is contagious? How does it spread?"

"For now, the virus must be inserted into the tissue directly, but you know how viruses can evolve. These two think they are masters of everything. If he had just listened to me..."

"Mother, what can I do?" Daniel interrupted, trying to pull her back to the situation at hand.

"The damage is ... irreversible. I'm afraid if we don't remove the injured areas soon, he will die," she couldn't even look in the direction of her son as she spoke. "We have everything you need. He's on 30 mg of morphine already and 100 mcg of Propofol. We have methohexital ready too ... Please, I can't lose him!"

"You want me to remove his legs?" Even though everyone in the room was technically a doctor, he was the only one who had ever performed surgery on a living being.

She nodded.

"I brought a few things myself. Deep down I knew something like this would happen, eventually. He has always been reckless," Daniel said scornfully while

94

pulling out his gear and donning latex gloves. His glanced over to see his strong, easy going and proud mother sobbing so hard that she was hiccupping.

"I will help him. It will be over and done before you know it. Maybe this will teach him to listen to reason, and his mother, for a change," he said while holding her close for a hug, rubbing his hand up and down on her back to try and comfort her. "Hold your breath and then have drink, it will clear up those hiccups. At least, that is what my mother always told me," his effort at cheering her up was rewarded with a faint smile, interrupted only by more hiccups and tears.

"Get a drink," he said sternly and moved quickly towards his brother's bedside, sliding on a mask as he marched forward. He needed steady hands – that took a clear mind right now. And focus. Focus on the task at hand. He took a deep breath then walked through the opening in the plastic tarp hanging from the ceiling.

His father promptly stepped aside and pulled the blanket back to show Daniel the extent of the damage. Both legs were black as charcoal, with bulging dark veins and skin that was like petrified wood from his calves up to almost mid-thigh. Cliff was conscious, but he was glaring at the ceiling with a blank stare and set jaw. Daniel knew Cliff didn't want to hear 'I told you so' but expected exactly that from his older brother.

"We'll have to cut from here to start," Daniel pointed to the middle of Cliff's thigh, an inch above the damaged area. "We'll place the tourniquet here. You know what all these are," he showed the clamps and tools he had brought, Martin nodded. "Where is the blood?"

"I have four pints of o- available, will that be enough?" Martin asked.

"It'll have to be," Daniel replied, it might not be enough. Anything could go wrong.

"Put me out, now. I don't want to hear this, I don't want to know. Please," Cliff begged. His father immediately went to the drip and turned up the Propofol and started prepping the barbiturate. He had Cliff out in less than 2 minutes while Daniel laid out and organized the equipment.

After placing the tourniquet on the right leg, they began cutting the skin where they would peel it back for post operation wrapping of the femur stub. They clamped the peeled flesh just below the tourniquet. Martin lifted the leg and found that on the back side the dark streaks had begun to move closer to the area they were cutting and the muscle beneath was beginning to blacken.

"Will it be sufficient to cut here?" Martin asked.

"We're cutting up here, we just need the skin in that area."

"Was zur Hölle?!?" he heard his father exclaim, realizing how high his son had planned to cut. They were cutting almost to the tourniquet, which was just below the groin. Cliff would lose both entire legs.

Daniel began digging his fingers into and pulling the muscles back to clamp down the major arteries. "Hand me another clamp," he said, reaching a bloody hand up while concentrating on stabilizing a delicate vein.

When he was done clamping, he pointed to the groin area and said, "I will need you to ensure that stays out of the way of sharp objects as we proceed. If a clamp slips, or a tendon pops, muscles could spasm and he could jerk around. I am pretty sure you want grandchildren and he will never forgive either of us if we screw up. Also, keep a close eye on his vitals and the drip. Let me know if anything changes and if we start running low on meds. Are you ready?"

Martin nodded, somberly.

He could hear his mother cry out from across the room as he turned on the electric blade. All the animals in the cages cried out with her. Daniel put it all out of his mind, he had to focus.

Over an hour later, they were done. All four pints of blood were needed, but both legs were successfully removed. It hadn't been easy, he'd even had to chase a disappearing tendon in the left leg. But, Cliff was now stabilized and on a saline drip, his morphine at 60 mg.

His mother had gotten coffee, and she'd stopped crying and hiccupping. She was at a lab counter across from his father who sat quietly sipping coffee too. He was jotting down the day's events in a scientific journal with one hand while holding her hand with the other.

Daniel stood looking at the monkeys in their cages; they never had monkeys when he was a kid. "I bet you wish you were swinging from a tree, Lulu, don't you?" he said to the female, dark eyed, black and white capuchin in the cage in front of him labeled 'Lulu.' She showed her teeth by pulling her lips back and biting the cage bar, then she held onto the bars with all fours and bounced up and down. "Yeah, me too. I always did love trees."

"Thank you, son," Martin said, one hand resting on Daniel's shoulder. He had come to stand next to him in front of the monkeys. "You did amazing work."

"Thank you, I..." Daniel started to say but found himself choking on his words. He wanted to scream, "it should never have come to this!" but there was no point. His father had always encouraged Cliff to push barriers and take risks. It was his fault and he knew it.

"You like the monkeys? They are proving to be particularly useful. We should have had them years ago."

"Sure, is that why there is added security? Did you steal these from a zoo?"

"Steal? You know we would never steal anything."

"Just do illegal experiments involving deadly viruses and bacteria. Now on, what I suspect, are illegally acquired primates."

"Not everything that is illegal should be. The rules set in place are for profits by the pharmaceutical industry. The bureaucracy in this country is rooted in greed, at the cost of human lives."

"Oh? Is that what you told Cliff? Before you allowed him to inject a highly experimental drug into his own body?"

"Allowed him? He didn't even ask me what I thought ... I ... your mother..." Martin peered over at Beth for help, but she looked away.

Daniel didn't even want to look at his father, who was holding his head down staring at his feet. Lulu started jumping up and down, and wailing.

"The added security isn't for the primates and it isn't to hide illegal work. It is due to the threats we've been getting from the local tribes. Didn't Tsintah tell you?" Martin said as he reached his hand in to comfort Lulu.

"No, what threats?" Daniel couldn't believe Miss Tinny wouldn't tell him something like that.

"Your mother has been stalwart at the city council for development of her business, and we have been expanding in the tunnels. We needed more lab space. Some of the natives are unappreciative of what we are doing with the land. We had to fire Tsintah, we caught her trying to get into the labs."

"No wonder she never mentioned it. Why didn't you tell me?"

"The phone lines may be tapped. We are contemplating installing a fiber optic system throughout and encrypting all communication. We are not sure who we can trust right now."

"If they only knew what else you were doing here..."

"We are being safe..."

"Oh, you are?!? Do you call that safe?" Daniel turned his back to the monkeys and was pointing at his brother.

"It is crucial work ... we are so close to a cure for so many things ... We have not had an incident in all these years, and your brother was so hopeful."

"I know father, I know."

"How long will you stay," Martin asked and Daniel knew what he was going to ask next. He wanted him there, to help with his research; his all-consuming search for a cure for cancer and a cure for MD.

"No longer than I need to in order to make sure he recovers well. Hopefully just a few days. I have patients that need me in LA and I have..."

"She is never going to wake up Daniel, give-up!"

"Would I ask you to give-up on your research? Have you found a cure for cancer? For MD? Simply because I haven't found a way to wake her from a coma yet, doesn't mean she won't wake up."

"My research has already helped millions of people's lives and will save billions of lives once I find a cure. Cancer kills 22% of the population and just about everyone on my side of the family. She is just one girl."

"I help many people, one at a time. It is my life."

"Schwachsinn! What kind of life is that? You have no friends, no girlfriend. You don't have a pet ... I suspect that you do not even have a plant!"

Daniel knew he was right. He had inherited his dad's obsessive nature, and his drive to want to solve the impossible. Unlike his father, he didn't have a woman in his life that did what his mother did – pull him out of the lab and into the world. He loved a girl who was in a coma. He really did have no life.

"I know a marvelous young woman I met at a conference, she would be perfect for you, honey," his mother said as she came around to his other side. He was now cornered by both parents, with monkeys at his back. That heart pounding feeling of dread he felt earlier was returning. She continued with, "I was thinking about hiring her to run my new department, researching and perfecting bat guano for a new cosmetic line. We've finally found a bat cave and I want to make use of it."

"You finally found a bat cave, huh? You're in a bat cave, you're both batty!" Daniel exclaimed. "Look" he pointed to his sleeping brother. "Will you never learn?"

"He made that choice himself, and he paid the price." Martin declared.

"Will he stop?!?" Daniel shouted. "Will he ever stop?!?"

"Yes," a faint cry came from the bed. All three standing turned at once, in unison, to face the now awake Cliff. "Daniel ...if you had been here ... I know you ... I know you would have stopped me ... I need you."

Daniel didn't know what to say, there were tears forming in his eyes and he felt pressure in his throat rising up to choke him as his breath was caught in his chest. He knew it was true, deep down, he knew he was the only one his brother ever listened to ... and if he had been here ... maybe his brother would still have his legs.

"Okay ..." Daniel could hear his mother gasp at the simple but poignant word. He glanced over at his father, who was smiling proudly. "I will need to go ... to make arrangements..." he couldn't let himself think about what this meant for Amy. He was sandwiched again by both parents, only this time with hugs.

With the two of them this close he couldn't help but notice that they appeared as if they hadn't aged a day since the last time he saw them. It had been 8 years. Some signs of aging should be present. Not to mention, he couldn't quite tell how old they were. From the lack of wrinkles around their eyes to the tightness of their skin, they could both pass for early 30's. But, they were technically in their late fifties. Daniel had been in LA long enough to spot plastic surgery, so he knew there could only be one explanation.

"I have one condition," he said and his parents looked at each other, concern flashing between their eyes. "We can't have any secrets between us, understood?"

"Of course, son." Martin insisted, and Beth nodded in agreement.

"We would never keep a secret from you," she said.

"No secrets? Okay, then you have to tell me what is in that coffee."

Chapter 7

Microchips and Membranes in Men's Brains

Susan Aldean spent the last three years doing nothing but writing letters to universities and institutions across the world. She was sick of writing and even more sick of waiting on responses. On a whim, she decided she was going to walk right into an office today, to talk to one of the local doctors who had not given her an answer. Maybe she could convince him if she was face-to-face. It was worth a try.

Dr. Jared Daniels was a professor in neurology at UCLA and specialized in Parkinson's disease and other disorders of the brain that her invention would be perfect to treat. She'd sent him an envelope containing a disc that had all the data on the successful tests her team had conducted on mice. It included photo copies of the accolades her ICMod had gotten in Scientific America, and a proposal letter explaining she needed human test subjects that he could provide.

Bravery was the name of the game today. She was willing to brave the two-hour stop-and-go traffic through LA, using it as an opportunity to practice her elevator pitch, over and over. She was willing to brave the Santa Ana's almost blowing her briefcase out of her hand as she struggled against the wind to close her car door in the parking lot of the medical center. She was willing to brave anything to have a chance to convince someone her research was worthwhile.

"I'm looking for Dr. Daniel Jared," she said to the woman in scrubs behind the counter at the neurology department.

"You mean Dr. Daniel Jarhen?" the middle-aged, dark-red haired woman replied with a quizzical brow while continuing her activities of marking-off papers and sorting folders.

Susan was taken aback, that didn't sound right. Had she said the wrong name? She was a bit dyslexic and English was not her first language. She was far more comfortable in her native French.

Before Susan could answer her back, the woman behind the counter pointed to the man walking in from the elevators down the hall and said, "You're in luck, there he is right now. Really good timing, he's been out for over a week with a family emergency." She held her hand over her mouth then continued, "Oh, I shouldn't have told you that!" She leaned over the counter and whispered, "Don't tell him I said anything."

"Hi Nancy, how are you doing this morning?" The male doctor who had just come in from the elevators asked. Susan's first thought was that he appeared as if he could be a movie star. He was tall and had a broad, muscular build. Plus, he had full lips, a chiseled jaw and dreamy hazel eyes. He also looked young enough that she would have thought he was an intern.

"Fine. Just fine, Dr. Jahren," replied the women in scrubs. "This lovely young lady is here to see you."

"Hi, I'm Dr. Susan Aldean from the ICModTech Research Group here in LA I've been writing to you for the last six months and I would like to discuss with you my research proposal," she said while shaking his hand firmly, to show confidence. Finally, it was time to use that elevator pitch she'd practiced, "I have an innovative, implantable microchip that can..."

"I've never heard of ICModTech, are you sure you sent your proposal to the right address? I typically send rejection or acceptance letters within ninety days of receiving them."

"I..." Susan began. Had her dyslexia struck again? She went to open her briefcase to check her copy of the letter. But, as she opened the right latch, the left latch flung open and all of her papers came flying out. She bent down to chase the pages, but her head struck against the young doctor's hard enough for her to see only stars. He must have bent down to pick up the papers at the same time. By the time she could see anything else, she saw that all of her papers were back in her briefcase and it was closed and on her lap. Did she black out?

"How are you feeling?" the young doctor asked as he handed her a cup of cold water. "You may have a concussion. Can you stand up?"

"I'm alright. I need to talk to you about my research..." she replied as she held onto her briefcase with both hands while Nancy and the doctor hoisted her up by each arm. She stood steady and said, "Thank you" as they released her to stand on her own. "I'd like to show you my proposal."

"You are persistent! I believe I can take a few minutes to hear you out. Come to my office," the doctor said with a smile. He was far too cute to be a doctor!

Susan sat down and couldn't help but notice the nameplate on the desk in front of her and then read it aloud, "Dr. Daniel Jahren." She knew that was definitely not right when she heard herself say it. She was pretty sure she needed a Jared Daniel. She might just die with embarrassment.

"You can call me Daniel. Please, let me see your research," he asked with an outreached hand.

Susan decided to hand him her papers even though she knew there would be the inevitable: "No, this is not at all something I'm interested in. Good day, maim." Her head was pounding, and she kept sipping the water as he shifted through her papers. She started to notice that she would take a sip every time he turned a page and then had to stop herself and tried to look around the room for a distraction.

The office was bare except for an impressive array of awards, diplomas and certificates on the wall. There were a few rocks, and oddly, a dream catcher, on his desk next to his computer and office phone. No family pictures. No girlfriend pictures. She checked his hand instinctively, no ring either. How can a guy this handsome and successful be single? What is wrong with him? He was probably married to his work, like her.

Nancy came in quietly and handed her an ice pack for her head. Susan thanked her and went back to staring at the office furniture and trying not to stare at the cute doctor.

"So, you have developed a promising implant to stimulate the dopaminergic neurons of the substantia nigra," he looked up and Susan nodded. "I am particularly interested in this part about 'improvement in motor response and overall brain activity' that you mention," he looked up again and Susan nodded again and he continued: "I have a patient, Charlie, that has been doing well with an electro-stimulation implant, but he continues to have significant motor loss in his left side. Could this device be altered to provide feedback to an electro-stimulation unit already installed?"

"Yes, of course. They have very similar modalities..."

"How soon can you have your equipment here and ready to go?" he interrupted briskly.

"Today! I can come back in an hour ...wait, maybe three depending on traffic." Susan couldn't believe her ears. She was going to be able to work on a real-live-human-test-subject for the very first time! She had waited so long! She jumped up and immediately had to sit right back down. Her head was pounding!

"Dr. Aldean, you have a concussion."

"You can call me Susan."

"Susan, you need to rest for today. If you are feeling better, come back tomorrow. I'll still be here. Take some Tylenol and rest, agreed?" he said gently. He shuffled her papers neatly back into the briefcase and securely set the latches.

"Thank you, I'll be back first thing tomorrow," she picked up her briefcase from his desk, getting up much slower this time. She was having trouble looking into his eyes and was feeling that same nervous feeling she always got when a cute guy was around. Great, I have a silly crush! She thought as she headed out the door, trying not to run.

~ ~ ~

Susan had spent the last two days in a lab at UCLA near Dr. Jahren's office. She was matching her implant with a rudimentary electro-stimulation device. Most of her time was spent writing the code needed to provide a feedback loop between the two and a mock-up to represent neurotransmitters. Apparently, Dr. hottie-Mc-Jahren (that's what she was calling him in her head anyway) wanted her to provide stimulus simultaneously at multiple locations and increase the implant output based on measured EEG activity in the left hemisphere of a brain trauma patient. It was a novel approach, and ambitious. Exactly the kind of work she thrived on. It wasn't the ideal patient trail she had planned for the ICMod technology, but it tested the limits enough to provide significant data for forthcoming applications. And, if all went well, it was patentable.

"Is the system configuration complete, Susan?" Daniel asked, handing her plain, black coffee from the break room in a Styrofoam cup. He was drinking coffee from his usual container; a dark grey thermos that had his name on it and "Do NOT Drink" in big, red, bold letters. He was serious about no one touching his coffee, though she doubted anyone would touch it considering how awful it smelled.

"Yes, I just ran my last test simulation. Thank you for the drink," she said, carefully sipped the piping hot beverage. He was leaning over her shoulder to look at her Compaq Presario screen, he could apparently read C from the way he was scanning the code. This was the closest he had ever been and she couldn't help but notice he smelled like shaving cream and burnt coffee beans.

"I think it would be best if you were near during the surgery." He was looking at her for a response to something ... did he just say he wanted her near?

"During surgery? Are you sure you want me in the room? I've showed you all you have to do is press the spacebar ... it's fairly straightforward." Her specialty was the microchip and software, and her doctorate was in electrical engineering, not medicine. So, she typically wasn't in the room when one of her teammates installed the implant onto a mouse. Also, it didn't help that her hands weren't that steady when dealing with such delicate matters. Plus, she was a bit accident prone in general. "Are you really sure?"

Daniel laughed, he was starting to get used to her and was well versed in the plethora of little accidents that she was prone to already. The amount of accidents was directly proportional to the level of her nervousness, and in this case, the handsomeness of the doctor she was working with.

"Okay, I'm ready then. Prep the patient!" she almost shouted as she picked up her laptop, knocking her Styrofoam cup down and off of the counter. Daniel must have anticipated the sudden movement and had the cup in hand before it spilled a drop. He was pretty good at averting her disasters.

"I should keep you around all the time," she said without thinking, then blushed at the thought of him around all-the-time. Oh God, did he think she was hitting on him? She probably sounded psychotic wanting him around all the time, like Misery or something. Oh God, did he think she was going to be like Kathy Bates' character? "I didn't mean it like that I..."

"That's okay, I know what you meant," he interrupted, chuckling to himself.

He definitely thought she was flirting. That was a good thing, right? She was terrible at flirting, at least on purpose.

They first headed into the patient's, Charlie Abram's, room and began questioning him to make sure he understood the procedure and risks. He had limited speaking ability but was still able to verbally agree and sign a disclosure notice for the experimental procedure.

Susan set up her laptop and equipment in the operating room and waited for Daniel's team to prep the Charlie and initiating the gory stuff. There would be three other doctors and support staff involved, and they needed to go over the operation together before starting. She would basically be there to witness and ensure the feedback loops were operating before the implant went into his brain and then run a brief calibration program. Charlie would be under conscious sedation, with localized anesthesia, so they could get his feedback.

While the other doctors were in the hallway talking procedure, she looked around the room for anything she could trip over or knock off of something. She made sure any and all objects were far away from where she would be standing.

Once everything began, the whole process went by quickly and smoothly. The interface functioned well with the electro-stimulus device previously installed. The implant seated in the desirable spot of the cerebral cortex without damaging the surrounding tissue. All thanks to the remarkably steady hands of Dr. Jahren. It couldn't have gone better.

After Charlie was moved to recovery, Susan found herself standing outside the operation room door, in a daze. They did it! They actually did it!

"I'm impressed," Daniel said as he was washing up. "That went nicer than I thought."

"You're impressed with me? You're the one that just cut into a human being and..."

"Can you take a compliment?" he asked, and held her gaze with his gold-flecked hazel eyes that she found so mesmerizing...

"Humm ...?" she finally asked, not realizing she had spaced out, staring into his eyes.

He laughed. At least he found her quarks funny. Some people thought she was annoying when she was constantly knocking things over and spacing out. She even found herself annoying.

"Are you hungry?" he asked. "What are you doing for dinner?"

"I'm ... ummm ..." What was she doing for dinner? She hadn't even thought about what she would do after the surgery, except maybe lurk around Daniel's lab until she could run her full program on the patient.

Wait, was he asking her on a date?

"Do you like BJ's?" he inquired.

"Do I like WHAT?" she was scandalized at what he was suggesting.

"There's a BJ's Brewhouse right around the corner, it's one of my favorite restaurants. We should celebrate your achievement today. I'll even buy you a Pizookie." He had a confused look that spoke volumes about his innocence.

Susan was blushing red as a beat, but managed to get out, "What's a Pizookie?"

"It's a hot and gooey cookie topped with ice cream, delicious!" Daniel replied. "Let's go."

They managed to get to the restaurant alive and in one piece, but only barely. Walking a few blocks should not be a life-threatening fiasco. But, with how distracted she was today, mishaps were bound to happen.

The first accident was on the stairway leading down from the hospital. Susan turned around to talk while walking backwards, failing to realize there were stairs behind her until she almost went flying down them. Then, at the curb to cross the street, she tripped and almost fell right into traffic. Talking while walking was definitely not her best skill. She was merely trying to explain her fascination with Parkinson's disease and helping people like her uncle and Michael J. Fox. Both times Daniel saved her before she fell to what might have been her death.

"So, do you make a habit of saving the lives of falling women?" Susan asked as they were seated at their table in the restaurant. For some reason, that question had the opposite effect on Daniel she was hoping for – it produced a dark frown instead of a bright smile. He sat there, quietly, deep in thought.

"What did I say?" she asked, obviously she had hit a nerve. "I'm so sorry, are you ok?" Maybe he was finally sick of her bad jokes.

"I didn't ... I couldn't save her..." he said and glanced back in the direction of the hospital.

"Who couldn't you save?" She turned her head back towards the hospital and didn't see anyone. "One of your patients?"

"Amy ... she was my childhood friend ... we were climbing ... and she fell ... and..." he was speaking very slowly, controlling his words and taking deep breaths in-between as if it just happened.

Susan quickly realized the severity of her mistaken words. "Oh my god! I'm so sorry! I had no idea! I didn't know your friend died like that. I'm so sorry!"

"No, no, it's ok. She didn't die, she's in a coma. Here." He was staring in the direction of the hospital. "But, I couldn't save her ... I can't wake her up." He gazed at Susan with tears welling up in his eyes.

"Good Evening! My Name is Linda, and I will be your waitress. Can I start you off with something to drink?" said a bright and cheery, middle-aged woman with bleach-blonde hair pulled back in a bun and smile wrinkles three rows deep on either side of her mouth.

The cheerfulness of the waitress was in such stark contrast to the mood of both Daniel and Susan that they both took a breath at the same time. Then they focused all their attention on Linda.

"I'll have a beer," Susan said, "a Hefeweizen if you have it." She peered over at Daniel again and then asked the waitress, "Do you have something bigger than a pint?"

Linda shook her head.

Daniel cleared his throat, forced himself to smile and said, "May I have a water, no ice, with a lemon slice on the side? Please? Thank you, Linda."

"I'll be right back," the waitress said, scurrying off in the busy restaurant.

Normally, Susan would pick-on a guy that goes to a brewhouse and doesn't order a beer but she didn't feel like this was a good time. She was left not knowing what to say so she fiddled with her napkin nervously.

"I'm going to miss this place," he said, scanning the crowded restaurant with a half-smile.

"What do you mean?"

"I'm leaving in two weeks to go back home to Colorado. I've already put in my notice with the medical center. My brother is not well, and my parents need my help."

"Two weeks?!?" she exclaimed, dumbfounded. This was the first time he mentioned anything about leaving. "What about Charlie? We've only begun, what will..."

"The staff all know, and he will be in good hands."

Susan sat quietly stunned, completely speechless. They just met and he was going to leave her so soon. Leave her ... It all made sense, his research, his friend in a coma ... and he was finally giving up ... that's why it shook him so bad when he talked about her. He was going to leave his friend Amy too.

"What about your childhood friend Amy, in the coma? Are you leaving her here?" She wanted to add a "too" on the end of that question, but she bit her tongue.

"Yes. She has been in a coma for over 10 years, with limited brain activity. I can no longer waist my life hoping she will wake-up."

"But, the implant ... when I was doing my patent research I stumbled across another recent implant patent used for deep brain stimulation. It was specifically designed to wake people from comas ... they were stimulating the vagus nerve directly with various pulsed frequencies ... Is that something you've tried?"

"The vagus nerve, that is odd. I've looked into pulsed frequencies. But, no, we haven't tried them. It is all very new, very risky. I don't want to hurt her. I'm not going to try something on her that hasn't been well tested on others."

"But, you are willing to hurt Charlie? To take a risk on Charlie? The ICModTech implant can be easily adjusted to emit similar frequencies to the patent I saw ... if the tests go well with him, would you be willing to help Amy?"

"What do you mean, you can easily adjust the frequencies? I have only tried DC on my patients ... isn't your implant DC based?"

"No. My paper clearly states that it produces a time-varying electric field through electromagnetic induction."

"Ah..." Daniel said, he looked a bit embarrassed and Susan got the impression he wasn't as familiar with electrons and neutrons as he was with electrodes and neurons. "I think I was confused when I read 'increase the levels of dopamine in the brain through direct neuron stimulation' and assumed that meant direct current like the devices we are having so much success with presently."

"I did hit you in the head right before you read my research proposal."

"Yes, you did," he chuckled. "Or I hit you? I think it was a mutual bashing. Though, I think you got the brunt of it because you were out cold for a few minutes and ended up with a concussion."

"Ouch, was I? Wow, all I remember was seeing stars. Come to think of it, you didn't even get a bruise, you must be very hard headed!"

The waitress came back with the drinks, and asked, "Are you ready to order?"

Neither of them had even looked at the menu. A burger with a beer at a brewhouse was probably a safe bet, "I'll have a cheeseburger and fries," Susan said.

"May I have a steak, medium rare, and a side salad. Please," Daniel replied with a less forced smile this time and handed the waitress both menus. "Thank you, ma'am."

"Coming right up," Linda's big smile was accentuated with a golden-brown lipstick that she must have been trying to match with the brown scrunchie in her hair.

"So polite, that is a rare trait in a man these days," Susan pointed out.

"It must be my country upbringing," said Daniel. "I grew up in a small town. By the way, where are you from? I couldn't help but notice an accent. I would say French but it almost sounds Spanish."

"I'm from Toulouse, in the south of France. So, you were very close."

"Oui? J'ai toujours voulu aller en France!"

"Tu parle français? C'est encore plus rare que d'avoir des manières pour un Américain."

"Yes, well ... I speak several languages, but most Americans feel it is rude to not speak English all the time, especially in public." He scanned the room pointedly – they had already gotten a few glares as they spoke.

"Well, maybe you should go to France. I could show you some fantastic restaurants in Toulouse where they love it if you speak French." Susan couldn't believe she had said that. Oh, I just met you, cute doctor, let me take you on a trip to Europe!

"I'm sure you could. I don't think I'll have much time for site seeing anytime soon though. I need to go home and help my family in Colorado."

There it was again, that mention of leaving that left a pit in Susan's stomach and made her mouth dry. She took another sip of her beer, a gulp really. Where did half of it go? Maybe it was the beer getting to her brain already, be she realized she couldn't let him leave.

"What about Amy? What about trying the ICModTech implant on her? Are you going to leave her here and let the other doctors work on her? Or, do you not want to work with me anymore?" Okay, that last part was definitely the beer talking, she needed to slow down!

"You're incredible truly. Somewhat accident prone, but incredible. Honestly, I mostly decided to work with you because I thought that at least if Charlie doesn't get his motor skills back, he will still be much happier. He has been fairly moody and depressed, and increasing his dopamine levels before I leave made me feel like I was giving him a nice going-away present."

"So, you are going to leave me here to wake up Amy, without you?" There was a look in Daniel's eyes, like a fire had been lit. It let Susan know she was right to guess Amy was the bait she needed to keep Daniel from heading home.

"Do you actually think it will work? We have to make sure that Charlie is ok, and responds well ... but, do you actually think it will work?"

"I would bet on it," Susan replied. Now all she had to do was figure out how to get her ICMod to wake someone up from a coma, and she had less than two weeks to do it or the dreamboat of a man sitting across from her was going to be gone for good.

Chapter 8

Oh Brother, Where Art Thou

Cliff dreamt he was flying up into a lavender sunset, with rockets for legs. Blue fire issued from his metal appendages, and he shot pulsed beams from his hands that created circular clouds radiating for miles, getting bigger and bigger as they dissipated.

He laughed as a giant eagle landed on his left shoulder, hanging on for the ride. He spun in circles to see if the bird would get dizzy and fall off. But it hung on easily, looking down at him calmly. When he stopped spinning, the bird flew out in front of him, leading him forward.

Cliff followed the giant, white faced, bald eagle with rainbow glimmering wings until it landed on a juniper brush jutting out from a red rocky mountain cliff. He immediately recognized the cliff when he looked down from it to see a young girl hanging on and screaming. He fired a pulsed blast at the eagle for taking him to this place but the bird had already disappeared.

The whole scene began to change as his anger welled up. The rocks around his feet started to levitate and the cliff broke apart as he screamed. The horizon in every direction was filled with floating rocks and broken mountainside until it all exploded into red dust.

What was left after the dust cleared was Cliff standing over his brother, who was sleeping at his desk at work at the UCLA neurology department. There was an object on his desk, a small microchip that Cliff held up to inspect. As he examined it further, a woman's face appeared smiling. She held his hand and led him forward to a world of bright shimmering light ... there were ships in the air flying around metal skyscrapers layered with trees ...

Cliff awoke in pain. His legs were still healing and he was trying to ween himself off of morphine. He looked down at the stubs where his legs used to be. He felt complete apathy. Maybe he should feel something, but he just didn't. He had hated his legs for so many years. They failed him and continued to fail him more each day until they were useless objects relegating him to a wheelchair. Now they were gone.

He lifted himself up onto the wheelchair next to his bed and rolled over to the lab to go straight to work. He began the day by tweaking a prototype leg that his mother ordered from a scientist she'd met at some conference. It was nothing like what he wanted. What it could be. What he imagined.

He heard his father come into the room but didn't turn around. Martin had been tip-toeing around him for over a week now and the super vigilance was annoying.

"I'm sorry to be the bearer of bad news. I received a call from Daniel, he isn't coming as soon as he planned. It turns out he has come across a new implant that may help wake Amy up and he wants to attempt it before he returns home," Martin sat next to Cliff, who was still not facing his father.

Cliff threw the small screwdriver in his hand across the room and exclaimed, "Why can't he just give up on that white trash, good-for-nothing tramp?"

"I am unsure son, I believe he loves her..." Martin reached out and gathered the other tools on the table, slid them into a drawer and was eyeing Cliff warily. "How is the morphine withdrawal? It is reasonable to add more if your symptoms start to get too much for you, you needn't be ashamed..."

"I can handle it!" Cliff yelled. He rubbed his temples and leaned over his workbench, head in his hands. This wasn't his first outburst since the incident, and it wasn't like him to lose his temper so easily. At least, not since he was a child. He felt like a child and hated being treated like one. But, if he wanted to be treated better, he needed to start acting like an adult. Maybe his father was right, maybe it was just the morphine withdrawal?

"I'm sorry dad." He turned to face his father, who's concern was evident. He looked away, he hated seeing pity. "Perhaps I do need to add a bit more morphine for a few days." The truth was the pain didn't bother him, it made him feel alive. But the withdrawal symptoms were turning out to be less manageable than he thought. Moodiness, irritation and outbursts of rage.

"The average person would crumble under the weight of the struggles you've endured and you've managed to thrive your whole life. One accident does not define a person," Martin put his hand on Cliff's shoulder. "I'm proud to call you my son. When you have completed these prosthetics, they will be the most state-of-the-art legs anyone could have..."

"Yes, anyone. Much stronger," he said as he thought than rotting flesh legs, and continued with, "capable of so much more. I'm fitting a power unit here," Cliff pointed to an area close to the top where they would attach to his pelvis, then continued, "and I'm planning to install an electro-gel membrane kneecap. I haven't decided on the hydraulic system quite yet."

"Brilliant work! Is there anything I can do to help?" Martin sounded genuinely pleased with the progress Cliff had made in such little time, and while getting over major surgery. It might be because he thought that the cocktail of enzymes, anthocyanins, and phenols he had injected was working well. He had immune supporting cocktails down to an art; after all, they were his bread and butter.

"Yes, fix Tribus. If I'm going to be strong enough to wear these things," he held up the prosthetic leg, "I'm going to need that formulation to work."

"I am unsure if that is the most ..."

"I know it will work. I need it. Dad, please?" he turned to look his father dead in the eye, still holding onto the leg and trying not to lose his temper again.

"Okay, son, but we need to initiate testing on human tissue, and thoroughly vet the stability. It may take a while to ..."

"Of course," Cliff interrupted, turning back to his work and pulling out a screwdriver from the drawer his father had slid all the tools into. He didn't want to hear it was going to take a while. Focusing on his work would help distract him from the set-backs.

"Well, we both have work to do it seems. I will get started." He patted Cliff on the back and then said: "I'm proud of you, son. I hope you know that, no matter what happens ... I love you."

Cliff hardly ever heard his father say he loved him. He looked up to see pride mixed with pain in his father's eyes, and a tinge of pity that was like a razor blade slowly going across a glass beaker in his mind. But, he managed to smile and say, "Thanks dad, I love you too."

Cliff had so many ideas of what he could do with cybernetic legs, but he needed his brother's knowledge of neuroscience. He didn't just want a prosthetic, he wanted legs that responded to his mind like they were his own. He knew that with his brother's help they could make exactly what he needed. There were universities all over the world already working on it, and if they could do it, so could he!

Dammit, why couldn't Daniel get over Amy! Daniel knew Cliff needed him, yet he was still wasting his time with her. What could he possibly be working on that could wake her up from a coma that she had been in for over a decade?

Wait, the dream he had last night ... it was already fading, but ... there was something ... he had had a dream of her ... and a microchip ... He learned a long time ago to pay attention to his dreams. Especially when he had a dream as vivid as the one he had last night. It always meant something important was right around the corner.

What if Daniel did wake her up? What would she say to him? Cliff quickly went online to buy a plane ticket, he needed to be there and make sure she didn't wake up!

~ ~ ~

This wasn't the first time Cliff was in public in a wheelchair, nor the first time he was in LA. But, it was the first time he was in a wheelchair in LA with no legs, and the looks of sympathy coupled with averted glances were driving him insane with rage. He bit his lip and continued on, ignoring as much as he could. By the time he and the cab driver (who was carrying all of Cliff's luggage) made it into his brother's office, he was humming a Buddhist mantra to stay calm.

"Cliff! What are you doing here? Is everything ok?" Daniel asked, getting up from behind his desk and rushing over to check on his legs as he wheeled himself into the room.

Cliff had to shoo him off, waving his hand away and then saying, "I'm fine. I'm fine. I heard you were staying here to wake that ... Amy. And, I just couldn't wait. I wanted you to see what I was working on and I knew you could help me."

Cliff motioned to the tall man in black, standing behind him holding several large suitcases and said, "Randall, you can leave those here, thank you."

"You never were very patient, little brother. What have you brought for me?" Daniel asked, curiosity piqued at the luggage being set down in the room and no longer focusing on Cliff's legs.

"Open that suitcase and see for yourself."

When Daniel unzipped and lifted the top, his eyes went wide and he pulled-out a large object. "Wow, and it's so light! What did you use?"

"I bought a prototype from a German manufacturer and re-designed it in carbon fiber. I used electro-gel for the kneecap and titanium for the hydraulic tubing. I altered the feet with my spring-loaded design I already had for my crutches."

"What is this area for? Is that a power supply? What does it power?"

"I was hoping you would tell me, for now it only powers some of the hydraulics ... but what I want is for those legs to feel like my own. I want them to work like my legs..."

"Cliff, I'm not sure that is possible..."

"It is possible! I've seen it. Look at those papers, there are studies. And all over the world..."

"But Cliff, I have never done anything like this before..."

"You can do anything you put your mind to Daniel. If you choose to use your mind for something useful like this."

Daniel was holding up the leg in one hand and the papers in the other, looking at the two. Cliff could see his mind racing, getting excited – he would solve this problem. Daniel could never back down from solving a problem.

"Wow, what is that?" said a soft, female voice with a slight foreign accent from behind Cliff's head. As she walked in front of him to reach out and take the leg from Daniel, Cliff had to catch his breath. He recognized her, from his dream ... and she was even more lovely in person. Soft brown hair, cut to her chin and doe brown eyes. She was the one with the microchip.

"Dr. Susan Aldean, meet my brother Cliff," Daniel said. Just as he said that it looked like she was noticing someone else was in the room. She turned backwards to look at Cliff, at the same time as bending to sit down on the corner of the desk, and also reaching out to shake Cliff's hand. It must have been a bit too much to do at once because she missed the desk and then spun around to try and catch herself. She realized she still had the leg in her hand and tossed it upwards so she could hold onto the corner of the desk.

This theatrical folly appeared as if it was normal to Daniel. He not only caught the leg mid-air, but also caught Susan within an inch of her face smacking right into the corner of the desk.

"Thanks, Daniel. Again. I'm sorry." She was smiling up at him and he was grinning down at her and he had his arm wrapped around her waist.

Cliff had to clear his throat to break the tension and let them know he was still in the room.

"Sorry, Cliff was it? Wow, good looks run in the family. It's a pleasure to meet you," she said, not even noticing the wheelchair or his legs.

Cliff was flattered. He wasn't used to compliments. He'd only had a few his whole life and only when he would go down to the tavern for a drink to get away and try to be normal for a day ... and mostly from drunken tavern whores that he wasn't at all interested in hearing compliment him.

"Cliff was just here to get my help with this prosthetic he designed," Daniel said.

"You designed this? It's amazing. Genius is another trait that runs in the family it seems." She smiled at

Cliff and he felt butterflies in his stomach. She had that petite librarian look that he always found sexy, and those little pointy glasses she had on just added to the effect. "What is the power supply for?"

"It is for the neural-interface network that Daniel is going to design for me," Cliff was staring Daniel in the eye and not breaking eye contact. He knew he needed to press him to keep him on track.

"I see. I could get this battery much smaller. And you'll need electrodes that interface directly with the nerve endings..."

"Susan, you don't want to help do you? Cliff will drag you off to Colorado if you keep talking like that and I need you here to alter the ICMod," Daniel said, half playfully, half seriously.

"ICMod, is that a microchip?" Cliff asked. This Susan was turning out to live up to his dreams.

"Something like that. It is an implantable integrated circuit I designed to create pulsed signals deep in the brain, stimulating neurotransmitters. Particularly the ones responsible for dopamine production. I'm making alterations to attach it to the vagus nerve so that we can attempt to bring Daniel's friend Amy out of her coma," Susan replied while running her hands along the prosthetic leg and poking at the gel in the knee. "This is brilliant, by the way."

"Daniel, if you don't marry her, I will!" Cliff heard himself exclaim before he even knew he had the thought. That statement made everyone in the room blush and look around nervously. "Sorry, I'm still on a lot of pain medications from my recent surgery. I don't usually propose to women I just met, usually." He gave

Susan a wink, and she glanced over at Daniel, who was scowling at Cliff.

"Oh no, it's fine. I need to go get back to work. Daniel, I should be ready to run the full program on Charlie by 2:30 this afternoon, if I leave now anyway. It was nice meeting you Cliff!" she attempted to walk out of the room while saying all of that but only managed to trip over a suitcase and then catch herself on Cliff's wheelchair.

He held her hand so she could steady herself as she got up, and he couldn't help but notice how soft, delicate and warm to the touch her skin was. He also couldn't help but notice she wore heels. "You know, it would be easier to walk if you wore flats."

"You would think so, but no..." she whispered loudly, shaking her head. "Besides, I love heels, and I just wouldn't feel very French anymore without them."

"French? Parlez-vous français?" he asked.

"Bien sûr!" she replied.

"Yes, of course you would speak the language of love."

Both Cliff and Daniel watched as Susan exited the room. "Now that's the kind of girl Mom would want you to take home, Daniel," Cliff said when the door closed.

"What does that mean? As opposed to who?" Daniel stated indignantly.

"You know who," Cliff said with disdain. "Look what you've done. You've made me come all the why out here to beg you to help me. Do you know what kind of debacle I had to put up with at the airport? I couldn't bring any of the vials father made with me, TSA took them all. I sure hope he didn't put anything … you know … risky in them."

"Are you kidding me?" Daniel shouted, "Cliff, you're joking, right?"

"You wouldn't come to Colorado, so I had to come here."

They both sat in silence, staring each other down. Daniel broke the gaze first, his eyes sliding down towards Cliff's legs for a mini-second and then away quickly.

"I want to help you right now, Cliff. I do. But, I made a promise to myself, and to her, that I would do everything I could. If the tests go well with Charlie today, we'll start on Amy soon after. Since you're here, and if it takes Susan a while to configure the ICMod, while she does that I can help you with your prosthetics. Deal?"

"Deal," replied Cliff. "So, what is the 'deal' with you and Susan. Is she single? Are you two, umm, together?"

"No, no, no. We just met a few days ago. Why?" Daniel replied too rapidly, he could be so naïve when it came to women. So, she was available. Cliff felt relieved. She probably had no idea how obsessed his brother was with that girl Amy, but she soon would.

"Can I watch her run the program on, Charlie was it?" Cliff asked. "This ICMod microchip sounds interesting. I have more questions I would like to ask her."

"I bet you do." Daniel said, peering sideways at Cliff, eyes squinting.

~ ~ ~

"It feels like ... warmth emanating from the inside of my skull, and I feel ... good? It's hard to describe. But hey, I'm describing it! Wow! Don't I sound good!" Charlie Abram said not long after they began the program. He had wires coming out of the back of his shaved head, electrodes on both sides of his skull and down his neck and he had on an EEG head cap.

"Yeah Dad, but you look like a cyborg," his three-year-old son said, sitting on his mother's lap next to the patient's bed.

"Yeppy, Cyborg Chucky they are going to call me, mwarrrr!" Charlie exclaimed as he tickled his son's belly, leaving the kid squirming and giggling in his mother's arms.

"You do sound like yourself again, and look, you are using your left arm!" his wife said, overjoyed.

"We're going to step down the power now. We need to see what maintenance level we are going to have to keep to continue to see benefits," Susan adjusted the stimulation and continued stepping down the power levels and checking Charlie's response until he showed visible signs of deterioration in speech or movement.

"600 milliwatts, I can work with that," Susan said. "I'll have my contacts in Idaho generate a compatible power unit. If we're lucky, it will be here in less than a week. When we are done hooking that up we can remove most of the wiring and" she looked down at the three-year-old and smiled "he'll not look so much like a cyborg anymore." Charlie's son giggled when she said 'cyborg' as he apparently loved the word.

"You have friends in Idaho that can make an implantable, micro-sized power supply in under a week? That's impressive," said Cliff.

"It's a microchip manufacturer that has a research and development division working on novel product lines. I help them with fresh markets, they hook me up with some of their latest tech. And, because they already have all the manufacturing and production set up for solid-state devices, most of the hard part is already in place for fabricating the necessary components. This makes it easy for ICModTech to acquire one-offs for our wide-ranging uses. For instance, right now they are generating an integrated circuit for cell phones that can capture photographs to the same resolution as a 35 mm film camera."

"Who would want to use their phone to take pictures? I'm more interested in the power supply. You mentioned earlier that you could get me a better power supply for the prosthetic. Is it from the same manufacturer? Are you thinking lithium-ion?"

"Yes, we'll have to evaluate your needs to configure your..."

"Stop right there, we are working on configuring the ICMod for deep brain stimulation at the vagus nerve next, not for prosthetics. I told you both, we can work on that later," Daniel interrupted, visibly perturbed at Cliff.

"Daniel's right, one thing at a time..." Susan began but Cliff didn't want to hear her agree with his brother, so he interrupted.

"Don't you have to make sure there are no negative side effects with Cyborg Chucky here first before you open up Amy?" Both Susan and Daniel looked at Cliff questioningly, they weren't biting on his bait. Charlie's implant was the epitome of success, after all. "Fine. But, Daniel, you promised to get started helping me with the prosthetic while Susan works on configuring the ICMod."

"Okay. Let's get started then. First, we need to know what we're dealing with." Daniel took hold of the back of Cliff's wheelchair to wheel him out of the room.

"Here," Cliff reached over before Daniel could stop him and removed the EEG head cap from Charlie. The he put it on his own head. "Go ahead and run some tests..."

"Sorry, Charlie," Daniel apologized. "My brother here is very curious about what we are doing with your implant, it is state-of-the-art." He then sat back down at the computer and removed the leads to the electrodes on Charlie's head. "Cliff, Susan's software only works if it is talking to her ICMod, and this particular set-up is special. The EEG you put on your head, though it may make you look like a cyborg," Daniel smiled down at the giggling little 3-year-old who loved the word 'cyborg' and then went back to the computer and continued, "it can only tell us so much, it has a feedback loop to ..."

Daniel was deep in concentration, he had stopped talking in mid-sentence.

"Daniel? Are you okay?" Cliff asked.

"Your frontal lobe ... I've never seen anything like this ... what are you thinking about?" Daniel asked, in awe.

"Nothing, I was just imagining being a cyborg..."

"Well, you are either using far more of your brain than a typical human being or you have far more neural connections in your cerebral cortex. I want to get an MRI done ASAP. I've never seen anything like this before, it's amazing!"

"What are you seeing?" Susan asked. "You do work with mostly coma patients Daniel, so your basis of comparison is low." She said as she was putting away her equipment and walking over to Daniel's computer. "Wow, you weren't kidding!"

"Susan, don't let this distract you. I will see you in the lab later, go..."

"Geeze, has he always been this bossy?" Susan asked Cliff.

"You noticed too?" Cliff laughed. "And stubborn to a fault once he sets his mind on something he wants."

"I'm not the only stubborn one here," Daniel chimed in.

"That kind of neural activity would be perfect for..." Susan began but Daniel interrupted with, "Susan, don't you need to reconfigure the ICMod for Amy?" He turned away from the computer, crossing his arms on his chest and tapping his foot.

She was obviously intrigued. Cliff wanted to know what she wanted to use him for, but Daniel was not happy with her attention on Cliff. That only made him smile even bigger at his older brother.

"You're right, Daniel. I'll get started right away," she said and patted Cliff on the shoulder. "It'll have to wait until later then. Charlie, thank you for being such an ideal patient. I'll be back in a few days with the upgrades."

Cliff watched Susan leave the room then noticed Daniel was glaring at him. That made Cliff wonder if the EEG could read his mind and not just his brain activity.

Chapter 9

Amy On An Escapade

It was here! Susan held the highly anticipated yellow envelope in her shaky (caffeine-induced) hands. I'd been three weeks of 12-hour days, 7 days a week and multiple test configurations. And an ungodly amount of coffee. But now she was finally able to try-out her adapted ICMod on a coma patient.

All she'd had to go on was the diagram for a recent USPO patent, and her knowledge of how the nervous system interacted with micro-electrodes. She was trying something different, not just simple pulses of DC energy, but waves of complex signals at varying frequencies and power levels. She wanted to have the option of both simple DC and complex waves just in case one worked better than the other.

It took everything she knew to make it work. She'd needed to get the specifications to her friends in Idaho at least a week in advance of when they planned to put in the implant. Since then there'd been nothing to do but tweak the software and anxiously wait for the updated ICMod to arrive. And it was finally here!

"Ready?" Daniel suddenly said from behind her, startling her and making her drop the package in her hands. Thankfully he had good reflexes and was able to snag it before it hit the ground.

"Yes, when do you want to install the implant? Knowing you it will be this afternoon." Susan was talking rapidly due to caffeine jitters. It also made her voice have a bit of a squeaky vibrato. Plus, lack of sleep always made her a bit talkative. "It's this afternoon isn't it? Now, I bet it's now? I bet you want to install it now. I'm ready, let's go! You're ready, right?"

"Yes, we can go immediately. I've had two interns and another doctor on call for the last few days waiting on your package. When they can get here, we can begin. I've already paged them."

"You're very, umm, how do I put it? In control?" Susan said. He was so commanding, competent, efficient ... he wasted no time and he seemed a step ahead of everyone else. Everyone except his brother of course. She still hadn't quite figured Cliff out.

"Is that a bad thing?" Daniel asked, intrigued and sipping on his coffee.

"No, quite the opposite." Indeed, his ability to command any situation practically drove her crazy with desire and she wanted to tear that white coat off of him and ... Wow, pull it together Susan! She thought as she pulled the rubber hair band she kept on her wrist and let it go. "It's probably a good trait for a brain surgeon to have – being in control, having everything figured out."

"Ha! Yeah, you don't say?" he laughed. He looked sideways at the rubber band on her wrist, he still hadn't asked why she started wearing it over a week ago. "Where is Cliff? I thought I would find him with you, it seems I have no control when it comes to him."

"No one does, he's all over the place. We should call him wheels, though I'm not sure he'd like that," she said and then saw Daniel shaking his head vigorously.

"Well, he was here earlier, asking a million questions about the software updates ... I don't know where he went."

"I'm sorry, I've been trying to keep him away but..."

"No need to be sorry, I like his company. He's very sweet."

"Oh?"

"Yes. The other day he brought me flowers, lilies. Oh, and he also got me chocolates – my favorite Belgian ones. And he's always getting me lunch and asking how I'm doing, how my work is coming along. He's attentive..."

"He's just trying to distract you."

"Oh? Is that it? Just distracting me?" She didn't know what was going on between the brothers, but it seemed they were fighting over her these last few weeks and she liked every second of it.

Daniel opened his mouth to say something but a vibration at his waist caught his attention. He pulled off the little, black, square pager clipped to his belt and said, "It appears as if the other doctors are ready, it's time."

The two headed over to the patient quarters and ran into Cliff about to go into Amy's room. "So, you got the news?" Daniel asked as they approached, holding up the package in his hand.

"Yes, of course. I thought you were already in here, actually. I was looking for you," Cliff said, positioning himself between them and the door to Amy's room.

"Well, whatever you have in mind for me is going to have to wait. We were about to move her into the operating room," Daniel declared impatiently.

"Already? Are you sure you don't want to run a few more tests?" Cliff asked, then looked to Susan for support. "You're ready?"

"Yes, we're ready. Hopefully we'll all be celebrating tonight when it's over. Don't worry, we're only installing the device today and turning it on to make sure it works. We don't want to stress the patient too much in one day," she answered, dropping her mouse into his lap when she leaned over to console him by patting him on the shoulder. Then she went to grab it back but thought better of it – reaching for his crotch was not exactly lady-like.

Cliff breathed a sigh of relief, while Daniel had the opposite reaction – clenching his fists and putting on a strained smile. She looked from brother to brother, a bit confused. Daniel reached down into Cliff's lap to retrieve her mouse then handed it to her along with the package.

"Let's go," he said, walking around to behind Cliff's wheelchair and moving it out from in front of Amy's door. "Cliff, shouldn't you be wearing your mods? Why are you still in this thing?"

"The god forsaken legs are too bulky and unresponsive. I hate them. I want something that feels like my own legs, in my mind and in my body."

"What you are asking for simply doesn't exist..."

"Yet!" Cliff interjected. "Daniel, I know if we work together we can make them!"

"Yes, yes, of course ... but for now at least try to wear the ones we have created so far to get used to them, okay? Have some of my coffee here if you need a smidge of, you know ... nerve." Daniel said, giving his brother a wink and handing him his grey thermos.

"Nerve, right..."

Was that an inside joke? she thought.

"Next time I see you, you'd better be in the prosthetic mods," Daniel then pushed his little brother down the hall in the opposite direction saying: "Now go, we have work to do!"

~ ~ ~

There was a whistling sound, like a train in the distance coming closer and closer. Except, it never came. Amy tried to open her eyes, to look around and see if the sound was coming from behind her and found that her entire body was paralyzed. Fear gripped her. Her whole body was now vibrating to the sound of the distant roaring whistle in her ears. She felt her breathing, her heart beating hard in her chest and the numbness of pure immobility. Behind her eyes she imagined the train or whirlwind that was making the sound coming for her, but it never came. Her mind was trying to make sense of the vibrations in her body, she felt out-of-sync. Then the frightening roar surrounded her and she wanted to scream. After a few seconds she realized she was still alive. It had consumed her and she still felt her body vibrate but it was in sync with the roar in her mind and ringing in her ears.

Why couldn't she move? She wanted desperately to move something. She focused on her eyes, but nothing. What kind of monster was holding her eyes closed? It was as if each inch of her body was made of lead, sealed in cement. She wanted to weep in frustration, to cry out.

She started to hear voices echoing around her, getting clearer through the whistling roar and ringing rush that filled the dark void in her mind. A male voice, almost familiar, was speaking. She focused on his voice. He was saying something about increased brain waves ... Another voice, a woman, chimed in excitedly asking to ... continue testing?

Amy felt a sharp jolt in her head that left her wanting to scream but she couldn't. She couldn't even weep. What had they done? Was there something in her brain??? She felt her skull vibrating, the vibrations getting stronger and stronger and then her body began to convulse uncontrollably.

She felt herself bite her own tongue and could taste the blood, acrid and filling her mouth. She wanted to shout for them to stop but couldn't even control her tongue to stop it from getting bit again and again. The blood and her tongue were choking her.

Hands came from nowhere, touching her body, holding her down. They were foreign and felt plastic. Gloves? They shoved something into her mouth. Her eyes flung open on their own and started to move side to side. She could hardly see anything. A light above, blurry. It was stark and glaring, and it hurt as her pupils tried to adjust. She tried to blink and couldn't.

The jolting vibrations in her head abruptly ended, and her body convulsed a few more times and then stopped as well. She was still paralyzed. Her eyes were left open, but she could still hardly see and she had no control.

The familiar male voice was talking again. Was he talking to her? She could barely make out what he said from the ringing echoes in her ears and head. But, she concentrated all she could on his voice. Then she heard him say clearly "I think she is locked-in. We need to stop!" and afterwards there was nothing as her consciousness faded in a pleading whisper.

~ ~ ~

"I'm so sorry, Daniel..." Susan began but Daniel raised his hand to stop her from continuing. He was merely sitting there next to the hospital bed, staring at Amy, holding her hand.

"It's ... it's ok," he said at last as he stood up slowly, laying Amy's hand softly on the bed. "We are making progress, it will all be worth it when she's back with us at last."

"I can make some modifications ... I read something about music being particularly effective and..."

"Yes, I've tried music therapy on some of the less severe cases. Occasionally it seems to be effective, but it was never very reliable."

"It isn't exactly music therapy I was going to suggest."

"What do you have in mind?"

"Well, I was wondering what would happen if we played music transposed to lower frequencies that resonate within the brain cavity?"

"Go on."

"Maybe couple that with similar frequency combinations coming from inside via the ICMod, say in the Theta or Beta brainwave range? On very low power, of course."

"Yes, I was going to suggest lowering the power as well." The scowl he was shooting her was probably in reference to the jolt that had caused Amy to go into convulsions. She had no idea how an extra o ended up in a few lines of her code that ran the process of stepping down the voltage. Instead of going down, it had gone up to an unsafe level, one that could have caused permanent damage with the amount of current it was drawing. She'd had to frantically take manual control over the program to bring the voltage back to a safe level.

"By introducing sound with lower resonate waves in a familiar pattern we might stimulate a varied response across the brain. How does that sound?" Susan asked, then laughed at herself. "How does that sound, ha..." Daniel did not look amused. "See, I'm talking about sound and said 'how does that sound'..."

"Yes, I know. It's just not funny." Daniel was still upset, clearly. He usually found her banter somewhat amusing, or at least pretended to. "When can you start the modifications?"

"No need, I built-in the capability already. I simply need to select a musical arrangement and do the transposition. I anticipate it would be ideal if the song was something familiar to her, that she knew from her childhood. Do you know a suitable song? As her childhood friend?"

"I'll need to think about that. She should rest for today. It must have been frightening for her to be locked-in like that."

"I can only imagine ... I'm not even sure what 'locked-in' is, exactly." To her it looked like they had awoken Amy. She had moved and opened her eyes. Just when she thought it was successful, Daniel had gotten frantic and made her stop the program completely.

"It is a state of consciousness between a coma and full awareness. Like purgatory in the body. Where you are aware of your body and your environment but completely incapacitated. Some patients can control the movement of their eyes, but it seemed she couldn't even do that. Her brain was showing close to normal activity, a conscious level. So, she was aware ... for the first time in over a decade. And yet, unable to move or talk. That must have been terrifying. I would hate to put her through that again, or worse, leave her in that state."

"Tomorrow then?" Susan asked, but instantly felt callous at the suggestion when Daniel's shoulders visibly slumped and he looked back over at Amy ... longingly? "How close were you two, exactly? Sorry if I'm being too personal. I get the feeling you are very connected."

"She was..." he began to speak but looked like he didn't know the words or didn't want to admit something. "She was my first true love. We met as children and became especially close. I didn't have too many friends growing up and she was my best friend. She is special to me."

Wow, was he in love with Amy? Susan thought. It was starting to make sense why he was so protective and sensitive when it came to her.

"Did you wake her up?" Cliff said loudly breaking the silence between them as he entered the room. He was wearing his prosthetics and the clanging sound they made on the floor was a sharp interruption to the tense conversation Susan and Daniel were having.

"Those look fantastic! And look, are you taller than me?" Daniel said as he stood adjacent to his brother and put his hand above his head to measure the height difference with his fingers. "Wow, I'd say a full inch taller. How is the movement? Walk around!"

"Yes, sir," Cliff replied, sarcastically, and smiled over at Susan.

Susan gave him a shrewd nod – she knew how commanding Daniel could be.

Cliff regulated the forward motion of each leg with a small red button he had embedded into his fingerless, leather gloves. There was a rhythmic pulse to the movement from the hydraulics, and it was somewhat jerky. So much so that Cliff was visibly straining to keep from wobbling. He moved about the room quickly though, taking large strides. "I can work out the hydraulics to smooth out the motion, but the delay is bothersome between the switch and the leg."

"I told you, I will work on the neural interface when Amy is awake," Daniel said, looking perturbed again and sitting back down at his chair next to Amy's bed.

"We're close. She opened her eyes and moved today. We have a plan for tomorrow." Susan explained.

"She moved?"

"Convulsed, really." Susan was still ashamed that her program almost killed Amy. "There was a small glitch in the program. It won't happen again, I promise."

"She looks fine though, Susan. I'm sure you can easily fix whatever went wrong with the voltage."

"Did she say something went wrong with the voltage?" Daniel looked up at his brother and his jaw was set, fists clinched.

"I think he could gather that from the fact that she convulsed, Daniel," Susan wasn't sure why he was so suspicious of Cliff. Did he really suspect intentional foul play?

"What is the plan for tomorrow? More electro-shock therapy? Isn't that what you are, in essence, doing?" Cliff asked, with the typical disdain he always showed when it came to Amy.

"We're going to use music synergistically. But we need a song that will work. Something familiar to her, and I can't think of anything," Daniel replied, forlorn.

"What about that Janet Jackson song 'Escapade' that she loved so much?" Cliff offered. Daniel tensed up and become visibly angry at the suggestion, staring at Cliff with daggers in his eyes. "What? That might shock her back into life."

"What's the matter? Why is that song..." Susan began but was quickly interrupted by Daniel.

"Cliff knows exactly why," he said.

"If it is a strong memory, that could be enormously helpful Daniel. We should try it." Susan explained. The more of a connection someone had with a song, the more brain activity would be stimulated when listening to it. Everyone knew that who knew anything about music therapy.

"Okay ... if you think it would work, we can try it tomorrow," Daniel said tentatively.

"Why tomorrow?" Cliff asked.

"She needs a break, we have put her through an unforgiveable ordeal today," Daniel replied.

"So, you can push me around and make me do whatever. You have me running around in quasi-formed prosthetics and drinking 'coffee' just to move them but your precious Amy gets a break just because she had a few extra jolts?"

"She was locked-in..." Susan began and was interrupted by Cliff. These guys really liked to interrupt her!

"I don't care. All you're doing is playing music. Waiting is just wasting an entire day of my life where we could be moving forward. Have some balls!" Cliff ranted.

"Wow, you're a selfish ass, aren't you?" Daniel retorted, standing and walking up to be face to face with Cliff.

"Play the music! Wake her up! Get it over and done with, now!" Cliff demanded. "I'm sick of waiting around and wasting my time here."

"Cliff, remember I still need to find and configure the song," Susan said. The guys were about an inch from each other's face and had their fists ready. She had no idea how to calm them down.

"I have it on my iPod, we can download the mp3 right now." Cliff pulled out the small white device from his pocket and held it up. Neither Susan or Daniel responded, they were both speechless. So, Cliff took the opportunity to head over to the computer and begin downloading.

Daniel was still tense, and the latest bit of information made him look even more angry with his brother. But, he sat back down on his chair next to the bed. He kept staring at Amy with a longingness that Susan was starting to find irksome. "Do it," he finally said.

Why would he be mad that his brother had 'Escapade' by Janet Jackson on his iPod? It must be another inside thing between brothers that she didn't get, like the coffee.

"I'll start the transposition," she took control of the computer from Cliff after he finished the download. She thought she saw him quickly close another screen, though it might have been iTunes.

Cliff stepped away and back towards Daniel. "The sooner this is over and done, the better, for everyone."

"We'll play the song from the speaker at the same time as I generate the respective internal waves," Susan said. "The combination, along with a micro-shock to the neural network near the vagus nerve, should have some effect. So, prepare yourself."

Both Susan and Cliff were looking at Daniel for a command, or a movement, or anything to say he was ready. He was as still as granite. This was unlike him to not take charge. But it seemed that when it came to Amy he was a different man. Unsure, unsteady.

"Oh, come on!" Cliff said and then reached across Susan to hit start.

The music began to play. There was no response. Susan was too afraid to touch the voltage regulation after last time, so she simply let the program continue.

Cliff was staring at her with a blank expression and Daniel's eyes were locked on Amy.

About a minute into the song, Susan decided to increase the microcurrent intensity manually, being extra careful about how many 0's were involved at each step up.

Amy's hand began to twitch and Daniel leaned over her, taking hold of her hand. At about 3 minutes into the song, when Janet yelled 'Let's Go!' Amy sat straight up, screamed and reached her hand out into the air so fast that it hit Daniel right in the face and knocked him off of his chair.

Daniel was on the floor and Amy was sitting up, looking around the room. When she saw Cliff's legs, she gasped in a raspy voice. "Oh my god! What happened? Who are you? Where am I? What happened to my voice?" Her speech was barely more than a horse whisper, but discernable nonetheless.

"You were in a terrible accident Amy. What is the last thing you remember?" Daniel asked, sitting back in his chair and holding onto his bloody nose. "Cliff, can you get me a tissue?"

Cliff brought him the whole box and remained standing between Amy and Daniel. Daniel shoved one tissue up each of his nostrils and then held his head back.

"Cliff? Like little Cliff? You ... your legs ... and you're so much older ... Daniel? Is that you, Daniel?" Amy asked, in shock while squinting her eyes and blinking repeatedly. She then held her head and laid back down onto the bed with a soft moan. Her voice was getting louder but still sounded extremely horse.

"Yes, you've been in a coma for over a decade," Daniel explained.

"A decade? Where are my parents? Mimi? Oh my god, Mimi?" Amy was crying in between words.

"Your parents died in a car crash not long after your accident. Your dog Mimi, I don't know ... she was old even then, so I don't expect..." Daniel stopped talking. Amy was already enormously upset about finding out she was in a coma (who wouldn't be?) and telling her about her parents and Mimi dying was probably not the first thing she should be hearing right now.

"My parents are dead?!?" Amy wailed in between guttural, choking sobs. It sounded odd with the bright music of 'Escapade' still playing in the room. Susan didn't want to shut the music off just yet, because she didn't know what would happen if she did.

Everyone in the room was silent, except for Amy. No one knew what to say.

"What? What happened to me?" Amy asked, after weeping for a short time and then feeling the top of her shaved head.

"You fell off of a cliff chasing that stupid dog and hit your head." Cliff insisted. Daniel hit him in the leg and then regretted it instantly as the clang against his knuckle sounded like it would leave a solid bruise. Cliff just looked down and smiled as Daniel tried to flick the pain away while biting his lip.

"I did?" Amy asked, closing her eyes and wiping her tears. "I fell off of a cliff?" she opened her eyes and squinted at Daniel, "I can't remember, why can't I remember?"

"It will all come back to you in time, don't worry," Daniel said soothingly while rubbing his bruised knuckle and scowling at his brother.

"Well, she did hit her head pretty hard. I'm sure not all of her memories will come back. Some won't be correct either, I'm sure," Cliff said. "Who knows what kind of jumbled mess her mind is in, or what crazy things she might think."

"Actually, we should see what happens without the ICMod stimulus," Susan said. "Daniel, Cliff? Ready?" Both guys nodded together so she hit the off switch on the computer.

There was dead silence in the room, no one was even breathing. Amy lay there with a blank expression on her pretty face, tears rolling down her pink cheeks and pouty lips. Susan never realized how much she looked like Goldilocks until now.

"I felt a buzzing in my head, and it stopped. What was that?" Amy asked, forehead scrunched. Everyone let out a sigh of relief, breathing again.

"It's a microchip we inserted to stimulate brain activity," said Susan. "It is what brought you out of your coma."

"Who are you?" Amy asked, peering at Susan quizzically. "Do I know you too?"

"No. My name is Dr. Susan Aldean, and I'm the one that designed the microchip," she answered, proudly. "Daniel is the one who installed it though."

"Wow, you must be super smart," Amy said, swallowing hard. "Thank you for waking me up. Thank you both."

"Yes, she is remarkable." Cliff kissed Susan on the cheek, unexpectantly. She blushed and looked over to Daniel for a reaction but he was just staring at Amy, in awe. Were those tears in his eyes?

"Well, it looks like my work here is done. Daniel?" She didn't know what she was hoping for, but at this moment her heart was breaking because Daniel wouldn't even look at her.

"Come on Susan, let's leave them alone. I have an idea for what we can do with the ICMod next," Cliff said as he put his hand on the small of Susan's back and led her out of the room. As she walked out of the door, she turned her head to see that Amy and Daniel were now holding hands and looking at each other, longingly. It was all so sickeningly sweet.

Chapter 10

Wedding Bells and Cells

The weather was always pleasant in California, and Susan needed a break from the lab. So, a jog in the sunshine was perfect medicine for the dark mood she'd been in. As she was coming back home from her run, she decided to stop and check the mail. Her endorphin levels were high as she thumbed through the contents of her mailbox, humming to the music in her headphone. That is until her fingers stopped on a fancy envelope. She opened it to find an invitation to the wedding of Dr. Daniel Jahren and Amy Shipley. She almost threw the letter in the trash instantly. Then she thought about stomping on it – burning it maybe? The runner's high she had was now gone and all she felt was rage and frustration.

She walked into her house and laid down flat on the couch, tossing the mail on the coffee table and staring blankly at the ceiling. Six years and she still felt the same. Would she ever get closure? The more she thought about it, the more she thought she should probably go to the wedding. Maybe she would be able to finally move on? Cliff had been begging her to come to Colorado for years to help him with his family business. But it was his family, particularly his brother Daniel, that she didn't want to have any business with!

After they had awoken Amy, it was as if Susan no longer existed in Daniel's eyes. What a prick! She thought.

She was perfectly satisfied with her life in LA She had been enjoying great success with her ICMods being implanted to help Parkinson's patients and had even gotten FDA approval. Now, ICModTech was using her devices everywhere and for various application. The company was at the leading edge in the research of patients with severe and un-responsive ADHD, anxiety, depression and even epilepsy.

Cliff even had her design a modified ICMod for amplifying his brain signals to control his prothesis. It was working out well, at least that is what he kept saying. She steered clear of him, mostly because he reminded her of his brother. Daniel the prick! Urgh!

Why couldn't she just feel the way she did about Daniel, for Cliff? He was brilliant and handsome too. His brain was fascinating – she had never seen anything like it. It made her want to do more research on dreamers, which is what she had been studying for the past few years. The only thing that stood out about Cliff was that he had strong, frequent, lucid dreams in comparison to most people. He was more intelligent too, but this was beyond that. The anterior of his prefrontal cortex was dense, and when he slept his brain lit up like the fourth of July.

After conducting an open call for lucid dreamers, she found that her intuition was correct. Many shared the same metacognition abilities and brain density. None so remarkable as Cliff's, but all similar. She was thinking about looking into Native American dream-walkers next, because Daniel mentioned once that his Native American nanny said Cliff was a dream-walker.

With a new microchip, she might be able to project what these strong dreamers where seeing onto a computer. Basically, because they had such conscious and vivid dreams, their brain waves were more stable and focused. The strong signals would help her to hone in exactly what algorithms she needed to project thought. It would be the next step in human evolution, projected thought!

Susan heard the song 'Dreamweaver' play from the kitchen, that could only mean one thing. Cliff was calling her cell phone, again. Likely to ask her to come work for his company, again. She grudgingly got up and picked up the flip phone from the counter and put it on speaker. "The answer is 'NO,' Cliff," she said before he could say anything.

"Hi, Susan. It's Daniel." With those words Susan's heart skipped a beat and her mind went blank. "Are you there? Hello?" She went to sit down on the stool next to her kitchen counter, almost falling off but then catching herself.

Susan had to clear her throat, it felt like it had a knot. "Hi. Yes, I'm here."

"Good. I am sorry we haven't kept in touch. I've tried calling, but you always seem to be busy."

"Yes, I am very busy."

"I'm sorry, Susan. I never meant to hurt you."

Tears started to well-up in Susan's eyes. He waited six years to call and tell her this? "I'm fine. Why are you calling?"

"Well, I knew you would answer from Cliff's phone and I had to talk to you. It would really mean a lot to Amy and me if you came to the wedding. She adores you and she thinks you are 'The Angel that saved me with microchips' she says." He said this with such joy in his voice that Susan almost threw the phone. "Did you get the invitation?"

"Yes, it came in the mail today."

"Good, will you at least think about coming?" he waited for a response but Susan was biting her lip, trying to hold back a torrent of words she wanted to say. "Cliff misses you, he would love it if you came. He might try to kidnap you and make you work in his lab, ha ha."

Susan was shocked, did he really just say that? Cliff probably would try to keep her there!

"I'm just kidding. I wouldn't let him kidnap you, Susan. I promise. Honestly, he does miss you. We all do. Will you at least consider coming to Colorado for the wedding?"

"I'll think about it," she said at last.

"Good, I'm glad. Amy almost wanted to make you a bridesmaid, can you believe it?"

Susan scoffed. She could believe it. Amy was so adorably innocent that it was hard not to love her, even if she was the only thing standing between Susan and the man of her dreams.

Daniel continued with, "but I talked her out of it."

"Thanks!" she exclaimed, the last thing she wanted to be was a bridesmaid.

"It would mean so much to her if you came. I'll let you go now. I know you're busy."

"I'm..." Susan began, but was at a loss for words. "I'm glad you called," she realized she was as she said the words. "Goodbye," she said and it felt like letting go.

"Goodbye."

Susan sat there, stunned. She felt like a weight had been lifted off of her shoulders. Did she finally let go of her feelings for Daniel? Could she move on?

Dreamweaver started playing again and she picked up her phone, this time with less confidence as to who was on the other end and said, "Hello?"

"It's me, Cliff! So, you're coming to Colorado?!!?"

"Wow. Patience is not one of your virtues is it, Cliff?"

"You know it. I've been dying to show you around our new facilities. We've been hiring like mad lately, getting the prosthetics into manufacturing. We could most definitely use a brilliant engineer like yourself on our staff and I would ensure a weekly bonus of Belgian chocolates was on your desk."

"Daniel said you were going to kidnap me."

"Oh? Daniel said I was going to kidnap you, did he?"

It sounded like Daniel got hit with something. She heard an "Owe" and something or someone falling to the floor with a thud. "Hello!" she finally said to get Cliff back on track with the conversation.

"Oh. Sorry, Susan. Daniel accidently knocked over a vase just now. I'm so happy you will be coming up! There is so much I want to show you. How have the studies on the dreamers been going? Found anyone as good as me yet?"

"No, you're still the odd ball out. But I have found a few interesting … similar ones … but…" She wanted to say that she hadn't decided to come up yet when Cliff interrupted, as usual.

"Good! I've been talking to a guy in Japan named Pat Morichi, who specializes in harnessing the power of blood flow for nano devices. We might be able to start powering your ICMods with something far more sustainable than lithium-ion batteries. What do you say?"

"That all sounds very interesting, but I have a life here in LA and…" And what? she thought. She had a Siamese cat named Franklin and an aloe Vera plant that she sometimes called Bo-Bo … both would be fine in Colorado. If she was finally over Daniel … It did sound like compelling work and she could do her dream-walker studies anywhere. Heck, she would probably find some in the large Native American population near their facility. But, was she over Daniel?

"Just promise me you'll give me a few days when you come up for the wedding and I promise you I won't have to kidnap you to make you want to stay, okay?"

"Okay…"

"Fantastic, see you soon!" he said, gleefully.

Urgh, did she just agree to go to the wedding?!? Wow, Cliff sure was manipulative! She always seemed to say 'yes' when she meant 'no' with him. That's why she liked to start the conversation with a 'NO' to get it out before he could stop her. At least she had six months to decide how she felt about Daniel before the wedding and prepare herself.

Did Cliff say nano blood motors? Or machines? Was it chemical or physical? That sounded intriguing and would help with some of the heating and power problems she'd been having with the smaller mods. Maybe she should email him now, just for a little more information.

~ ~ ~

Daniel couldn't be happier. He was sitting in the hotel lobby bar, sipping on a glass of sparkling water and greeting family and friends as they stopped by to check into the hotel for his wedding. He had everything he had ever dreamed of. A beautiful bride to be. A nice house on a hill. He'd even convinced his family to stop doing dangerous and illegal work – except for the coffee, they couldn't give that up. They had a legitimate research and development company now, focused on prosthetics development. It was much better than the mud wrap and mask company that his parents had used as a front for their illicit research for years.

Tomorrow he would be married and starting a whole new chapter of his life with Amy. When she had first awoken, her mind was that of a 15-year-old girl and she was all alone in the world. He had no idea how to take care of her himself. So, he had sent her to a boarding house for women. A place where she could learn and adapt to the world. Their feelings for each other only grew stronger over the distance. They would email each other every day like they had written to each other as children.

She still didn't know about his family's ... umm, unique? ... ways of viewing research, but she never needed to because they had all promised to do the right thing when Daniel came back to help with the prosthetics neural networking. As far as she was concerned, they were all ethically saints and Cliff had lost his legs in a car accident.

"So, do you want the best man speech tonight at the rehearsal or tomorrow at the wedding?" Cliff said, walking up to Daniel and putting his hand on his shoulder with a tight grip.

"Ouch! That's quite the grip you have there," Daniel replied. "Are you nervous?"

"Sorry," he responded, loosening his hold. "Not really, there isn't much to say: 'Glad you're awake Amy. Now go have fun making babies with my brother?'"

"Funny."

"Seriously, what do you want me to say?"

"I don't know. I still have to work on my vows."

"What? Aren't you mister 'poetry?' I would have thought your vows were written months ago!"

"It's just that these words are more important than any other. It is a promise for the rest of my life, and I keep my promises."

"That you do, and she is lucky to have you!" Cliff said, patting Daniel on the back so hard it made him cough.

"Cliff, are you trying to crack my back?!?

"Sorry, umm ... I need to go started writing my speech. See you later tonight!" Cliff hurried away, pulling down his sleeves as if to hide something on his arm. He was behaving oddly and that was never a good sign, knowing his brother.

"Is this seat taken?" a soft, female voice asked next to him.

"Susan!" he exclaimed, turning to see his old friend. He thought about giving her a hug but it felt awkward so he just put out his hand for a handshake. That felt even more awkward so he pulled it back at the last minute. She went to take the hand while she was about to sit on the bar stool and when he pulled it back she fell forward, almost landing in his lap.

"Sorry!" They both said at the same time. You could cut the tension with a knife.

She had been in town for a week. But it practically seemed as if she had been avoiding him because she hadn't said a word past "Hi" when passing through the halls of their new facilities with Cliff.

"Your research laboratory is amazingly state of the art. You must have good investors," Susan began and hailed the bartender with, "I'll have a scotch on the rocks, make it a double. Thank you!"

"Yes, the funding is ... not important. How have you been doing? Has Cliff convinced you to stay?"

"He is trying, he can be very convincing."

"Tell me about it!"

There was awkward silence again. The bartender returned with the drink and Susan downed it in one gulp and said, "Another!"

"Wow, are you okay?"

"Fine. I'm fine. I just spent the day with Amy. Looking at all the flowers and wedding décor. She even had me and a few other ladies from the boarding house she went to making these little fans that have the wedding program on them. Adorable. Really, quite adorable."

The bartender was back with another drink and this time Daniel put his hand over the top of the glass before Susan could gulp it down. "You don't look fine, Susan." She looked like she was about to cry, actually.

"Did I ever even have a chance, Daniel? I know I was just too successful. If I had waited, maybe no woken Amy up..."

"What do you mean? You saved her life! I had given up on her and was going to leave ... who knows what UCLA would have decided to do."

Susan slid the glass from under Daniel's hand and started to sip the scotch, not taking her eyes off of him. She appeared as if she was wondering something about him. He was completely muddled and felt anything he said was wrong. He had apologized for leading her on. He hadn't meant to. He had started to have legitimate feelings for her before Amy was awake but once she was back Amy was all he could think about. It wasn't his fault. It wasn't her fault. It just was. He had spent over a decade, losing hope every day, working to get Amy back. How could he explain that to Susan?

"You're a remarkable and beautiful woman," he said at last. "I'm sure there have been plenty of men who have tried to make you theirs, right?"

Susan scoffed, sipping her scotch. "There is this one guy. He's a dream-walker, like your brother. He volunteered for one of my research projects. He is part Native American, part Irish. He's a charmer. He'd asked me out a few times before I finally said yes about a month ago. His brain is unlike any other and surpasses even Cliff's."

"Don't tell Cliff! You know how competitive he can be and how proud he is of that special brain of his. Why is it that you two never got together? He has been pinning for you for years!"

"I don't know … I guess I don't trust who I am around him?" she stopped to think for a minute, taking draws from the scotch. "I get caught up in his schemes and ideas so quickly. I don't want to be another one of his li'l groupies. Have ya seen the lates set? Those three scientis tha never leave hisside at the facilaty? Is … issa … is like they worshap him or somethan, is kinda creepy!"

"No, I never noticed. Are you sure you're ok? Are you coming to the rehearsal dinner? I need to start heading over to the restaurant now."

"No. Is think I'ves had enough weddi…" she hiccupped and continued with, "excuse husme, 'stuff' for the day. I'lls see ya tomorrow," she said as she shot back the last of the scotch and stumbled back towards the lobby elevators.

"Do you need help getting to your room?" Daniel yelled after her, concerned because she was obviously drunk and upset.

"No, no, no … iz fine! Go! Go to yur Amy!" she exclaimed as she got into the elevator and left.

The hotel was fairly safe, but he asked a bellman to go check on her just in case before he headed out the door.

There was a garden patio set aside for the wedding party at Dominic's steak house and it looked like he might be the last to arrive. The summer air was warm in the Colorado desert even this late in the evening and today was particularly hot. There were misters and lights hung along the beams overhead that cast a foggy shadow over the area. Three large banquet tables were shaped in a U for the party, and every seat was full. His bride-to-be was sitting right in the center. She was in a delicate, pink, ruffled, mermaid shaped dress with a low back and no sleeves. He long curly blonde hair was set in a twist to the side and her bare, tanned shoulders shone in the candlelight from the table. She was handing out gifts to her bridesmaids when he came behind her and kissed her gently on the cheek, whispering in her ear, "You look exquisite, my dear."

"Oh, you finally decided to arrive?" she replied back, jabbing him with one finger in the chest. "Where have you been? Someone said they saw you in the hotel lobby bar with another woman, getting drunk!"

"Me? Getting drunk? I've never had a drop of alcohol in my life!" he laughed.

"Oh, that's right," she said, abashed. "Well, you're still late. Sit down so we can get started." She motioned to the wedding planner they had hired, and that must have been a que for the activities to start. Daniel had no idea what was going to happen. He had left the planning to Amy. She had very specific ideas and he did not want to get in the way of making her happy by throwing in any of his ideas in the mix, even if everything did turn out pink – which it did.

"Tonight, we celebrate the union of our two most beloved friends, Amy and Daniel," the neatly dressed, pant-suited planner said. She then clapped her hands to generate applause from the crowd. "We would like to start off the night showing a video prepared by the family to highlight their very special relationship." She pressed a button and a white screen came down. She turned on a projector and it showed pictures of the two of them as children.

Watching the display, Amy went from laughing out loud to giggling and back, and Daniel found it hard to not look at her dimpled smile the whole time. "Your mother found some hilarious pictures of the two of you boys as children. And Miss Tinny, I had forgotten about her! Where is she?" she whispered to Daniel.

"She had a falling out with the family a few years back..." he didn't want to tell Amy that Tsintah had found out what really happened to Cliff. Then, after getting fired for snaking into a lab, had refused to go anywhere near them. When she found out where they had gotten some of the viral compounds used to derive Tribus they almost had a full Native American uprising on their hands. He had to think of something to say to Amy, quick. "Cultural differences. About how we were using the land near the mine."

"That is sad, I liked her very much. Maybe I can work out an environmental plan that the native tribes will like? It could be my thing. I could be, like, an ambassador or something."

Daniel kissed her on her forehead, he treasured her optimism. "That sounds lovely, dear."

The pictures continued, until a delightful shot of Amy's old Chihuahua 'Mimi' showed up. Amy gasped, holding her hand over her mouth. Daniel put his arm around her, he could feel her shaking.

"Are you alright?"

"I..." she was fixed at Cliff, eyes wide. Cliff was scowling back at her, fists clenched. He never did like her, but he could at least have some empathy for his soon to be sister-in-law's weak mental condition. They should have never included her dog in the slideshow!

"Turn it off!" Daniel yelled. The planner quickly hit the stop button.

"I..." was all Amy could get out. She started scanning around the room in a daze as if she was lost. "I'm sorry. I think I need to go lay down. Excuse me," she said as she got up to leave.

Amy's maid of honor, Amanda (a pleasant, black lady she had met at the boarding school) got up and said, "I'll make sure she gets safely to her room." She was used to Amy's sudden spells. Even after all these years Amy's mind never fully healed.

Amy reached over and squeezed Daniel's hand, "I'll be alright, I just need to rest." Then she shot a glance over to Cliff and shuddered visibly. Daniel looked at Cliff in confusion, had he done something to Amy?

Cliff noticed Daniel was staring at him and quickly pulled away from the table. He tossed his napkin in his seat and then stormed off.

The wedding planner didn't know what to do. The bride, maid of honor and best man had just left the table. She was just standing there completely flabbergasted.

Thankfully Daniel's mom stood up and gave a toast to try and ease the tension. "My handsome son was able to awaken sleeping beauty; but, alas, she still needs her beauty sleep!" she said as she clanged the side of her champagne glass with a spoon. "To young love, and real-life fairy-tale endings!"

Daniel's father followed with another speech about how proud he was of his son and how he hoped to have many grandchildren. The night continued with him having to engage with relatives he had never heard of before and colleagues of his mother's he had never met. The entire time he was worried about Amy. He was also disturbed that his brother had not returned so he could ask him why Amy seemed frightened of him so suddenly. He was able to excuse himself eventually and hurried straight to Amy's room.

Amanda was sitting next to Amy, brushing back her hair with her hand and singing a lullaby when Daniel walked in.

"How is she?" he asked.

Amanda got up and picked up her purse, readying to head out. "She's fine. Simply a little frazzled, you know."

"Yes, I feel better now. Amanda has such a sweet voice. I love hearing her sing." Amy smiled, eyes still closed as she lay in bed.

There was a knock on the door. Daniel opened it to find the bellman with a package. "Another wedding present arrived," he said, handing Daniel a white box with a dark red ribbon. The note just read, "Congratulations!" and nothing else. The bellman was gone before Daniel could ask who it was from.

Amanda took the package and declared, "Oh, how lovely! Amy, do you want to open this one now? I know how much you love presents, it might cheer you up."

"Are you sure that is a good idea? We don't know who it is from." Daniel insisted.

"I'm sure they merely forgot to put their name on it," Amanda scoffed. Amy was already opening the present. Inside was a beautifully decorated ceramic tea pot. "Oh, isn't that a nice gift!"

"Yes, I love tea!" Amy said as she was trying to open the lid but couldn't.

The mental spells left her a bit weak sometimes. Daniel took the teapot and placed it on the counter, saying, "We'll make tea later, dear. Get some rest!"

"I'll be going now. See you tomorrow, Amy! Goodnight!" Amanda exclaimed, sauntering out the door.

Daniel sat down next to Amy and she started to open her mouth to say something when his phone began to ring. It was Cliff. He had a few choice words he wanted to share with him, so he flipped open the phone and walked out into the hallway.

"What did you do to Amy?" he demanded.

"Nothing, what did she say I did?" Cliff replied.

"She didn't say anything. It was just that look you were giving her ... and she was trembling..."

"She has brain damage Daniel, and you know I have never liked her."

"Why did you storm off?"

"I was just mad that I had spent so much time trying to figure out the best man speech and she had to go and ruin it with her little episode."

"What? You're that mad about a speech?"

"Yes, and I'm mad she wouldn't even let you have a bachelor party too. What kind of best man am I anyway that I can't even throw my brother a bachelor party?"

"You know I don't drink Cliff..."

"Well, I do! And you could at least meet me in the lobby bar for a drink, pretend we can have a bachelor party."

"I don't know, Amy is out of it..."

"Oh, let sleeping beauty sleep!"

"Ok, I'll go. Just one drink." Daniel acquiesced.

"Ok, are you heading there now?"

"Yeah, I am already in the hallway."

"Good, see you soon!" Cliff said, hanging up.

Daniel hung up the phone and started to walk towards the lobby but remembered he hadn't said goodbye or given Amy a kiss before leaving. He went back towards the room and right as he reached for the door he heard a loud explosion followed by ringing in his ears. The next thing he knew he was pinned between the door and a hallway shelf. The mirror behind him had shattered into pieces showing thousands of reflections of fire and smoke cascading around him. The pain in his legs was intense and the door holding his body down was on fire. The last thing he saw before losing consciousness was the arm he had used to reach for the door. It was three feet down the hallway, still holding the handle.

Chapter 11

Mindful Mind Full of Mods

There were voices talking in hushed tones. Two women and one man, arguing. The chatter awakened Daniel's mind. The grogginess in his head transitioned to awareness of a heavy body laid down on a hard bed. He opened his eyes to look towards the sounds and could barely make-out three blurry figures coming in and out of focus above him.

"He should have the right to decide what he wants. Just because you are his father, doesn't mean you have the right to make decisions for him," Daniel's mother's voice could be heard clearly from across the room now.

"She's right, let him decide," Susan's voice was subdued, but distinguishable and coming from one of the three figures above him.

"I'm overruled, apparently. It is a moot point, he is awake now regardless: observe," Martin's voice announced from the blurry figure on the right.

"What ... happ ... happened?" Daniel asked. He saw all three figures looking down at him, heads almost touching in a triangle blocking-out the glaring florescent light above and turning them to shadows.

"There was an explosion, son. It appears there was a remote detonation device inside a ceramic container in the hotel room. You're lucky to be alive," Martin said, in somber tones.

"Yes. We're all glad you're alive, honey," Beth said, coming up to his right side while his father was talking, and taking hold of his hand. He realized he couldn't feel his left hand. He winced as an image of his arm in the hallway suddenly flickered in his mind.

"Amy? Is Amy ...??" Daniel already knew the answer before anyone could say a word. Tears began rolling down his cheeks and his chest began to ache.

"I'm so sorry, honey. It was swift, and painless. She was such a lovely girl. She deserved so much more in this life." Beth was unable to hold back tears herself as she spoke.

"Bellman ... he ... he brought us ... a ... a ceramic tea pot ... he might know..." Daniel was having trouble getting out the words. His throat kept clenching and it felt like his vocal chords where collapsing.

"Yes. Amanda already told the authorities. The bellman said he didn't remember coming to the room when he was held for more questioning by the police," Martin explained. "They did a lie detector test and also found a heavy dose of flunitrazepam in his system. Consequently, they presently have no leads."

"We were all hoping he would remember something for the longest time, but..." Susan said.

"Cliff ...where is Cliff?" Daniel demanded.

"I'm right here, brother," he heard his younger brother's voice coming from the shadow next to his father. "I've been here the whole time. I'm so sorry for what happened to you ... I'm ... so glad you're alive!"

"Did you ... did you..." Daniel couldn't quite bring himself to ask the question that was burning in his brain. Cliff never liked Amy and his actions had been suspicious. But, could he accuse him of such a horrible thing? Of murder?

"Cliff came up with some great ideas for modification for you Daniel. He's quite the wizard when it comes to prosthetics. I can have a master ICMod made for you in no time. It'll have the new nanogenerators we've recently developed. It'll make it to where the mod can be completely hidden, no wires coming out. I will have to go to Japan with Cliff to work it out, but from the papers he sent me..."

"That's right. Susan and I are working together again and we'll have you better than new ... you'll be invincible!" Cliff interjected.

"I promise I'll do everything to make you feel whole again, Daniel." Susan's words were like ice in his chest, highlighting his loss ... not of his body, but in his heart. Amy was gone, he would never feel whole again. Tears rolled down his cheeks without restraint.

"We should let him rest," Beth said.

"Right, we all have work to do," Martin said and the four shadows were gone, replaced by the blurry, bright light of a hospital ceiling.

Daniel closed his eyes and wept until the void of sleep eased him into an oblivion he never wished to wake from.

~ ~ ~

Months passed into years, and years faded away the pain. Everything took longer than anticipated. Technology and the heart never reacted as expected. While Cliff and Susan worked the nanogenerators in Japan, Beth and Martin worked with Daniel to accept his new life. To accept the pain and loss in his heart and in his body. The love they showed him, and to each other, was inspiring. By the time Susan and Cliff came back from Japan, Daniel was ready to try again. To live again.

The new prosthetics they had him try finally trying on today weren't that bad. In fact, they felt like extensions of his own body, only his body felt bulky, heavy. "I see what you mean, Cliff, about the weight," Daniel explained. "I never understood before; but, you're right – it's cumbersome."

"How about the Mod?" Cliff asked. He had started to call the ICModTech microchips Susan created 'Mods.' They'd just gotten back from Japan two days ago with the latest version and installed it within the hour of arrival. Cliff's small team of scientists had spent the last 48 hours calibrating the controls with Susan's direction.

"I feel ... better, and of course it provides seamless control of the prosthetics," Daniel answered, proudly. He didn't know how to explain it, but he felt happier these last few days then he had ever felt in his life. Did Susan add an extra dopamine stimulus package to his Mod? Knowing her, she would, for him, he thought. "I feel too good, really."

"Yeah, the neurotransmitter stimulation can have that effect. You'll get used to it," Cliff smiled.

And then you'll want more!

That was a strange thought, where did it come from? Daniel thought, looking at Cliff, who was grinning like a Cheshire cat. "Did you say something?" Daniel felt Cliff's attention focus inward and away from him.

173

Is he reading my mind? Daniel heard in is head, only it 'sounded' like Cliff's voice in a strange way.

Are you reading my mind? Daniel asked in his head.

"No," Cliff said aloud. Then realized what had just happened and looked appalled, eyes wide and mouth agape.

"Has this happened to you before, Cliff? With any of the other Mods?" Daniel asked, concerned they had gone too far this time, or that his brother had been keeping the side-effect secret.

"No, I swear!" Cliff exclaimed.

He answered that maybe too quickly? Daniel thought, staring down his brother.

"Why are you swearing?" Susan asked, entering the room with her laptop, glasses having slid down her nose. She was dragging wires behind her that she would no doubt trip over any second and ... Daniel caught her as she tripped. He also snagged the computer she had flung from the air too. "I see the neural network interface is firing well. That arm speed was just as fast as your normal reaction."

"Oh, so you tripped to test the Mod?" Daniel laughed. He had missed her quirkiness, she always kept him on his toes.

"Right, I'm that good," she winked, sarcasm seething.

"Cliff and I were just noticing ... Umm, how can I put this? An unexpected connection? Cliff?" Daniel hoped he might have a better idea of what to ask.

"Our minds ... they appear ... linked..." Cliff was talking too slowly, he was obviously struggling with how to describe it ... or didn't want to.

"We can read each other's mind, Susan. Is that an intentional design element?" Daniel wanted to get directly to the point.

"Holy Mother of God!! No!!!" Susan exclaimed while falling back into the chair behind her and grabbing her forehead. She was in complete shock and disbelief. "What is it like? Do you hear a voice or is it just a perception of thought? An image? Oh My God, this is incredible!"

"I heard him ask me a question as if it was aloud," Cliff relinquished.

"I heard him thinking to himself," Daniel expanded.

"You did?" Cliff asked and Daniel nodded.

"Yes. If I think about it, I can feel a measure of what you are feeling..." Daniel started to concentrate on the impression he had in his head that he was starting to identify as coming from Cliff.

No, no! Please give me my privacy! he heard Cliff scream in his head. The echoes in his skull were deafening. But, what was even stranger, is that it shook him physically as well and the lights began to flicker in the room.

"What was that!?!" Susan asked, looking from brother to brother and up at the flickering lights.

"I ... I don't know..." Daniel said, sitting down next to Susan and rubbing his forehead. It felt like Cliff had punched him with a sonic boom in the center of his brain. Not nice, little brother, he said in his head to Cliff. "What have you done, Susan?" he asked aloud.

"Nothing! I well ... I added a few modifications Cliff and I discussed that might be beneficial for you..."

"Beneficial?" Daniel interjected. What kind of crazy augmentations had Cliff convinced her to put into his brain?

"Yes, but this is unexpected and..." she stopped mid-sentence, eyebrows scrunched while she sat there thinking for a minute. "I'm guessing here ... but, I think because you are so genetically similar, your brain waves may sync better. I saw a study on it once, I think it was on the Discovery Channel? It was on genetically similar people. Identical twins. For instance, they tend to almost be able to read each other's minds ... some say that they do read each other's minds. The Mods enhance your brainwaves to control the prosthetics, and they must be amplifying more than just the ones for motor control."

"I'm not so sure I like this," Daniel finally said, after letting all of that sink-in.

"I'm not so sure I like this, either," Cliff declared, staring at his brother and sending out what felt like a threat to not go into his head or he might be sorry. Cliff then strode out of the room, fists clenched.

"So, you think it is only because we are brothers that this is happening? Are you positive?" Daniel asked.

"No ... I ... umm," she was staring in the direction Cliff had gone. "Maybe ... You can try it on me, let's see," Susan faced Daniel, gazing intently at him and obviously thinking hard about something. Daniel could sense nothing, except his own heart beating faster while peering into her eyes. He felt drawn to her, an attraction that he hadn't felt in a long time. Was it the Mod?

He shook his head.

She moved her chair closer to his and then continued, "Okay, I'm thinking of a number between 1 and 10." Daniel did not hear a single thought, or feeling, or anything coming from Susan other than the warmth of her body and the scent of her orange blossom perfume. It was intoxicating and he suddenly wanted to kiss her but stopped himself.

"Maybe it is the duel Mod interaction? It is probably only because you BOTH have an amplification Mod for your prosthesis. That, combined with the fact that you are genetically similar, could explain the odd interference the two of you are experiencing. Most of the Mod's I've built are for stimulation, not amplification. So that would explain why we haven't seen this kind of thing before," Susan explained, appearing worried. She got up and was checking the hallway Cliff had stormed down.

"Perhaps. We can try-out your theory on another prosthetic patient who has a Mod right now. Do you want to see if Bill can read my mind? It's worth a try. I want to see how far this goes." Daniel had a pretty good idea of what Cliff might have done with the Mod technology, and none of this was likely an accident. He always wanted more – more amplification, more control. Though it was hard to believe that even Cliff was chasing mind reading technology.

Susan nodded and followed him reluctantly down the hallway towards the main facility.

Bill was a veteran who had lost his legs in Afghanistan and volunteered as one of their initial trials a few years ago. He now worked at the facility as one of the operators on the manufacturing line. As they approached, Daniel said in his mind Turn around.

Bill turned around from the shipping bins and greeted them with a big smile, "The miracle-working geniuses! What do I owe the pleasure of your company?"

Say 'Monkey wrench' Daniel said in his head, projecting his thoughts towards Bill.

"Monkey wrench ... sorry, I think I am developing Tourette's! Ha, ha," Bill laughed and looked embarrassed, staring at Daniel quizzically. Daniel could feel Bill's embarrassment, could sense his troubled thoughts.

"I just wanted to check on you and see how you're doing, you look well!" Susan said, then gazed over toward Daniel, unsure of what to say next. She, of course, had no idea what was going on. Daniel wasn't about to tell Bill that he could not only read his thoughts but control them. He did have to give Susan an indication that he was trying-out her theory.

"I'm thinking of a number between 1 and 10, got any idea?" This time Daniel wasn't projecting his thoughts, he was just thinking.

"Three?" Bill guessed. "That was an odd question, was I right? What's up?"

Susan opened her mouth to say something but Daniel put up his hand to silence her. He'd been thinking of the number seven. Now he thought I need to get back to work and projected it at Bill.

"I need to get back to work," Bill said while walking backwards away from them. "It was nice seeing the two of you again. Thank you for the legs, I'm forever grateful!" He turned around and hurried away down the assembly line towards the optical inspection booth that he normally operated.

Daniel waited until they were out of earshot in a nearby hallway, away from any doors or cameras for him to let Susan know what had just happened.

"That can't be right, are you sure?" Susan whispered, loudly.

"I'm sure. I could practically control his mind and he couldn't even read mine. I heard his every thought when I focused on him. I could even feel what he was feeling!" Daniel exclaimed in hushed tones.

"Shushh..." she said, looking around and then up at the camera at the end of hallway. "We need to talk somewhere else, somewhere private."

"Why?" Daniel asked, suspiciously now wondering exactly what special modifications she used in his Mod. He wouldn't put it past Cliff to slip something into the programming, but he also felt that the good mood he was in (despite all of this and everything before) had something to do with her.

She tiptoed close to him, raising her chin to his ear and the euphoria that ensued could not be natural. Did he feel this way about her before? "The lake. Noon. Tomorrow. Come alone. It is important. Tell no one and guard your thoughts," she said as softly and as close to his ear as she could before rushing off.

Daniel watched Susan walking away and tried to sort-out his feelings. Was she always this beautiful? His heart was pounding and his skin was flushed, he felt excited but not worried or anxious. This didn't sit right in his mind, but he couldn't quite place why.

What were you two talking about? Cliff demanded in Daniel's mind. His heart jumped at the sudden invasion but he kept calm.

We were talking about the new Mod, we may need to make an adjustment, Daniel said back in his mind, looking down the hallway to where his brother was standing, only 20 feet away.

I want to show you something, come with me, Cliff said in his head. Daniel felt compelled to follow him, compelled! It made him wonder how much control Cliff hand over his mind after the interaction with Bill.

What interaction with Bill? he heard Cliff ask inside his mind.

I just wanted to see if Susan's 'genetically similar' theory was correct, which it seems to be Daniel lied as he projected an image of Bill being completely confused and thought about him guessing the wrong number. He then tried to guard his thoughts as much as he could by focusing on the objects and things around him. On walking. On the feel of his new legs and arm.

I see, Cliff replied casually in his mind.

Daniel almost felt amusement coming from his brother before there was nothing. Cliff was either good at muting his thoughts or he had none. Daniel tried not to think about protecting thoughts or Bill or Susan or anything and just focused on his new legs as he came closer to Cliff.

They were walking side by side now, toward the elevators in the back that led to another, deeper facility. The rhythmic pulse of their legs was in sync and the metal on metal clank of both of their appendages was ominous entering the dead silent elevator.

Cliff was guarding his thoughts so well that Daniel was having trouble following them and every time he tried he felt a push backwards, almost physically. He glanced over to see a small smile creep onto the side of Cliff's lips that sent chills down his spine as the elevator plummeted to the depths below.

"I want you to meet our onsite propulsion engineer, Ran McNaulty." Cliff was talking aloud now as he strolled out of the elevator.

"Why would we have the need for a propulsion engineer, Cliff?" Daniel asked aloud as well, following in stride.

"One of the benefits of the new Mods is that they generate their own energy. But, you'll notice we kept the larger power systems on the prosthetics," Cliff stated nonchalantly, walking down the hallway before he reached a steel door. He punched in a code and opened the door wide, with a hand out to usher Daniel in first.

"Dr. Jahren, and Dr. Daniel Jahren, I presume? It is a pleasure to finally met you!" An older gentleman, about 60, with peppered grey hair and a stubbly, matching beard said with hand out to shake Daniel's. He was wearing the blue cotton overalls with company logo that was the standard issue uniform for engineers in their facility.

Daniel shook his hand and was looking around the giant room that gave the impression of being an airplane hangar dug into the mountain. Even smelling of jet fuel. It was filled with what appeared to be small rocket engines and other devices that could be grenade launchers for all he knew. What is this!! he yelled at Cliff in his head.

Cliff shook his head and rubbed his temple but before he could say anything Ran started to talk.

"Now that you have gotten used to your prosthetics, I'm sure your brother has told you about the enhancements we have been developing for the military," Ran announced.

"A secret military funded project, Cliff?" Daniel said, aloud.

"Yes, need to know only. I wanted to show you how much more you will be capable of, and you deserve to know what your hard work has led to."

"What has my work led to?" Daniel asked, concerned and annoyed. All he ever wanted to do was help people, not blow them up. Everything in this room looked like a weapon.

"Attachable robotic propulsion systems and sonic blasters mostly, but the latest enhancement device is my favorite." Cliff beamed as he walked over to an arm that lay on the table. "Go ahead, switch it out."

Daniel immediately removed his left arm and placed the one on the table over his interface. He turned it left to lock it in and then could feel it sync into his mind. He opened and closed the fist, noticing a hole in the middle of the hand than was wound-up like a solenoid inside. It wasn't until after he put the arm on that he even realized he was going to do it and Cliff was smiling like he was up to something. He tried to put those thoughts out of his head.

"You'll want to be in a narrow passage, or hallway when using this one ... here, we have a test range built." Ran led them over to a room on the right wall. It was filled with tennis balls and bowling ball sized objects of different weights and materials. "Hold your arm out and concentrate on the center of your hand," Ran directed.

Daniel held his hand out and there was a buzzing in his arm, followed by a sonic wave that pulsed in the room at a low frequency that he could hear and feel. The objects scattered about the room started to levitate, tennis balls first. As he focused harder, the larger objects began to levitate higher. It was amazing! He could feel the pride and exuberance flowing from his brother and couldn't help but mirror the feeling.

I almost want to cut my own arm off, just to be able to have this one, he heard Cliff say in his mind. He understood, the power was overwhelming.

"What else do we have?" Daniel asked, unable to control his excitement and unsure if the source was him or his brother. He would be keeping this arm though, no matter what.

"These legs use liquid hydrogen fuel and can fly for about 30 minutes on full burn; but, we have modified them with a sonic interrupter that helps maintain altitude and can generate a glide for up to 2 additional hours," Ran explained showing off a pair of 'legs' that looked more like rocket thrusters.

Daniel felt Cliff's heart beat faster and his pride double as Cliff stroked the metal legs. Titanium additive manufacturing he heard his brother say in his head.

"This is what I like to call a 'sonic sickener.' It can generate tones that cause severe headaches and induce vomiting." Ran pointed to the first hand on a table with three different metal hands. "This one is fundamentally a Taser, and this one shoots off bullets from the pointer finger like a gun. They are all exchangeable with the one you have now. Look and see."

Why wasn't I told about any of this before, Cliff? Why am I just now finding out? Daniel asked in his mind, turning to face Cliff.

You were so preoccupied with Amy and wanting a 'normal life,' he said in his head with dripping disdain and ... hurt?

Did he feel hurt that he wanted to be normal? Daniel thought, completely confused.

"I didn't think you would understand," Cliff said aloud. His emotions were wild. One minute he was staring at the hardware around the room with pride and excitement and the next he felt hurt and guilt. The rollercoaster of emotion was overwhelming and Daniel was starting to have trouble breathing.

"Am I missing something?" Ran asked the two of them. He'd been gazing from brother to brother, who'd been staring at each other, not saying a word (from his perspective) for the past few minutes.

Cliff smiled, then turned to face Daniel.

Suddenly all Daniel could think of is how much work went into making these dreams come true and how state-of-the-art each and every device was. "This is legitimate, government work, right?" he asked, aloud.

"Of course!" Ran and Cliff both exclaimed at once.

"Well, then, lets test these babies out!" Daniel said, excitedly removing the levitation hand and replacing it with the sonic sickener. "Who wants to go first?"

"Whoa, very funny!" Cliff laughed, holding up his arms as if he was being accosted by a cop, but in his head he was calling his brother a few curse words.

Ran held his arms up too, not wanting to volunteer either.

Daniel laughed, until he noticed something on Cliff's arm. Black streaks going down the muscles in his forearm. Cliff quickly pulled down his sleeve.

"Cliff!!" Daniel yelled, the lights in the room began to flash and all three men looked around. He took Cliff by the arm and ripped back his shirt, revealing the extent. "Tribus? Really?"

It isn't Tribus, father fixed it. He's calling it Quinta, he added two more ingredients to stabilize the reaction. Cliff was looking at Ran and back to Daniel, speaking to Daniel's mind. Ran doesn't know about this. This is not sanctioned. I know. I'm sorry but the prosthetics were too heavy and my body was still ailing. The MD was too much and Quinta is the only thing that could stop it.

"Am I missing something? What is Tribus? What is wrong with your arm Cliff?" Ran asked.

"Just a bad tribal tattoo," Cliff lied as he tried to fix his slashed sleeve to cover the black streaks.

"I'm guessing Mom and Dad know all about this, am I right?" Daniel asked, aloud.

"Of course," Cliff answered, aloud.

"Yes, your parents helped set-up the contract years ago. It was your mother who hired me," Ran proclaimed. "We actually went to school together. She hasn't aged a day since I met her. That mud business must be working-out well for her."

More like coffee! Daniel thought, hearing the echo of Cliff in his head. They both chuckled.

"You have quite the remarkable family," Ran said. "Most of the ideas for this technology came from Cliff, I just put it together."

"Yes, we have quite the family!" Daniel said. It was hard to be mad at his brother when the brilliant work around him was so extraordinary. Maybe it was the new Mod, but he felt more connected to Cliff than ever before. And, now he was sure Susan had added an extra dopamine enhancement to his Mod because he knew he should be angry or upset or even disgruntled with his family's usual breaking of every known law and ethic. But, he just felt exhilarated.

Cliff was smiling, and Daniel couldn't help but match it with an equally big grin.

Chapter 12

Arrested Development

Susan sat cross-legged on a wooden park bench, gazing out at the lake and nibbling absentmindedly on a bag on Funyuns when Daniel arrived right on time, right at noon. He placed his hand on her back as he sat down next to her and said, "Hi Susan." He had a smile so devastatingly handsome that it made her heart melt but also made her painfully aware of her own onion breath. She packed away the snacks into her backpack, uncrossed her legs and looked around to make sure they were alone.

"I think the coast is clear," he whispered to her, with barely muffled amusement as he feigned to look around as well.

"Did you talk to your brother after I left? Did he tell you to do anything?" Susan asked, unabated and serious.

Daniel was not the same. He was acting different and it was slightly unsettling. He was so happy, unnervingly happy. She hadn't seen him happy in years, not since Amy's death. The new Mod she'd placed had an extra stimulus package to help drive him out of his depression and an extra bit of amplification based on Cliff's feedback. But, it was having a far different effect than she'd anticipated. Were his emotions being amplified by hers?

"Yes, and yes. Why?" Daniel asked, still smiling like a buffoon and leaning closer to Susan. She could smell his breath. See the gold flakes in his hazel eyes. Feel the heat of his body next to hers. She was starting to forget why she was here – he had that effect on her. Unfortunately, she wasn't wearing her rubber band on her wrist to snap herself back out of it anymore.

He asked, "Are you ok, Susan? You look ... dazed?" as he hugged her next to him and rubbed his hand up and down her back to comfort her. That didn't help. The closeness and heat of his body took over her mind.

"I'm fine ... how are you?" was all she could think to say as she stared into his eyes, leaning towards him, pulled in by his magnetism.

"I've never felt better, truly! What did you put in my head, Susan?" he asked as he straightened her glasses. "Do you want me to fix these? The left side is crooked." He didn't wait for an answer as he removed the glasses and bent the frame back. "There, that looks more even," he said, placing them on her face while softly brushing her hair back behind her ears on either side.

"What did you put in my head..." she repeated out loud, not quite catching on, staring at his full lips. "I'm not..." she began but was interrupted by those full lips on hers. It was a full minute before she could catch her breath, much less try to finish her sentence. He had kissed her! How did that happen?

"I'm sorry, was that ok?" Daniel asked, still inches from her face and holding her close with his right arm around her waist. The endorphins released in his warm breath were making her giddy and her glasses a bit steamy. She had to take them off again and wipe away the condensation.

Susan wanted to stay in this moment forever. She had dreamt about it. Wished for it. Wondered how those lips would feel on hers for so long. Years! She'd wanted him to kiss her for years! It did not disappoint. He was an incredible kisser, as gentle and as adept with his tongue as he probably was with his fingers during surgery. Before she knew it, her finger was touching his lips, gliding over the contours ... But, this was not ok! Not in the least ok! What was happening??? She should have better control over herself!

"I can't!" she said at last. "I'm seeing someone, and this isn't right – it isn't fair to him."

"Who?" Daniel asked, unfazed and going in for another kiss. She couldn't help but dissolve into his arms and relinquish control to his thorough hold on her. He moved her, body and soul, and she didn't even feel like she was in reality anymore.

A few minutes later, or an hour? Time had stopped. Susan pulled herself together and pushed Daniel away enough to catch her breath. They sat there, foreheads touching. His hand on the back on her neck holding her fervently. Her hands on each of his shoulders, keeping him at a safe distance.

"This isn't right, Daniel."

"This feels very right to me, Susan," he implored, looking her straight in the eyes, which, at the distance they were from hers, melded together to make him look like a cyclops. That funny thought helped pull her back to reality.

She took his hand from her neck and held it in between hers. Such a large, strong yet delicate hand. She looked down at his left hand and finally noticed he was wearing a new prosthetic she had never seen before. "What is that?"

"Cliff showed me this yesterday, after you left. It is a secret prototype for the military. You'd love what it does. But, if I told you, I'd have to kill you," he said, teasingly. "I'm kidding! It affects gravity. I'd show you, but it has to be used in a confined space for the waves to build up enough to lift anything."

"Cliff making secret weapons for the military, great! I thought things couldn't get any worse! Daniel, there is something I have to tell you." She tried to get every word out before she lost her train of thought again to his full lips. "Cliff is controlling people and has been for years! I'm not sure he knows it, but he will probably figure it out soon after what happened yesterday."

"Cliff has always been manipulative, Susan," he replied. "What makes you think he is 'controlling' people? We tested out the Mod, it only affects others with a Mod, right? Is he..." he stopped and looked a bit annoyed, then continued with, "do you think he is controlling me?"

"Yes, Daniel. I do. I'm sorry."

"How? Why? Right now?"

"No, not right now. Of course not right now! Unless ... is he here? He's not here, right?" she said as she looked around to make sure Cliff wasn't hiding in the park or waiting in Daniel's car.

She was pretty sure that if Cliff was close, he wouldn't be too happy about them making out and would have stepped-in a long time ago. He'd been asking her out for years and it took everything she had to tell him 'No' because of how persuasive he had become. But it was exactly his manipulative tendencies that made her not want to go out with him in the first place. He had been even more persistent and aggressive ever since she came to Colorado, and she was afraid to even bring up the guy she was dating.

"How can I know if he is trying to control me? How can I stop him? I felt like I had a fairly good handle on him yesterday," Daniel stated.

"I don't know. You probably won't be able to tell. Plus, he might not even know he is doing it. The Mod is amplifying more than what was intended, that has become very clear today."

"What do you mean?"

"I mean, have you ever felt this way about me before, Daniel?"

He pulled back and thought for a minute. "I've liked you since the day I met you, Susan. If it weren't for Amy, I think we would have been together a long time ago. I think you know that too."

Susan was shocked. Hearing him say aloud what she had thought for so long seemed surreal. Could it be he was just finally over Amy and ready to love again?

"Why do you think it is amplifying my feelings?"

"Because you have never kissed me before..." she was not able to finish her sentence before he kissed her again.

"It feels right to me," he said, smiling and caressing her cheek.

"As much as I want it to be real, I don't know..." she began but was having trouble putting a finger on what was wrong. "I don't trust it, it feels ... sudden. And, I know Cliff has more control than you know."

"I am in control." He was getting angry. "You know I am always in control."

"I don't think so, Daniel. I ran some tests while we were in Japan that I found disturbing, like source code in the microchip that shouldn't exist. After what happened yesterday, I realized it was that his brain figured out how to integrate and use the Mod for telepathy."

"Yesterday, you told him that the telepathy was only due to our genetic similarity."

"I had to think of something to say. I don't trust what Cliff will do once he knows his capabilities."

"I have the same capabilities too, right?"

"Not exactly. Your Mod is a different, an advanced version. It has more capacity and enhancements, so you will likely not be as susceptible to his control as say, Bill. But, we both know Cliff's prefrontal cortex is ... special. He could override yours, you might not be able to stop him," Susan explained. "Once he truly realizes the extent of his abilities, there may be no stopping him from doing whatever he puts his mind to."

Daniel did not look very happy anymore. The lightheartedness, and lovi-dovi-ness of the new Daniel had been replaced with a grim look of determination that she had seen often before when they had worked together years ago. In a way it was comforting to see him back to himself. But, her heart still sank and her lips were aching for his. It wasn't meant to be, though, and she knew it. She took a deep breath, let it go slowly and tried to focus on the dilemma at hand.

"I've been working on designs to enhance the output of similar patients, for imaging purposes. I think I told you, I've been working with dream-walkers?"

"Yes, I remember. You were a bit drunk, so I wasn't sure how much of what you were saying should be taken to heart."

"I wasn't that drunk!" Honestly, she didn't remember drinking that much, but couldn't remember much else of that night. That bartender had given her a strong scotch on the rocks. She only remembered ordering two drinks. She'd never been drunk on only two drinks.

"You stumbled away and fell into the elevator, Susan. I had to send the bellman to go check on you."

"Is that why the bellman went to my room?" She had wondered about that, and continued with, "huh ... ok, anyway, dream-walkers seem to have the same brain patterns as your brother. Remember, I told you I found one that was stronger, better than Cliff?"

"Yes, where are you going with this? That is the guy you are seeing, isn't it?"

"Yes, it is, but that isn't the point. The point is that I think that if I work with him, I can develop a microchip that can stop Cliff from controlling you. Or, at the very least, allow you to overpower him. I need to understand more how it all works with Darren..."

"Darren, that's his name? So, you want to leave and go back to Darren?" Daniel asked, holding her hand tightly, then pulling her close for another kiss. "Does Darren make you feel like this?"

"I ... I can't ... But, we both need to leave! Get as far away from Cliff as we can. He's probably already figured it all out by now and it is dangerous for..."

He kissed her again, holding her close before saying: "How about we just run away together instead, Susan? Get as far away from here as we can together. Leave Cliff to his own devices."

"Run-away together?" The thought had never crossed her mind. Of course, she never expected Daniel would ever reciprocate her feelings for him – not after what happened with Amy.

"Yes, just me and you. Maybe, Seattle? Though, I might rust with all the rain." He laughed and held up his left hand. "Or, you could finally show me your hometown of Toulouse."

"But, my work. Your family..." as much as the idea of running away appealed to her, she had never been one to run away from a problem. Or leave the world with a legacy she never intended to create. Did Daniel not understand the implications of Cliff having telepathy?

He tried to kiss her again, but she had to stop him. And as much as it hurt her to do it, she had to bring up the hard truth he was unwilling to face. "Who knows what Cliff will end up doing ... are you sure you trust him? The incidents surrounding Amy's death, the way he always despised her ... I ..." Susan felt the tension in Daniel immediately, his posture went ridged and his jaw was locked. "I ... I'm not saying that he..." Susan couldn't continue. She wasn't the only one who speculated that Cliff might have had something to do with Amy's death, but no one would say it aloud. No one dared. The whole town didn't. Cops and all.

"He couldn't have ... he is my brother, he couldn't have..." he was staring out at the lake, void of emotion on his face and eyes looking like they were seeing miles away.

"You can't..." Susan didn't know how to finish that sentence. Daniel, with his current Mod, might be the only one with a chance at controlling Cliff. And Cliff just couldn't be left to do whatever he wanted ... not after what happened with Amy.

If only Daniel could learn to manipulate the Mod the way Cliff did, and focus his mind. If she could get him an improved chip, that would be even better. But, for now she had to help him as best she could. "Do you ever dream, Daniel?"

"Not in a long time, not that I remember. When I did, it was only bits of nightmares. Why?" he asked. He had moved away from her already, and the aching distance felt like a deep cold chasm.

"There are some that believe that in a dream state we can access the 'collective consciousness' of humanity. It is where all human minds can connect, have you heard about this?" Susan asked while looking around for an ant pile ... there had to be an ant pile around the lake somewhere ... ah ha! She got up and walked over to kick the ant pile, causing complete chaos for the ants.

Daniel had been following Susan around, confused at her sporadic behavior, "So you think this access to the collective conscious by dream-walkers is somehow tied to the ability to use the microchip for telepathy?"

Wow, he didn't miss anything! He put that together quick! she thought as she nodded.

Susan pulled a Funyun out of her bag and placed it down next to an ant that was all alone on the sidewalk and placed another Funyun a few centimeters away but not next to any ant. "Watch. Look how this little ant can't pick up the snack ... and look, here come several family members to help out."

"They probably smelled the onion."

She was suddenly self-conscious of her breath, but she cleared her throat and continued, "No, see how none of them went to the other Funyun, even though it was just as close to the group as the one here. The only difference was there was a single ant here – he called for help. This experiment has been done before, several times in labs. The ants, they can sense when other ants need help. They have a communal mind. They use it all the time and that is how they are able to accomplish so much together."

"So, this is your collective conscious experiment? Dream-walkers are ants-like humans?"

"Yes, I think people who are dream-walkers are more in tune with the collective conscious, and make much better telepaths if ... say, their abilities were enhanced. The Mod pushes and amplifies brainwaves. Yours uses the energy of the blood to produce the power needed, and it is limitless. You haven't had it for very long, so there is no telling what you will be capable of."

"I never wanted this, Susan. And Cliff is the last person on Earth who should have this capability." He was watching the ants intently and then looked to her and said, "You truly believe I can stop him?"

Susan couldn't meet his look, she glanced away. 'No' was the answer she had in her head but instead she said, "Cliff's Mod is still regulated by the outer power controller, but he wants a new one installed. He asked for it the other day and I said I would get him one made once I went back to LA. Honestly, I never intended to give him any upgrades. I could install a less advanced version instead ... but we would have to keep it a secret from him until then ... and that might be possible."

"Do you think it is just the latest versions and dream-walkers that it would do this for? Or could this affect everyone with a Mod? Did you design this on purpose, Susan?"

"No, of course not! You know my intentions. I always wanted to help those suffering from debilitating illness and disease. Not mind control!" she was offended he even suggested she had purposefully unlocked human telepathy.

"I'm sorry, you just seem to know a lot about it for someone who says they didn't do it on purpose," Daniel inquired. "I know the EEG was originally designed by a doctor wanting to explore telepathy. Did you know that? His experiments failed, and I never expected that anything would come of your Mods besides the shortsighted, personal goals I had."

"My goal was Parkinson's, you know that ... everything else has been an accident," she replied while thinking of all the sideways twists and turns in her research that had led to this moment.

"You are prone to accidents," he chuckled.

"I'm worried about you Daniel. Now that you have this new Mod installed, your brain is more open, it's like a doorway. Cliff is far more advanced than you, he's not only a dream-walker, but he has had years with his Mod. If you want to resist his persuasion, I think you'll need to work on your dreaming skills. Learn to become a lucid dreamer. It's your only chance."

"How would I do that?"

"For one, try and remember your dreams every morning when you wake up. Have a diary, and write down what you remember and..." Susan stopped what she was saying, standing up at the sound of police sirens coming into the park.

"They are coming to arrest you for kicking over that ant pile," Daniel joked. "And littering with those Funyuns. Better hide the bag and clean the dirt from your shoe."

"Very funny." Susan couldn't help but feel concerned, and Daniel stopped smiling when four police cars stopped right in front of them, lights on and forming a barrier to any exit.

A Sheriff, middle-aged, lean and grizzly got out of the foremost vehicle. He had his hand over his holster, the other hand with cuffs already out, and gruffly stated, "Are you Dr. Susan Aldean?"

"Why, is there something the matter?" She stood still, looking at the group of men in uniform forming around her. Their faces were graven and intent as if they expected her to flee at any second.

One of the officers opened the backseat door of his car and Cliff appeared as if summoned. "Yes, that is Dr. Aldean," he remarked. "It is best that you not resist, Susan."

"I'm afraid I'm placing you under arrest. You have the right to remain silent, anything you say or do ..." The sheriff continued but Susan didn't hear a word he was saying, she was in complete shock as her arms were being forced behind her back and the hard, cold handcuffs were being placed on her wrists.

"Sheriff Osbourne, there must be some mistake," Daniel began. "Look, you've known me my whole life. I tell you this woman is innocent of whatever it is you think she has done!"

"She is being charged with the murder of your fiancé Daniel. We have found compelling evidence that she is the one who planted the bomb."

"WHAT?" both Daniel and Susan said at the same time.

"That is absurd! Why would I want to kill Amy? Daniel, you don't believe this, do you?" Susan pleaded, gazing up at Daniel for defense while he was merely standing there gaping.

"How? What evidence?" Daniel finally asked, holding the Sheriff by the shoulder with his mechanical arm. The Sheriff's eyes went wide, seeing the formidable prosthesis for the first time.

"I, umm..." Sheriff Osbourne took a deep breath and continued, "I received a call yesterday, from the bellman at the hotel. He said he finally remembered who he had seen last and where he had seen the suspect 'present' before – in her room. He still couldn't remember much else, including how he got home or even delivering the present. It is clear he was drugged, that was established. We did a check of her credit card transactions and found the purchase of a ceramic tea kettle the day before, one that matched the description the bridesmaid, Amanda, gave."

Daniel's grip on the officer got tighter and the Sheriff was now wincing and bent forward, holding onto the metal hand with both of his own. "Please, Daniel!" he yelled.

"It's true, Daniel. It's all true," Cliff said, coming over to stand next to his brother, placing a hand on his shoulder.

Daniel released the officer, who dropped to the ground. He then glared at Susan with the coldest expression she had ever seen in her life, with eyes like black holes. "You wanted me to think it was my own brother? You almost had me convinced! Amy trusted you, she loved you! I loved you!"

Susan's heart felt like it was going to pound out of her chest. Her head was spinning and her lungs felt like iron. What was happening? Think Susan, think! "The bellman did come to my room. You sent him, you said so yourself ... I did get a teapot for Amy, but ... I was so drunk, I don't remember anything after the bellman came knocking, asking how I was ... I could never have ... I would never have ... you must know that ... Daniel?"

"Take her away, I can't even look at her," Daniel said, walking away with Cliff by his side. Neither man even turned to look back at her as they got into Daniel's car and drove away.

Sheriff Osbourne had his hand on her head and was pushing her into the back of his patrol car before Susan could open her mouth to plead her innocence. How could he believe that she could kill Amy? How could anyone believe that she could kill anyone?

They all had to know it was Cliff ... he must have figured out that she knew and ... she never should have asked to meet Daniel alone yesterday! Cliff must have overheard, he must have gotten the bellman to call the Sheriff!

She should have run yesterday. Her instincts had told her to run. When she saw what happened between Daniel and Cliff, and what Daniel could do to Bill ... she should have run! But, she had wanted to help Daniel, to warn him ...

How in the world was she going to get out of this mess? She was staring out the window of the back seat of the cop car, out into the red rock desert that was beginning to look like hell to her. She should never have come to Colorado!

Cliff had complete control over everyone, and no one could see through it. Or chose not to. Did he set her up from the beginning? Did he take her present and drug the bellman? He had to have! Which meant there was more to this than just overhearing a conversation yesterday.

What motive could he possibly have in trying to implicate her in all of this? Jealousy? She could see that he might be annoyed or frustrated that she would chose Daniel over him ... but not to this extent.

Think! What happened in the last 24hrs??

He had always wanted her close, wanted her to come to Colorado and work for him. She had just told him yesterday that now that Daniel was fully recovered she would return to LA ... Was this an attempt to keep her here? A sick, sadistic attempt to force her into some kind of agreement to work for him? That bastard!! Whatever he wanted, and whatever it took, she would never, EVER, EVER give it to him!

Chapter 13

Dreams and Things

Daniel stood on a cliff, overlooking the grand desert valley below. He came back here often in his dreams. He was pulled to it, as if his soul was not through with it. His subconscious wanted him here. He hated coming here, this is where Amy had fallen so many years ago. He sat down on the red rock, cross-legged, waiting for what this dream would bring him next.

"You know the truth, dear Daniel. Admit it and you will be free," the familiar voice of his old nanny, Miss Tinny, could be heard from behind him. He turned around, but she was not there ... only rock fading to more rock.

He turned back around to face the edge and saw Susan, one hand outreached. She was holding on for her life from the precipice, like Amy had been so many years ago. She begged him to help her. He refused to move, to get close to the edge, and then she fell screaming.

Daniel awoke bolt upright in his bed. He picked-up a notebook from the nightstand and jotted down everything he could remember ... his mind already reaching for details that were slipping away. Was it Susan or Amy falling? Was it his mother or Miss Tinny's voice he had heard? How did he get to the cliff?

He was getting better at remembering, but it was still difficult for him. It didn't come naturally like it did for his brother but he knew it was important for him to get better at it if he was to have any chance to find the truth and face it. To ease his troubled mind.

Susan's arraignment seemed like yesterday. She had the motive, the means, no alibi, and all the evidence pointed to her. He still couldn't believe she did it though, not fully. That she was the one who murdered Amy. His recurrent dreams kept reminding him that deep down he thought she was innocent. He knew that is what his dreams meant. But, he also knew that if she didn't set the bomb then ... he didn't want to think about it. There was only one other person that it could be.

And, if it was Cliff, how could he have ...? How? How could he get himself to admit he thought his little brother was capable of murder?

His mind kept bringing him back to the day in the park Susan was arrested, and all the words she'd said. How he felt when he was with her. How close he had been to running away with her ...

If Susan was right, and innocent, working on his dream skills was the only thing he could do for now to prepare to face Cliff. And eventually challenge him mentally to force-out the truth.

In the meantime, he had been struggling to not let anyone know that he still suspected Cliff. Because if Cliff found out Daniel suspected him, who knows what he would do. If he was capable of doing the things that he may have already done then more murder was not out of the realm of possibility. He shuddered at the thought and pushed it out of his head.

Daniel worked with Cliff every day on prosthetics for new patients. Often veterans who could not afford care. They also worked on weapons for the military, and for personal use. Side by side, and with his parent's support. The family had never been closer. And when they were working together it was so easy to forget the past; to shove the horrors aside and focus on the help they were able to give so many.

Today they were testing out an acid solution his mother designed for one of the projectiles used in the launch packet Cliff had developed. An ideal family gathering for accusing your brother of murder. Right. Best to keep those thoughts out of his head.

When would it be the right time? When Susan was in prison for another year? Ten more years? If Susan was innocent, how could he do this to her? Every day she was in prison would be on his hands forever, and the guilt and conflict were eating him up inside.

Daniel had just reached the research facility when he guarded his mind. Then he set to thinking about the work at hand. His father greeted him at the entry to the military bunker where they would be doing their testing today. He had two thermoses of coffee in his hands and handed one to Daniel.

His parents still didn't know about the telepathic link between the two brothers, or the Mod's opening the mind to manipulation by those with more advanced Mods or more advanced cognitive abilities. Cliff never mentioned it and Daniel figured with Susan in jail and unable to fix the problem that it was better to not bring it up either.

"Thanks, Father. How are you today?" Daniel asked while drinking from the welcomed thermos of steaming energy.

"I have been having troubling headaches, to be frank. I may step out for a bit today," Martin admitted, uncharacteristically, then continued walking forward as if he has just said, "I'm fine."

That admission stopped Daniel in his tracks. He had never known his father to be ill. The coffee was invented by him for that sole purpose! To keep the cancer at bay that plagued his brain and it had worked for decades to prevent any kind of illness, including even aging. His father never had headaches. Was this his way of him telling him the cancer was back?

"What?" was all Daniel could get out.

Martin ignored the question and kept walking. He was such a proud and stubborn man. Admitting the cancer relapsed was admitting failure. The last thing he ever wanted to do was admit failure.

Daniel's mother was waiting for them in the back of the hangar-like complex within the mountain that they had reinforced for weapons testing. She was wearing a jet pack with an attached flame thrower nozzle converted for acid spray. The goo-ified remains of rubber dummies were oozing in front of her. Their stench was noxious and that was with loud fans blowing out into sizable ventilation shafts at the furthest wall to the south of the great open room.

"You're too late, boys!" she yelled over the noise of the fans. "These guys are deep-fried slimers now!"

"I see, honey. You couldn't wait?" Martin asked his wife, leaning over to give her a kiss on her cheek right below the chemical goggles she was wearing. Her hair was pulled back in a blonde braid that hung down to the middle of her baggy, blue coveralls and she had on giant black chemical gloves that came to her elbows as well as large, black boots that came to her knees.

"I tried to stop her, but she simply felt like those dummies deserved to get it this morning," Cliff said, coming from one of the locked research rooms and carrying another chemical bag and nozzle. He was dressed similarly to his mom, but with goggles on top on his head. "I was working on getting this one to create a mist. I added a nebulizer; but, we would have to contain it in another room. We need a smaller area if we are to test out a mist."

"You'll need a full suit and mask as well, for a mist. Not just these cotton threads," Beth suggested. "I probably should have worn a mask, this stuff sure stinks and those blowers are barely pulling the fumes out! Likely I inhaled a good dose of carcinogens I'll regret later."

"Is it because Father is sick that you are being more reckless than normal, Mom?" Daniel asked.

"You told him?" Beth said, throwing off her gear and gloves. She reached over to Martin to check his pupils with a small flashlight that was sitting on the counter next to him. Even she knew it must be bad if he was admitting any symptoms.

"It has advanced unpredictably fast, honey," he said. "I don't think we can hide it anymore."

"Told him what? Father is sick? What's going on? What are you hiding?" Cliff demanded.

"Dad has a glioblastoma that he has been self-treating for years, Cliff. Didn't they tell you?" Daniel said, shocked that his parents were able to keep something like that from Cliff all these years. Daniel had figured part of it out when his parents gave him the formula for the coffee, and the rest by confronting his father. He'd asked him if he could examine him, possibly operate if needed and Martin had refused help. He had his own methods of treatment and felt like brain surgery was a last resort.

"No! But your research, oncolytic virology ... isn't there a cure in there somewhere, in all those viruses you dug up?"

"No, there isn't son. There are treatments, enhancements, remedies..." Martin seemed to lose his train of thought, and sat down, somewhat wobbly. After a deep breath he continued with, "there is one virus that we haven't tried..." he gazed at Beth and she shook her head. Then he said, "your mother would never let me test it on myself. And, it has to be altered to my DNA first ... it is a particularly virulent strain, prone to shifts."

"If the virus evolved after mixing with his DNA, it could become highly unstable and even kill him. And, it is extremely contagious ... we decided this a long time ago, that we would stop working that strain." Beth looked forlorn and wasn't unable to take her eyes off of her husband. "But, I never expected that we wouldn't find anything else after decades of research ... and that the coffee would stop working."

"How bad is it, father?" Daniel asked, realizing the gravity of the situation, locking eyes with his brother Cliff, who's jaw was firmly clasped in the shared rage and helpless frustration they felt so strongly in the moment together. He could feel his brothers surprise and ... betrayal? He felt betrayed they had never told him. You have to know that father is too proud to admit failure, Cliff.

"I'm just happy to spend any moment I have with my family," Martin said, in a humbled resignation that sent despair into Daniel's heart like a knife and he felt the anger well up inside Cliff to a dangerous level.

"That is unacceptable, Mother, that we can't try this virus of his. Simply unacceptable! If there is any hope, we have to try." Cliff was focused hard on his mother, and Daniel could feel the determination in waves pulsing through his anger and frustration. "You know we can keep him in quarantine until he stabilizes; and, if the strain evolves we can deal with it when it comes. This is an acceptable risk, we have to try!"

Surprisingly, Beth was nodding her head as he spoke. She appeared to be in a daze.

"Yes, you're right Cliff ... we have the facilities now to contain this ... and the alternative is just as unbearable to me as the risk," Beth explained, both hands holding her husband's head gently. "We have to try."

"Are you sure, honey?" Martin was gazing into his wife's eyes, which were filling with tears as she nodded.

Daniel couldn't believe what he was hearing. He was no expert in viruses, but for his father to be this hesitant about using one, at the risk of his own life, meant that this strain was very dangerous indeed. He would have to ensure everything went smoothly. "How long will it take to prepare the sample with the altered DNA? Will you be able to perform the alteration in your condition, father? Can I help?"

"Yes, I will need to move everything to the quarantine labs. I think, 48 hours? I'll know more then," Martin explained.

"I'll bring in a team. I have three scientists in mind that can help..." Cliff began.

"Not those three that keep following you around, Cliff? Ferris, Dawson and Lobbs?" Beth was flustered and more annoyance entered her voice with each name she dropped.

"Yes, they are the best we have and I know I can trust them. I'll have them help you set up, Father, and prepare the chambers in case you need to stay for a while," Cliff insisted. "It will be good to have help."

"Right, and which of them knows about the dangers of not following the proper protocols around viruses?" Martin asked. "How to determine if there has been an antigenic shift?"

"Lobbs is a microbiologist, and I am sure Dawson and Ferris took some biology, they are doctors, after all," said Cliff. "It matters more who we can trust now than anything."

"I'll show them where to go then. Daniel, can you clean up this mess?" Beth said as she led Cliff and Martin out of the room and left Daniel standing there in disbelief.

He stood in silence for a while. Then cleaned up the rubbery ooze, placing the remains in large hazmat barrels.

As he was leaving the room he glanced over at the rocket legs Cliff had been developing ... which gave him an idea. His family would be distracted over the next 48 hours ... What if he broke Susan out of jail? He could be out and back before they even noticed anything was missing. This might be his only opportunity!

He didn't know for sure if she planted that bomb, but his heart sank at the thought of her in prison for life knowing that her love for him is what put her there. Maybe if he finally helped her, his recurrent nightmares would go away and the turmoil inside of him would subside.

Daniel took the rocket legs, a laser blaster, and one of the black Kevlar suits and then headed out the ventilation shaft.

~ ~ ~

Susan was settling into her top bunkbed with a self-help book called "Let. It. Go." She had heard of other martyrs going to jail and becoming wise by reading a ton of books, and she thought that maybe improving her mind was her best bet to keep her sanity.

Her bottom bunk mate, Lana Perez, was a Hispanic woman who had robbed a bank with her ex-husband, thinking they would be the next Bonnie and Clyde; but, they hadn't even made it past the first heist before being surrounded and tasered.

Lana was nice. She'd been here a year already and had taken on the hobby of doing hair for the other ladies in her corridor. She'd offered to give her some blonde highlights and Susan didn't dare refuse. She wanted to fit in because it looked like she would be here for a while. The highlights turned out more pink than blonde, but her hair was the least of her worries.

The night was drawing on, and she was beginning to fall asleep when she noticed an odd smell, like burning electric wires. Then she felt the heat coming from the wall next to the window. She looked over to see there was a bright orange, square outline forming on the wall and it was getting brighter. There was a low hum, getting louder.

"Christ! Lana, get back!" she whispered loudly as she jumped down and pulled her dozing roommate out of her slumber on the bottom bunk. She got as far back against the far wall as possible, pulling the half-asleep Lana close.

The square outline was now completely formed, and then the wall burst forward, revealing a metal hand extended. On the other side of the wall, floating in mid-air, was Daniel of all people! He was dressed all in black, with a jet stream coming out of his legs. She was more surprised at who was there than that there was a cyborg outside her jail cell – she'd thought it would be Cliff who would eventually come for her. She was convinced Daniel hated her.

"We have to go now, we don't have much time," he said as he lifted her into the air and out into the desert nightscape with the surprised Lana waving 'bye' from the open 3rd floor cell wall. They were moving at incredible speed, and she had her face buried in his chest because the wind was blasting her eyes. He had on a protective helmet and goggles, and he held her tight enough to almost crack a rib but she didn't mind. He had come to save her!

They stopped in a wooded area near the highway and he landed down gently, debris flying in all directions.

"Here is some money and a dress," he said, handing her a wadded-up cloth over a purse. "Down the road about a mile, you'll find a greyhound bus station. I suggest you take a bus and disappear."

Susan was not sure what she had expected him to say, but 'take this and disappear' was not it. It hurt that he was so cold.

"Why are you helping me, Daniel? Do you still think I killed Amy?" She asked as she pulled over the dress while pulling off the tan and black coveralls underneath. She kicked the coveralls into the bushes.

"I don't know, but..."

"Right, Cliff has you believing whatever he wants..."

"I don't know what I believe, Susan!"

"Did he tell you he came to me, in jail? Several times, actually. Offered to get me out if I would work for him. Saying he forgives me for killing Amy, but that you never will. As if I didn't know that he did it, that he set the whole thing up!"

"He visited you in jail? What did he want you to do for him?"

"He's out of his mind, Daniel! Can't you see that? He has figured out that the Mod's could be altered to control people, to control everyone, not just people with Mods. He wants a master Mod to control everyone! He wants me to develop it for him and I refused."

"I don't know if I can believe that, Susan."

Susan was looking at Daniel in the low light of the crescent moon: half machine, half a broken human being who had lost so much at the hands of someone who should love him the most – his own brother.

"I'm so sorry, Daniel," was all she could say. He was so broken, in so many ways.

He reached his human arm out to her and pulled her close for a kiss, a kiss filled with tears from the both of them.

"I'm sorry too, Susan. I have to go, before they find out I left. And you have to get out of this state."

"Thank you, Daniel. For everything."

He blasted off, leaving her coughing on desert dust. She looked down at the cash in the small purse, it had to be over $400,000! That should buy a bus ticket or two! She wondered if her cellmate had jumped out of the hole in the wall. Maybe Lana thought she was still dreaming. Seeing a cyborg appear and jet out had to be fairly un-expected after waking up from a nap. Hopefully she knew better than to tell anyone who had broken her out of jail.

Daniel was always so prepared. Dress, purse, money ... he must care about her. If only he could admit that his brother was pure evil, sent from hell to inflict harm on all humanity! Okay, maybe that was too much. Cliff was an evil bastard though, for putting her in this predicament!

Now she was a fugitive and had no idea where to go. All she knew was that she wanted to get as far away from Colorado, and the Jahren family, as she possibly could get and never come back!

~ ~ ~

Daniel finished replacing and cleaning all of the gear he had used just in time for Ran to come into the bunker.

"Trying out the goggles?" Ran asked, pointing to his head.

"What? Yes, the visibility is great. IR was a nice touch for night vision," Daniel replied, removing the goggles he had forgotten to take off and trying to play it off. He realized the dirt on the goggles was likely all over his face as well.

"Yes, the night vision can come in handy. Where is your family? I thought you were testing the new acid wash technology today?"

"Something came up with my father, he's sick," Daniel explained, heading towards the door to avoid any more questions he had no idea how to answer without further implicating himself. "I should go check on him now, in fact."

"That explains why your mother has been acting strange lately..." Ran began, obviously wanting to continue talking despite the fact that Daniel was walking away. Daniel made it to the door before hearing. "Please, stop, there is something I need to tell you!"

Daniel halted and turned around to see Ran biting his lip and wringing his hands, completely unsure of what he was about to say next but desperate to say something.

"Your mother and I ... umm, no, let me start over ... Cliff, he ... he can be quite persuasive, you know, and ... we know Daniel, we know what happened. I'm sorry," Ran was stammering.

"What are you getting at, Ran? What is it that you know?" Daniel asked, more confused than ever.

"There is another bunker. Your mother had me work on it and keep it a secret. She never trusted Cliff, and I can see why. Please don't tell Cliff! He can't know. Here, take this key. The door is in the far wing of the third level basement. There is a cut-out in the side of the rock that if you go past, you'll miss it," Ran explained. "You'll understand when you see it."

"I don't understand." Why would my mother build another bunker and keep it secret from Cliff? What did she know? Daniel thought.

"Cliff has an insatiable appetite for power, Daniel. None of this will ever be enough for him ... can't you see that?" Ran looked scared, and as if he might be regretting telling him any of this.

"I think I know my own brother, Ran." Daniel took the key from Ran's shaking hand and hurried off in a metallic-clanking fury down the hallway to find this other bunker.

The third level basement was not fully finished, there was more chopped rock tunnel than hallway as Daniel walked around looking for an enclave in the mountain that could hold a door. He walked by it three times before he noticed the opening. He pulled out the key and unlocked the door.

This was not a military weapons bunker! There were computers, beds, and barrels of the family brand coffee. It had supplies enough for a small city ... and incubation pods? Was his mother planning for World War III?

He strode over to one of several 7ft long tubes that he was guessing was an incubation pod. It had a touchscreen display with temperature controls and tubes coming out for liquids going into the ground. No liquid nitrogen as far as he could tell and the temperature only went down to -20 degrees centigrade. He pulled-up one of the floor panels next to the pod and there was an intricate system of tubing underneath. He opened one of the tubes and recognized the black liquid by the smell. This pod was definitely designed to sustain someone indefinitely.

This was not what he expected to find tonight. Ran and his mother must know something he didn't. This explained nothing! He was now more confused than ever.

He locked the room and put away the key, heading up towards the main facility to find his family. How many secrets were they keeping between them? Communication was not their best family trait, it never was. But this, this was on a whole new level. Plus, he had to keep this from Cliff as well? Another tangled web to navigate.

Chapter 14

A Reckoning

Beth sat anxiously waiting next to her husband's bedside. She was dressed in full bio-hazard gear and it was excruciating not being able to touch him. But, they were taking no chances until the virus ran its course, which was carrying on longer than expected.

She had never seen her husband like this, and it felt like it was killing her to look at him. Martin appeared to have aged a decade in the past week and lost a significant amount of weight. His face was wan, with dark circles under his eyes and his breathing was shallow and labored. They had been together so long, and part of her thought they would both live forever. She never wanted to think about life without him, she just couldn't.

She held his hand as best she could through her thick gloves and closed her eyes, focusing on breathing deeply. "Follow my breath, honey," she whispered. He followed her breathing, taking in deep breaths. "Breathe from your stomach," she explained, while putting her hand on his abdomen, "here." His breathing got stronger and longer, and he smiled up at her lovingly. The thin-skinned cheeks and frail lips drawn was enough to make her heart break at the same time as give her hope.

"How is he today, mom?" Cliff asked, coming in to sit next to her in full gear as well.

"Better, I feel like he is getting better. How are you?" Beth couldn't help but notice the dark circles under her youngest son's eyes that were evident even through the plastic mask.

"I don't know why this is taking so long to work … it's maddening!" Cliff had both hands balled into fists on his lap and was staring down at his own mechanical legs.

"You of all people should know, some things can't be rushed. It's barely been more than a week."

"Yes, of all people," Daniel said, coming in the back door with a rhythmic pulse and the sound of metal on the floor. He began donning his suit to enter into the cordoned-off bed chamber. When he got to his father, he began the usual routine of checking vitals and listening to heart and lungs.

"He's improving. And I have more good news. The last scan came back with no evidence of the tumor, so the virus has wiped his brain clean," Daniel was staring down at his father and trying to smile while delivering the good news, but it was obvious it hurt to see him in this condition. "Father, is there anything you would like us to get you?'"

"Coffee!" Martin exclaimed, with a half-smile and a twinkle in his eyes. In a shallow, wheezing voice he said, "Also, approximately 2mg of SAL-157 twenty minutes proceeding a booster of BR-76 and 25 mg of Benadryl." He took a few shallow breaths, coughed and continued, "And, my brain is not wiped clean, son. Hand me a Sudoku, honey. I'll prove it!"

"Honey, a Sudoku won't prove anything!" She should never have brought those into his bedchamber.

He was obsessed. Plus, he was solving all the good ones before she could get to them. "We all know you are still smart as a whip."

"He's improving? Then why does he look so..." Cliff started but didn't want to finish the sentence after he caught her concerned glance.

"The virus has taken a toll on his body, it doesn't just attack the cancer. Biomarkers are all getting better though ... at least than they were a few days ago ... he's stronger than he looks," Daniel was once again trying to make everyone feel better, but she wasn't sure he wasn't lying about the biomarkers based on Martin's appearance.

"We should give him Quinta. He will get stronger, much quicker," Cliff suggested.

"No!" everyone said at once.

"Why not? Daniel, you took it. I took it. Look how much stronger we both are with minimal side effects. He would get better so much quicker if..."

"Daniel, you took the Quinta virus?" This was the first Beth had heard of it, she thought her first born son was wiser than that. She thought Cliff must be lying. Her mind was frozen in a panicked rage waiting for Daniel to answer her question.

"The prosthetics, they are heavy and Quinta makes them feel like nothing," Daniel explained. "I guess I felt like I had nothing to lose, mom, after what happened..."

"Nothing to lose? How about me? Or your father? Or your brother? I can see Cliff doing some hair-brained thing like injecting himself with that monster of a concoction, but you Daniel?" Beth was standing, hands on hips and fully irate before she could stop herself.

Losing her temper was the last thing Martin needed to witness, so she began taking deep breaths to calm down. "It was bad enough when I found out your father and Cliff were working on that behind my back, but when I found out Cliff had injected himself ... and now you!" The deep breathing wasn't helping, and her temper was mounting. She felt like a deep breathing purple monster about to explode. "I can't deal with this right now," she said while exiting out of the bedchamber. She tried to let out a little of the anger she felt by throwing pieces of bio-suit into the donning booth with voracity.

Maybe it was the thought of losing her husband, and seeing him in such a horrible condition, but her ability to deal with Daniel's negligence was just too much right now. He was supposed to be the responsible one in the family! The only other one she could trust. She felt like everything was spinning out from under her control, and she needed to be in control.

Planning. Planning made her feel in control. If all things fail, go to plan B! She always had a plan B, or C, or D. And if that failed, E.

When life throws you a reckless maniac for a son, you have a responsible son who can keep him in line. Now, what did she have? A husband barely alive, and two senseless sons. Calm down! she said to herself. There must be more going on here.

This was not like Daniel, and she needed to figure out why he would do something so reckless. The Quinta virus was barely stable and had unknown side effects.

However, one known side effect that was not to be taken lightly was added aggression and instability, which Cliff had been displaying since day one.

Daniel knew better! But, he had changed so much since Amy's death, and there was something he was hiding from her, she could feel it. She needed to figure out what, now. But first, she needed to calm down so she could think straight. Breath! Count to 10 ... 1 ... 2 ... 3 ...

~ ~ ~

I would never have guessed you would break the woman out of jail who killed Amy, Cliff said to Daniel in his mind as they sat next to their father, who was now sitting up and sipping on a thermos of piping hot coffee.

Is that why you told Mom about the Quinta virus? Daniel asked, in his mind to Cliff. To expose my reckless nature? What are you trying to do, Cliff?

Why did you do it? Do you love Susan? Cliff demanded, pushing the question hard against Daniel's skull, enough to make him wince. You know I wanted her for myself.

Yes. Yes, I do, Daniel said, fighting back his brother's presence in his head, and at the same time realizing that he did love Susan. Wow, I love Susan, despite everything she's done? he thought.

Cliff was gone, he removed himself and it felt like a band-aid being ripped out of the inside of his skull. It was enough to make Daniel lose his balance and almost fall forward.

Susan is a special person, I wish things could have been different, Cliff said in his head, he genuinely felt strong affection in the statement. Daniel could feel it coming through into his own mind and mixing with his own thoughts so much that it was hard to distinguish individual feelings.

She's long gone now, Cliff. We'll never see her again, Daniel let him know, showing an image of her walking down the road towards the bus stop in his head.

I see, Cliff said, smiling and getting up to leave. Daniel felt a sudden panic, had he given away too much? Cliff would not be able to find her from only that simple image, could he?

"Where are you going?" Daniel asked, aloud.

"I'm going to find something I lost, brother. It should be a good distraction from all of this," Cliff explained, aloud, while swiftly taking off his suit in the donning booth and heading out the door.

"Good idea, Cliff. It will keep you out of trouble, I am sure," Martin said. "Daniel, can you hand me that Sudoku your mom left?"

Daniel tossed the Sudoku to his father and tried to follow Cliff out. He yelled, "Wait!" but Cliff was long gone, he moved quickly with the prosthetics and the Quinta virus giving him speed.

"Where is your brother hurrying off to, Daniel?" his mother asked, standing in the hallway, leaning back against the stone wall with her arms crossed.

"He is going to look for something he lost, that's what he said anyway ... are you ok, mom?" He knew she was mad at him, if her squinting eyes and pursed lips didn't say it themselves.

She seized him by the arm as he tried to head down the hallway in the direction Cliff had left. "Why do I get the feeling there is more that you aren't telling me? What other secrets are you holding, son?"

"My secrets?" he whispered loudly, looking down the hall in both directions. "My secrets? Come with me!" Now seemed like a good time to clear things up, with Cliff distracted.

He brought his mother down into the third basement, through the enclave and into the hidden disaster bunker. She followed, silent and sullen. "What is this, mother?"

"How did you find out about this? I told Ran not to show you unless..." Beth looked stunned. "You found out? You know Cliff killed Amy?"

"What?" Daniel was more shaken than he could stomach, and he suddenly wanted to throw up. He didn't know if it was hearing those words out loud or knowing that his mother knew that made him more sick. Ran knew. Others knew. The world was turning black. Was he about to pass out?

"Wait, you didn't know?" Beth looked thoroughly baffled.

"Of course I didn't know! Who else knows? Why didn't you tell the police?" Sickness was gripping him and he was trying not to hurl. He let his anger wash over him and held onto that to steady his stomach.

"I couldn't tell the police ... I'd just found out the day before he had injected himself again with the Quinta virus and I didn't want them to find out about that too."

"How did you find out?"

"He'd wanted to be strong for when Susan came to town. He was acting aggressive and irrational and I confronted him..."

"Not about him injecting the virus, about him killing my fiancé!"

"I'm sorry, it was obvious. His behavior ... his hatred for her ... and I knew where he got the drugs he used on the bellman ... Plus, Ran noticed some of the explosives were missing from the bunker. It just all added up."

"So, you have Ran keeping our dark family secrets too. How much does he know? I know he doesn't have a clue about the viruses. Now, I think he has another secret..."

"What new secret?"

"I had just gotten back from..." he held his stomach and felt dizzy, sitting down on one of the chairs next to the computer station. God, Susan had been innocent this whole time! "breaking Susan out of jail. When Ran gave me this key." He held up the square gold key for his mom.

"So, it was you who broke her out! I thought it was Cliff. I've been trying to figure out where he stashed her away. I assumed he was going to hold her prisoner until she gave him what he wanted, whatever that might be."

"What? Who all knows about Susan? Am I the only one who couldn't see she was innocent? How could you let him..." Daniel had no words, the amount of betrayal he felt was overwhelming, topped with the guilt for letting Susan go to jail.

"He is my son, Daniel ... he has always been troublesome. But I never expected for him to do what he did. I blame the Quinta virus for his erratic behavior, he took it right before the incident ... and it's a monster concoction ... He felt so badly afterwards and worked so hard to get you better ... he loves you."

"He felt badly?!? Erratic behavior? Amy was innocent! She deserved better."

Daniel looked at his mother, as if seeing her for the first time. Her eyes were filled with tears and her hands were clenched. She stood up straight and said, "There is nothing we can do for Amy. I am sorry, Daniel."

They stood there in silence, at a stalemate. Years had passed. Years of deception and now that the truth was out he almost wished he never knew. Daniel's insides were churning and settling until he said, "And this, what is all of this? What are you afraid will happen? The apocalypse?"

"Yes, after what happened. Yes! I didn't know where your brother would stop, or if he would stop. I don't know what he wants, but I have a bad feeling. When I have a bad feeling, I make plans, I prepare."

"Well, that you did!" he extended his hands out into the room of supplies, incubation pods, computers, beds and devices he hadn't even have a chance to fully inspect yet. It was enough to last his family decades, that much he did know.

"I planned to tell you about it. When the time came ... but it never seemed like the right time."

"Yeah, I know the feeling..." The rush of anger was gone, and the guilt. Now he felt empty and alone. Alone with his own dark secrets. Was he ready to tell his mother?

"Daniel, what is going on between you and Cliff? It is like he has control over you. It was always the other way around. And he got you to take Quinta? I can't believe it! What has changed? What happened to you?"

His mother noticed he was being controlled? Was he being controlled? Did Cliff have a hold on him? Daniel thought. Susan said he might not know if he did have control. Was Susan right about everything?

"It is the amplification type Mod. We can hear each other's thoughts, read each other's minds. Except he is much better at it than I am. Susan said it had something to do with him being a dream-walker, about the way his brain is wired and that it was better able to use and control the microchip in ways she never expected," Daniel explained. "I've been trying to learn, to fight back, but I don't know if I can tell my own mind anymore."

"I see, now that makes sense why Cliff would want Susan," Beth leaned back against the computer desk, one finger on her pursed lips, peering off into the distance. No doubt she was making more plans.

"So, Susan was right all along," Daniel said aloud. "And innocent."

"Yes. And you broke her out of jail thinking she was guilty? Why?"

"I ... love her," Daniel replied simply. "I couldn't let her go to jail for loving me, but I couldn't forgive her for what she did, what I thought she did ... and now Cliff is going to try to find her."

"What do you mean?" That made her sit back up in her seat.

"Susan is the thing that Cliff lost that he went to go find," Daniel explained. "She told me he visited her in jail. He wanted her to build him a master Mod, one he could use to control everyone. Not just people who have a Mod installed. She refused. So, he left her in prison until she changed her mind. She can be quite stubborn and she's better at resisting Cliff than most. Even without enhancement he is highly persuasive."

"I see. Well, don't worry. I am sure she is long gone," Beth said, reassuringly putting her hand on his shoulder.

"And if you're wrong, mom?"

"Let me deal with your brother. With the Mod, you are no match for him. I'm sorry but you have changed and not for the better. You stay here and take care of your father, get him healed!"

"And what will you do with Susan when you find her? Will you let Cliff do to her what you let him do to Amy?"

"What I let ...!!!" His mom was furious, but so was Daniel, eyes ablaze and locked on her in accusation. "I had no idea he would harm her, I had no idea what he was capable of..."

"But, now you know! Don't let him hurt her, mom, please!" Daniel begged. "Cliff has to be stopped. I've been in denial for so long ... but, I think you have been too."

"I don't know if I could..."

"Me either..."

They were both looking around the room, and both sets of eyes fell on the incubation pod at the same time.

They didn't have to read each other's minds to know what the other was thinking, and it was a good plan.

"Like I said, you take care of your father, and I'll take care of Cliff," Beth said solemnly.

~ ~ ~

It had been over a week since both his mom and brother disappeared and Daniel's father was not improving. In fact, over the last few days he'd actually gotten worse. He was going in and out of consciousness, losing more and more of his mind every day. The last Sudoku puzzle he completed was the day they'd left.

Daniel's three helpers, the scientist Cliff had assigned to work on the virus, had no clue what to do. They had been picked for their ability to keep the family's dirty secrets after all, and not for their expertise.

Dr. Steven Lobbs wanted to reformulate and try again. He was in his early thirties, self-assured, tall, dark and lean. He was younger than Daniel but thought that because he appeared much older that he was somehow in charge. The power struggle was annoying, but not something he wasn't used to. Daniel had stopped aging around 22, when he first started drinking the family coffee. So, people often thought he was much younger than he was. It was one of the only negative side effects of drinking the brew – so long as you kept drinking it an ignoring the taste anyway.

Dr. Brooke Dawson was a very attractive, tall brunette and a thoroughly respectable scientist who specialized in organic polymers. She had developed several new implants and had 14 patents, making her the top scientist in the company. She had a good head on her shoulders but was somewhat pessimistic. Her theory was that the virus had evolved and it was too late, they should let it run its course and start funeral arrangements. Daniel couldn't let himself come to that same conclusion, and he found himself frowning at her more often than not.

Dr. Jack Ferris was blue-eyed, red-haired, short and pudgy. A self-proclaimed genius, he'd come straight out of grad school in biomedical engineering at Cornell to work for Cliff six years ago. He was young and eager to test any and all new technology, at any risk. He was almost as aggressive as Cliff and wanted to inject the Quinta virus (of all things) into his father. That was an unacceptable solution. Cliff must have left him with that notion because he had been persistent about it from the beginning.

Thankfully both Lobbs and Dawson agreed with Daniel that the Quinta amalgamate was not something that should be mixed with another, possibly shifting, virus. Tribus had been extremely unstable and it had taken Martin years to fix it. It was likely anything could tip that delicate balance.

Between the four of them, they were at an impasse. None of them could agree on what to do next. Martin's consciousness had faded so much that he had no input to break a tie or offer a new suggestion. Daniel was learning towards Lobbs' idea of reformulation but wasn't sure how much he had learned from his father before his mental state had deteriorated. Lobbs was, after all, just a microbiologist. Likely they would try a new formulation today if Martin regressed further overnight.

Daniel entered the quarantine room and was beginning to don his gear when he noticed the bed was empty. He quickly ran over to the other side of the bedchamber, "Father?"

He heard a whimpering (interchangeably with fits of growling) sound coming from behind the curtain in the corner. He slowly pulled back the curtain to see his father curled up in the fetal position, rocking back and forth on the floor. He was wearing only blue cotton nurse pants, and there were black streaks all over his body.

Ferris! Damn you Ferris! Daniel couldn't believe he had gone behind his back and injected the Quinta virus. Martin's teeth were bared and his eyes were squeezed shut. There was froth coming out of his mouth as if he had rabies. He was jerking in spasms, snarling. His muscles were so wound up and he had lost so much weight over the last few weeks that his body was nothing but veins, muscles, bones and sinew hardened together.

"Father? It's okay. It's me, Daniel," he said while getting on his knees and approaching slowly on all fours. The whimpering was being replaced more and more by growling and he stopped moving forward because it was starting to sound more like a cornered wolverine than a human being. He got up and stepped back, hitting the emergency button on the side of the bed.

Where were those three buffoons? Where was Ferris? How could he inject him and then leave him like this?

The sudden movement of reaching for the emergency button caused Martin to open his eyes, staring directly at his son. It was the scariest thing Daniel had ever seen: eyes full of dark red blood – they were so bloodshot. There was something very frantic in the way he was sneering now, and animalistic. "Father?"

"What's going on? What is the emergency?" Lobbs said, entering the room, with Ferris and Dawson not far behind.

"Stay back!" Daniel yelled, turning to look at the doorway. His father growled and snarled at the abrupt sound which made Daniel jump back. His metal foot slipped sideways on the partially torn curtain on the floor, twisting and turning his leg. He fell down, hitting his head on the hospital bed, going dizzy, seeing stars.

When he opened his eyes, he was face to face with the froth mouthed, black streaked and bloody-eyed creature on the floor. The last thing Daniel saw were claws slashing towards his face. He experienced shearing pain in his skull as the beast gorged out his eyeballs in a clawing fury. Screaming, he kicked Martin back with his metal legs and heard him slam against the far wall.

His head was throbbing and all he heard was what sounded like wrestling and screaming as the three doctors attempted to reign-in Martin who was fighting like a rabid animal fueled by the power of the Quinta virus.

Cybrog Dreams: The Buried Past

Daniel felt his left eye dangling from his face and reached forward, blind, feeling for his right eye with his human hand. He eventually came across a bloody mass on the floor, squished. He swiftly passed out from the pain and shock.

Chapter 15

Fully Integrated Cyborg Functionality Test
Commence

Daniel saw bright flashes and twinged with the intensity. The flashes coalesced into a computer interface. There were screen selections in English. He opened his swollen and ripped eyelids to see light pour through, flooding out the interface.

"What is this?" he asked.

The voice of Dr. Brooke Dawson answered in her typical dead-pan monotone, "It is an organic light-emitting diode interface built into a willow glass, wrap-around backplane in a fully integrated visual stimulation virtual reality simulator I developed for blind patients."

"Oh, that's all?" Daniel answered, sarcastically.

"We'll need to calibrate it, as soon as you are ready, of course." Brooke replied. "It essentially uses the remote power and brainwave amplification technology you developed with Dr. Susan Aldean to aid in the ease of operation. Or, more simply put, we will be able to use your thoughts to calibrate the new eyes I have installed."

"Thank you for putting it simply for me, Dr. Dawson."

"You're welcome. Are you ready to start?"

"Should I close my eyes? I can barely see the interface with the light pouring through."

"I think it would be best if you kept them open. Any calibration would be better in the state in which you use the implants. Let's begin."

"Okay."

"Think 'Up' while saying the word out loud," Brooke said as she touched the up arrow on her computer, which was connected to both eyeballs via electrical leads.

"Up," Daniel responded.

"Good, now think 'Down' and say that as well," she continued, hitting the down arrow key. "Now 'Left', and 'Right.' Good!"

He acquiesced with all commands, though not particularly liking being told what to do. He hoped this would be over soon.

"Okay, think and say, 'Main Control' and now, 'Select'," she commanded.

"Now let's test out the interface. Think 'Main Control' and use the up, down, right, and left arrows to move through the commands. Think 'Select' to make a selection. You can always go back to the main control by thinking it as well."

There were ten different visual patterns to select from, and over a thousand languages. The vision system went from 20/20 to macro, micro, fish eye, and about 20 other versions of enhancement. "You developed this for blind patients, Brooke? Really?" he finally said aloud.

"I wanted to be thorough," she explained. "If you are going to do something, you might as well do it to the best of your ability. Don't you agree, Dr. Jahren?"

"Yes, thank you. This is exceptional work," he said as he sat up and looked at her. Her bright blue eyes were no longer blue, they appeared closer to violet, almost red. Though neither color described it, colors in general were muted. "Why aren't your eyes blue anymore?"

"The OLED has trouble with producing blues, unfortunately," she explained. "There is a German team working on it, but the technology just isn't quite there yet."

He couldn't help but notice a cut on her face, with black streaks coming out, and her arm was bandaged and in a sling. More black streaks were on her arm as well. Was she always that skinny?

"I am sorry about your arm, and your face. How is my father?"

She seemed a bit sweaty, and her eyes were bloodshot. Not a good sign, she was starting to look like Martin had right before he'd been found on the floor. "He's ... rabid. He's in quarantine. We had to put in a plexiglass confinement. We're all in quarantine, in fact. I don't think it is safe for us to leave. I put on a full bio-suit to go get those implants for you, and even then Dr. Lobbs was cautioning against it."

"Why? Do you think that ... that the virus has spread?"

"There is no doubt in my mind, Dr. Jahren. You are the only one who has not displayed any symptoms in the last few days. Dr. Lobbs and Dr. Ferris are in a worse condition than I am, and I am deteriorating rapidly."

"What do you mean, deteriorating rapidly?"

"The combined effect of all the immunotherapies ... maybe even the coffee ... it is unclear. We are not sure if it was the Quinta virus injection, but R.V. 321J-2017 has shifted and now produces something uncharacteristically violent, mind numbing and highly contagious. I sustained only a scratch on my cheek and arm nine days ago and already my mental capacity and health are greatly minimized."

"Nine days? It's been nine days?"

"Yes, Dr. Jahren. Dr. Ferris was not so lucky. He was bitten and went into convulsions within hours. Dr. Lobbs was able to confine your father but sustained several injuries. We worked together on coming up with a temporary solution for whatever this nightmare is that we are dealing with. But, Lobbs has not regained consciousness since yesterday. I will likely follow suit. As, although I was the least infected, I've still been symptomatic since the onset of this ordeal. It's inevitable, we are all doomed."

"I sustained more injuries than you but I feel fine. Why am I not sick?" Daniel asked.

"That is a very good question." Brooke was looking increasingly ill as she spoke. "I should probably go lay down and think about that," she said as she got up to go to one of the hospital beds in the fully crammed room, closing the plexiglass door behind her.

There were five plexiglass holding chambers within the room around five beds. The furthest one down had Daniel's father, snarling and growling at the doorway. Ferris was in the one next to his, curled-up on the floor and whimpering. Lobbs appeared as if he was sleeping soundly on his bed, but he also looked like he had lost weight and was covered in Quinta virus streaks. He must have gotten scratched in several places. They all looked terrible, sickly and thin.

Daniel didn't know what to think. He felt fine besides a bit of a headache from what must be eye strain. There was only slight pain from the sewed-up cuts on his eyelids. Understandable, given he had his eyeballs ripped out only nine days ago. Had he really been out for nine whole days? He looked at his bedside IV and noticed barbiturates. Dawson must have had him on anesthesia for the operation and had just kept him out for the pain until the implants were fully installed.

He had been entirely exposed when his father attacked him. Was it because he already had the Quinta virus that he was unaffected? Not likely, his father's health had deteriorated rapidly before the Quinta virus was administered. For all he knew, all that did was make him stronger, not less sick.

He stood there, looking at his father who was in a mindless rage, not even capable of knowing to reach for the door handle ... bloodied claws sliding down the plexiglass ... mindless, vacant, bloody eyes ... Mindless! Was it the Mod that made Daniel resistant? Was the Mod protecting his brain from the deterioration of the virus? Stimulating brain activity? There was only one way to find out.

"Wake up Dawson, I need your help. I think I might have found a solution," he said knocking on her plexiglass door. She looked like she was not doing well, but she was going to have to pull herself together, they had brain surgery to perform.

Ferris volunteered his father for the Quinta virus, so Ferris was going to get the Mod first. He was not exactly a willing patient. They had to shoot him with a tranquilizer and wait for him to stop writhing on the floor. Brooke was strong, having the Quinta virus running through her veins, and was more help than he could have hoped for, even being sick. She had been helpful in getting all the equipment while he went to get a handful of the latest Mods Susan had left. Both of them were forced to go out in full biogear, and thankfully it was after hours at the facility so they hadn't run into anyone.

Daniel had worked with Ran to develop what he called a 'surgeon-helper' robotic hand for a military contract that proved useful. This was the first live surgery for which Daniel had the opportunity to use it. It was more stable and precise than even his own hand, and that was saying something.

"Merely a simple upload, and then wait? Correct? I have never performed one of these before," Brooke admitted after the operation was complete.

"I've performed several. Yes, just hit that button once we are ready to go. I'll dose back the anesthesia and we will be able to tell if he can regain consciousness."

"Okqy, ready."

They waited for what felt like an eternity for Ferris to open his eyes, which were still fairly bloodshot. "What happened? What is going on? Why am I strapped down?"

Brooke was wheezing, but she said, "Oh, thank god!" as excitedly as she could. "Can I pass out now?"

She was one tough cookie, obviously giving it everything she had to hold it together until the end. Her adrenaline push must have worn off at the sight of success, because she was slumped over and barely holding onto her seat. Daniel helped her to her bed.

"One down, four more to go," he said, scanning around the room.

~ ~ ~

Beth had been searching for Cliff for weeks with no success. Always one step behind him. How hard could it be to find a man with metal legs? He hid them well, it seemed. Even Susan was better at hiding than Beth expected. She must have known Cliff would come looking for her and knew to stay out of reach. Smart girl!

She was beginning to feel more and more unsettled and had a strong urge to return home. She had a bad feeling about her husband, even though Daniel had said he was improving and the cancer was gone before she left. She got the feeling he might be lying to spare her feelings and keep her on track in the search. She hated giving up, but she couldn't shake the feeling that she needed to return back to Colorado, now.

Plus, Cliff was not answering his phone anymore. The constant questioning him where he was had likely given away her intent to follow him, and he was no longer engaging. She had tracked Cliff's last phone call to Seattle. She spent her days going from one coffee shop to the next, mostly near bus stops and crowded areas.

Today she was waiting in a small coffee shop on first avenue watching people pass by outside, hoping to see her son. Instead, she saw Susan. Recognizable despite the chopped pink hair and the fact that she had her face hidden behind some flowers she was holding up conspicuously. Was that a bouquet of wildflowers from the farmers market?

Beth ran out the door and yelled, "Susan, stop!"

Susan looked back, saw her face and bolted in the opposite direction, surprisingly fast in heels. It didn't last long though, as Susan tripped on a storm grate and went flying forward, almost into an intersection. Flowers scattered in every direction.

"I'm not going to hurt you dear, I'm here to help," Beth explained, helping Susan up off of the ground. "Let's get somewhere out of sight."

"How did you find me?" Susan demanded once they were in a parking garage stairwell. The bum urine smell made it clear what this stairwell was typically used for.

"I was trying to find Cliff..."

"Cliff! Is he with you? Is he here!?"

"He's out trying to find you..."

"I have to go!" Susan tried to run up the stairs but Beth caught her and brought her back down.

"I know, Susan. We all know..."

"Oh, we do? So, you know that your son is a murderer? Does Daniel know? Where is Daniel?" Susan's voice was breaking as she spoke Daniel's name.

Was she going to cry? Did she expect Daniel to meet her in Seattle? Why? Beth thought.

"My husband is ill, Daniel is taking care of him. He is no match for Cliff anyway, not after the Mod you put in his head," Beth accused. "Cliff practically has Daniel at his beck and call."

"I didn't know that it would do that, honestly. I was only trying to help people. How could I have known? I might be able to design something that can fix it, that can make Daniel more resilient. But I need my lab ... and another dream-walker," Susan explained. "And, I don't know how long it will take."

"I see. I may have a better plan. You'll need to come with me, do you trust me?" Beth asked.

"No! I don't. What would you do if Cliff showed up, right now? You let him murder Amy. Who would stop him from murdering me?"

"Like I said, I have a plan. I won't let him harm you, Susan,   I   promise."
"Does Daniel know about this plan of yours?"

"Yes, he helped me come up with it ... he loves you."

She could see Susan's eyes welling up with tears, even though she was trying to put on a tough face. "Alight, what is this plan of yours?"

~ ~ ~

Cliff had been scouring Seattle for weeks. In pursuit of the elusive Susan. This was the strangest city he had ever been in, and the greenest. It was a stark contrast to the harsh, desert landscape of his childhood.

The people were different too. Not a single person looked twice at his odd shaped legs under the dress pants he had thrown on over them in order to be more inconspicuous. Most everyone had their heads down under hoods – shuffling about in the drizzling, cold rain. Oddly, no one carried an umbrella. After the first week he tossed his umbrella too and bought a rainproof hooded jacket like the locals. The apathy of the people matched the dreary chill that reached through and into his bones.

Today he was settled in front of three large glass spheres filled with offices and greenery. It was a mix of technology and nature that reminded him of the dream he had where he first saw Susan and her microchip. Like the sparkling, green, futuristic city. A place he thought she might be drawn to.

As he stood there, he realized he'd made most of that dream come true. He'd awoken to the nightmare of his life and – through perseverance, vision and dedication – achieved everything he set out to accomplish. Rocket legs. Sonic blasters. Power in his veins that defeated his disease. He had the strength and ability to go wherever he wanted, whenever he wanted. In fact, he attained a level of ability far beyond human. Superhuman, in fact.

But, he wanted more. There was so much more the whole human race could achieve!

What was that world he saw in the end of his dream? Not one of divided, idiotic politics and old money families controlling the masses into destitution. For what? For the sole purpose of greed. His dream was so much more. It was one with flying vehicles, buildings like this one in front of him. With larger, spiral buildings up above and greenery all around.

The world needed to be led to it's destiny, and the idiots in charge were not at all capable ... at least not in his lifetime.

Susan was the key to bringing that world to life, and he knew it. His dreams always came true, one way or another. He was going to make it happen, and she was going to help him, like it or not. With her by his side he could do anything. They had come so far together already. The Mods. Nanogenerators. If only she hadn't fallen for Daniel. Why did he have to go and mess everything up? If only she had wanted to stay in Colorado. If only she could see his vision. See what they could be together.

She was proving to be better at hiding than he thought and he was not good at being patient in seeking her out. It was driving him mad. His fists were clenched at his side, rain dripping down his knuckles which were blue with the cold. Where could she be hiding? He hailed a cab and asked to go to Pike's Place Market. Maybe she was buying flowers, she always loved flowers.

~ ~ ~

"Ferris, what made you think that injecting me with the Quinta virus was going to help the situation?" Martin was lucid, sipping on coffee and almost back to his normal self besides the obvious toll the virus had taken on his body.

"Cliff demanded that I do it if things were not going well. I was following his last command," Ferris admitted. "He said it would make you stronger, and it did."

"Yes, well … I believe it had no effect on the mental depreciation, and only made the predicament worse for your when you tried to rein me in," said Martin.

"Thankfully the Mods are working. I can see that you are feeling much better. Your mental clarity is astounding, actually," Daniel could sense his father's mind working, and it was like a well-oiled machine. Focused and methodical.

"What do you mean, my mental clarity is astounding, son?" Martin was quick to catch his slip. Daniel was able to read everyone's mind in the room now that they had a Mod, and he was finding it difficult to tell what was said aloud and what was not. "I feel ... connected, to you, son. To all of you."

There were nods around the room. Can anyone hear my thoughts? Daniel asked in his head, projecting outward. More nods around the room. "Okay, try to speak to each other."

He felt a faint impression from his father, and the other doctors in the room were gazing in Martin's direction as well. There was nothing from the other three. The Mods they all had were of the older variety, not the more enhanced one Susan had created specifically for Daniel. They were closer to the one in Bill's head, just enough enhancement to run the prosthesis. Just enough to enhance brain activity against the virus. Martin must have a strong mind indeed if he was able to project thoughts with the older version.

"Well, it looks like I need to find a more suitable solution for this virus. I don't like having my mind in the hands of another person – even if it is my son's," Martin was quick to catch on to the situation. The other three scientists in the room took another few seconds for what he said to sink-in and then stared at Daniel in awe mixed with fear.

"Yes, I agree. Unfortunately, we'll need to be in quarantine until then. I'm not sure how fast this will spread if it gets out," Daniel added. "So far, we know that subcutaneous inject of bodily fluid is the fastest method of transfer. In addition, given Dawson and Lobbs only received cuts, and somehow ended up with the Quinta virus as well, there is more going on than I know. In the past, Quinta was only transferable straight into muscle tissue."

"You are quite correct. This combination of pathogens appears decidedly contagious and may even be airborne," Lobbs added. "I would say that it is deadly as well, given the only cure is brain surgery and how fast and thoroughly the illness took hold."

"I agree. The risk is too high to leave." Dawson eyes were the least blood-shot of the bunch and her pallor was improving. However, Daniel could hear her say in her head, We might as well work on our tombstones. He wasn't sure how much of that attitude he would be able to stand.

"You mean, we have to stay here until we find a cure? In this room? How long will it take?" Ferris demanded, unable to hold back his mounting panic.

"Calm down, I am sure with the five of us working on it, we'll have a solution in no time," Lobbs added. "Correct, Dr. Jahren?"

"On the contrary, only one of us has the expertise to establish even the protocols for such an endeavor. The rest of us are dead weight," Dawson concluded in such an indifferent tone as to make everyone in the room sink into depression.

"We have everything we need to synthesize a cure. I cannot guarantee a timeframe, but I will endeavor to deliver as efficiently as possible," Martin offered, but no one in the room felt any better about the situation.

"What happened here?" Beth said, entering through the chamber door.

"Stop, honey!" Martin exclaimed. "You will need to be in full gear to enter the room ... we have had an incident."

"What's going on? Why the plexiglass enclosures? Daniel! Your eyes! What happened to your eyes!" she said, walking toward her son.

"Stay back Mom, please!" Daniel yelled and Beth kept her distance.

"You're infected to? You like fine, except for your eyes. They look like mirrors, with flashing symbols, are those implants?"

"They look like mirrors? All I see is a computer interface. I haven't had time to work-out the intricacies."

"Yes, Dr. Jahren. There is a setting to project an image of more natural eyes. It is under the 'Eye' command, in 'Projections.' I uploaded a picture similar to your original hazel. Can you see it?" Dr. Dawson explained.

Daniel was able to find the picture and select the impression using his thoughts, it was seamless technology. "Is that better Mom?"

"Yes. Though, I think there is a bit more gold in the green than normal. What happened? Why did you need implants? Why can't I come closer?"

"Honey, the virus evolved to not only attack the cancer in the brain, but to shut off neural activity as well. In effect, it caused all but the most rudimentary of brain functions to be eliminated. Through deductive reasoning Daniel was able to find a solution and install Mods in all of us to re-stimulate cognitive function. However, we do not know how contagious we all are In addition, anyone who comes into contact with us may rapidly infect others before even showing symptoms."

"Do you mean a complete loss of higher order thinking?" she asked and was answered with nods. "Well, it was designed to attack glioma cells. It looks like you all have Quinta virus as well ... how did that happen?"

"Ferris," Daniel said calmly to his mom but in his head he was furious. He glared over at Dr. Ferris. Ferris held his head as if he had a headache, rubbing his temple and frowning sorely at Daniel. "He said Cliff commanded him to do it."

"Cliff? Is Cliff back?"

"No, and I'm guessing you didn't find him if you are asking that question." Daniel answered. For goodness sake, was there to be no good news today?

"He specifically ordered that if Martin took a turn for the worse I was to personally administer the Quinta virus," Ferris explained.

"Cliff ordered you to do that and you just followed him blindly?" Beth's voice let everyone know she was more than annoyed. "And you Daniel, you didn't want to tell me that things were going badly?"

"What could you have done? Everything happened so quickly ... and we just finished installing the Mods..."

"Do you ... um ... did you tell them ... the other effects of the Mod, Daniel?" Beth was trying to ask about the mind control without giving it away. Everyone in the room knew what she was saying though. They all nodded at once. "I see."

"I will find a cure, and we will remove these microchips, honey," Martin assured.

"Until then, Mom, you might want to make sure everyone stays clear of here, especially a certain someone..." Daniel knew his mother would catch on about Cliff. If Cliff knew he could control everyone in this room with a single thought, who knows what he would do with that kind of power.

"Right, well ... I will leave you to it then. Good luck!" She was backing out of the room, eyes wide with a strained smile on her face. She was never a very good liar.

Chapter 16

Buried Alive

Beth ran through the corridor, franticly trying to come up with a new plan. This news did not fit well with her current plans at all. She had just set a lure for Cliff to come back and if he came back now and found out what happened it could have devastating consequences that she didn't even want to think about. She needed Daniel's help getting Cliff into the incubation chamber, except he was now stuck in quarantine. Who could she possibly get to help her? Who could she trust? Ran!

Ran was in the military development bunker, as usual. He was toying with the acid wash tech when she burst through the door, huffing and puffing, "Shit just hit the fan, Ran!"

"Well, it was bound to happen. Which shit, which fan?"

"An out of control virus ... a homicidal madman, pick one?" she said between breaths.

"Same old news in your family Beth, what's new?" he laughed, likely thinking she was joking.

"Thanks," she said, stopping to catch her breath. "I found Susan, she's at the main facility upstairs as we speak. Cliff could be back at any moment. We need to get him into the incubation chamber before he finds out what happened to his father and the rest of the team."

"What happened to his father? Is Martin okay? What team?"

"I ... umm ... wow," she realized she hadn't told Ran about the secret oncolytic research utilizing deadly viruses. "Martin has grade IV glioblastoma..."

"My god, I had no idea. I knew he was suck but ... I am so sorry. Is that why you been gone? Everyone just disappeared..."

"Yes, and no. Daniel and a team administered a developmental virus that was able to clear out the tumor cells."

"That is good news then?"

"No, the virus shifted into something dangerous, deadly even. Then the whole team got infected, they're all in quarantine."

"I see," Ran's typical light hearted, humorous dispositions was beginning to turn as he realized the gravity of what she was saying. "And the homicidal madman? I am assuming you mean your son, Cliff? And why are we putting Cliff into incubation, Beth? What has he done now?"

Beth looked at Ran as if he were an idiot for a minute before she remembered that he didn't know about the Mod mind control problem. "I found out why he framed Susan. It wasn't what we thought, it wasn't to keep her from Daniel. Cliff wants her to build something for him, that he can use to control people's minds."

"Well, that is a problem. So, why did you bring Susan back here? Isn't that like bringing the sheep into the lion's den?"

"I had to get Cliff back here, where we can properly handle him."

"Putting him into an incubation chamber is the proper way to handle your son, Beth?"

"At least until I can figure out what to do with him, yes! I can't have him running around killing people and he has already figured out how to use his current Mod to control others. Who knows what he will do next?"

"He is controlling people already? How?"

"Yes. Susan tried to explain it to me..."

"Susan tried to explain what to you, Mom?" Cliff said, walking in behind her. "Where is Susan, by the way? I know you found her."

"I..." Beth's eyes were wide and looking at Ran for help. He was looking at her in confusion. She picked up the closest thing she could find, which happened to be the acid wash tech, and pointed it at her son.

"Whoa! Whoa! Mom, what has gotten into you? What did Susan, a convicted murderer by the way, tell you?"

Beth glanced down at the device in her hands, could she bring herself to pull the trigger? Ran was right behind her, but she knew he was no match for her son. Not only did Cliff have several weapons built into his legs, but he was about as strong as King Kong with the amount of Quinta virus in his body.

"She said ... that you were blackmailing her, to force her to work for you. Is that true?"

"All I did was offer her a way out of prison, if she would come work for me. Is that so bad? Mom, put the weapon down. We both know you could never use that on me."

"I let her come and get some of her things from the lab, she's in the main facility," Beth said as she slowly lowered the acid wash down onto the table. She was following Ran's movement from the corner of her eye, he was circling to the left of Cliff. Ran had an idea, and she knew it. So, she made sure to lock eyes with her son, and keep him for looking in Ran's direction.

A sonic blast left Cliff choking on vomit, Ran must have found a sonic sickener and activated it. That wouldn't stop Cliff for too long though. She picked up a wrench, thinking she might be able to knock Cliff out when he flung her back with a simple twist of his wrist. She could feel her ribs crack when she hit the corner of the metal table behind her, and her head was spinning from the pain.

Ran had reached the acid wash pack, but Cliff had him three feet in the air by the collar bone before he had even flung his mother aside like a rag doll. Beth was unable to see anything more from below the desk where she landed. But, she heard screaming from both men and the sound of breaking bones. The next sound she heard was the door slamming shut.

Her breathing was strained. She could feel a rib piecing her lung and it was getting harder to breath. She tried not to think about the extent of the internal damage, and especially tried not to move too quickly as she crawled over to where she had last seen Ran.

Ran's blank eyes were staring out from his twisted body, which was dissolving slowly into the acid on the floor. She quickly looked away, squeezing her eyes shut and trying to remove the image now seared into her brain. Ran had been a friend for over 30 years. How could her son have done that to him?

There was a trail of blood and green ooze leading out to the doorway, Cliff was injured. He would probably be heading straight for Susan though. She opened up her pocket to pull out her cell phone, no bars. Great! Well, of course not, she was in the bunker. What was she thinking? It was getting harder to concentrate on anything through the stabbing pain in her side. She needed to get help, she could feel her lungs filling with blood.

There was no stopping Cliff now. She hoped that Susan would turn out to be smarter than all of them and just run as far away as she could from this place.

~ ~ ~

Cliff needed to get to a medical room straight away. He removed his soiled shirt and wiped as much of the acid off as he could, but his chest and right arm were burning so badly it was hard to think. He didn't even want to look at his arm, he knew it wouldn't be salvaged.

Things had happened so quickly, he didn't mean for any of it to happen. Ran was dead. He could see his blank eyes staring at him through his skull. It was self-defense. Ran had tried to kill him. And his own mother? Had she tried to kill him too?

He found a wash station and rinsed ... the pain was excruciating. The water swirling into the drain was blood red, and he knew he had to stop the bleeding before he passed out. He took off his belt and wrapped it around his right shoulder.

In desperation, he reached out in his mind for his brother, Daniel. "I need your help, brother," he projected, sending images of his arm. He had never tried to reach him over such a large distance and didn't know if it was possible but he knew he had little time.

Cliff? Cliff is that you? Where are you? he heard Daniel respond in his head. He was only able to send jumbled images back to him. He tried to focus on his location. His mind was fading as he fell to his knees in the haz-mat shower. Help me, please!

When Cliff opened his eyes next, he was staring at lights on the ceiling. He was laying in a hospital bed. The pain was gone. He could feel his brother's presence in the room. And his fathers. Odd. "Father?"

"Yes, son. I'm so glad you made it. You lost a lot of blood," Martin replied from somewhere to the left of him. He tried to move to look over to his father but found that he was strapped down to the bed. His mind was a bit fuzzy as well, did they have him drugged?

Yes, Cliff. You are drugged, he heard Daniel say in his head. What did you do to Mom, where is she? I saw you hurt her. Where is she? The thoughts were like bullets in his head, pounding and ricocheting off his skull. Too intense, too focused.

I don't know. She attacked me. Ran attacked me, he replied in his head, trying to form the thoughts. She's in the bunker, the military bunker.

"Father, we'll need to gear up again. It looks like mom is injured as well and in the military bunker," Daniel said to Martin aloud.

"You have a military bunker?" Ferris said.

"I'm not surprised," said Dawson.

Cliff realized he could feel everyone in the room the same way he felt his brother. And, that meant one thing. He reached out to Ferris and told him to knock-out Daniel. He heard a smack, them a crumpled thud. He told Dawson to unstrap him. His brother obviously overestimated how much consciousness it took to exercise control over the earlier Mods. He could practically control these three without a Mod.

"Why is it that you all have Mods?" Cliff asked, sitting up and looking around the quarantine room while pulling out the IV in his left arm. His right arm was gone and he was bandaged from the neck down to his waist on his right side. "Put him in one of those rooms," he told Lobbs, who immediately drug Daniel into a quarantine plexiglass holding area. "What is the purpose of these enclosures?"

"The virus evolved, son. The effect was lack of brain function except primal necessity. Daniel was able to install Mods that invigorated our minds. Adeptly finding a solution before we all wasted away. Unfortunately, we are stuck in quarantine until we can come up with a permanent answer that does not involve invasive surgery."

"I see. I believe we need to go find out what happened to mother, let's go." Cliff said, and everyone in the room stood up at once, as if on command. Cliff smiled, it was nice when no one argued with him.

They reached the military bunker and Beth could not be found. There wasn't much left of Ran, just a pile of ooze on the floor. His mother must have gone to find Susan and warn her. They would no doubt be in the main facility upstairs.

"We should get in bio-hazard gear, son. We don't want an epidemic on our hands," Martin cautioned, putting his hand on Cliff's good shoulder. Cliff shrugged it off and walked around the room picking up pieces of gear.

"We don't, father?" He came across the interchangeable arm, he'd always wanted to try these out for himself. He had to use a Kevlar vest to strap it into place for now. Thankfully the pain medication was still working as he pushed the interface into his shoulder socket, hoping not to disturb the stitched-up wound before he could apply adhesive gel to seal it. Success, he felt his new arm come online. He opened and closed the sonic blaster hand, working each of the fingers one by one to get used to the control.

"That's right, son. If this virus gets to the facility above, it could get out. We don't have a cure. Who knows how many people could die."

"But, we do have a cure. We are the only ones who have a cure, the solution, in fact."

"The Mods are not a solution, son. I can develop a real cure, I just need time."

"Imagine, if you will, a world where no one argues with you. Wouldn't that be nice?" Cliff was imagining it himself, and it had so many possibilities.

"What are you suggesting?" Martin asked, gazing up as sirens began to go off.

"That's the beauty of it all, Father. I no longer have to suggest anything." Cliff ordered all four of the people to line up behind him and follow him through the door … and that is exactly what they did. He didn't even have to say a word.

~ ~ ~

Had it been days? Maybe hours? Beth finally made it up to where she had left Susan. Susan turned out to not be as smart as she had hoped because she was sitting there at her laptop, fiddling around with her darn ICModTech when Beth stumbled in and said, "You're lucky it's me and not Cliff, now run!"

"What happened to you?" the girl said back to her, still not running ... coming over to help her sit down.

"A little accident. Listen, things are worse than you can imagine. Wow, I don't even know how to explain this..."

"I've been watching the monitor. I saw Daniel bring Cliff into a quarantine room with his father and those three scientists that were always following Cliff around. Then everyone left Daniel and went into that room you came out of where there are no monitors. What's in that room? What's going on?"

"You've got to be kidding me?" Beth glanced over at the monitor in the quarantine room and saw Daniel laid-out on the hospital bed. She pressed a button and it sent a loud buzzing noise into his room and an intercom blared, "Daniel, wake up!"

"Mom? Are you okay?" Daniel said, rubbing his head and sitting straight up.

"Yes, I'm fine. What happened?" she lied but there was no time to talk about her injuries right now.

"The worst thing imaginable, that's what."

Beth knew what that meant and got up to reach for the emergency switch for the building, smacking it hard. She needed to evacuate everyone before Cliff made it up, virus in tow. Water was now coming down from sprinklers and the alarms were wailing.

"Susan, you need to leave. Never come back here, do you hear me?"

"What about Daniel, is he okay?"

"I'm sorry but Daniel has been infected with a deadly virus. Cliff is about to bring that virus into this facility. There is only one way to stop him, and you had better not be anywhere near when I hit that button, dear. Now, Go!"

"I can't leave him!"

"Susan," Daniel said from the quarantine room. "I need you to listen to my mom. Cliff is on his way, and if he gets to you ... please, you have to leave."

"No, I am not leaving! What can I do to help? There must be something I can do."

"Leave, go to your dream-walker, Darren. Forget about this place. Forget about me, it's too late for me."

Beth was finding Susan's inability to understand the gravity of the situation infuriating, she was not listening to reason. She would have to come up with something to distract the girl, quick. "There might be someone who can stop Cliff, another dream-walker who lives very close. Miss Tinny, the kid's old Native American nanny. She taught Cliff everything he knows. She's at this address." Beth scribbled the reservation address on a torn-off piece of paper and handed it to Susan. "It's not far from here. Go now and find her! Hurry!"

"That's right! Maybe she can overpower Cliff, or convince him to stop, she is the only one! Go!" Daniel said, aiding in the ruse to convince Susan to leave.

Susan looked like she wasn't sure. Buy it girl, buy it!! Every breath and every second she wasted was irksome, but Beth tried to keep her cool. "Please, you're our only hope." That seemed to make Susan put some pep in her step. She shoved her computer and equipment into her bag and took the slip of paper with the address.

"I love you, Daniel," she said, "I'll be back for you soon, I promise!" She blew a kiss to the monitor and left out of the room.

When Susan was safely out of earshot, Beth said, "Can you get out of there? I've got a plan!"

"Yes, Cliff didn't realize these chambers were only made to keep mindless people at bay," Daniel explained while opening up the plexiglass enclose to demonstrate.

"What would happen if I set off an EMP?" Beth asked.

"That would likely kill everyone with a Mod down here. If not instantly, then eventually because the virus would take over."

"So, it would destroy the Mods?" She asked, looking at the monitor outside the military bunker. Cliff had just opened the door and was leaving.

"Likely ... I guess it would depend on the shock of the blast ... where are we going to find an EMP? Don't tell me, I think I can guess..."

"I'm going to go try and stop them from coming upstairs, you hurry as fast as you can! They have just left the bunker."

Not very many people were in the building today, but she had to make sure everyone was out. She could feel her right lung filling with fluid, and she wasn't sure how much time she had left. The only thing that mattered now was stopping Cliff. She didn't want to die knowing she let lose an epidemic on the world. That would not be her legacy.

She spent all her energy and concentration on checking all the monitors and yelling over the intercom at the stragglers who thought it was just a drill. She saw Susan running out of the building and was glad that she had made it out. "Good girl," she said, and then she left to go downstairs. There was only one solution to dealing with Cliff now ... and it involved a big red button and not a nanny.

~ ~ ~

"Stop right there, Cliff!" Daniel demanded. "I don't want to have to use this!" Daniel meant every word. He really didn't want to use the round, glowing object in his hand. He didn't know if it would be completely ineffective or fry everyone's brains in the room, including his own. In fact, he really didn't even know exactly what it did, only that it was in the drawer labeled "EMP" in his mother's apocalypse room.

Put it down, he heard Cliff command in his head. Daniel resisted with everything he had, his body wanted to follow the command and he kept having to tell it to persist.

He looked to his father and felt a strong connection. Father, can you resist him? he said in his mind. Hold him back. I've got a syringe, if I can just inject him! He felt his father struggling to break free.

Daniel raised his hand and used the anti-gravity mechanism built into his prothesis to throw everyone off balance, hoping that would help his father distract Cliff long enough for him to free his mind. It worked! They were all in the air in the hallway. Cliff was caught completely off guard.

Martin had Cliff pinned to the side of the wall and Daniel almost reached him when Cliff kicked his father in the chest. Lobbs and Ferris took hold and started to pummel Martin mid-air. Dawson bounded towards Daniel in a rage, knocking the syringe out of his hand.

There was only one thing he could do now – set off the EMP. He pushed himself backward from the wall and threw the grenade-like device down the hallway, towards his brother. Cliff caught it in his hand and tried to toss it back before it exploded. But, Martin latched onto Cliff's hand, pulling him close in a tight embrace with the device wedged between.

A deafening explosion rung in all their heads and there was a flash of light before everything went dark. They all fell to the ground at once in a hard thud of flesh and metal on the floor.

Daniel, miraculously, retained consciousness despite the worst headache imaginable. Dawson had been flung on top of him in the blast, and he pushed her unconscious body aside. His vision was taken out by the EMP, and he could see nothing as he crawled down the hallway using his one flesh arm towards where he had last seen his brother. He felt through the bodies on the floor and he found the syringe. He then located his brother's mechanical arm, reached up to his neck and stuck in the needle delivering anesthesia that would make him unconscious for hours. That is if he ever regained consciousness from the blast.

"Good job, son," he heard his mother say over the intercom down the hallway, the blast radius must have been small. "You might want to try that remote power trigger I know you were smart enough to pick up."

"You do plan for everything, don't you, Mom?" he said as he opened up a small metal box and removed the battery-like object with a tiny blue button on top and held it down with his thumb. His vision came back online, the interface at reset. He still had an excruciating headache.

"Obviously, I taught you well how to prepare," she laughed but then started to cough and wheeze. "Check on your father, he isn't moving."

Daniel could now move all of his appendages, which meant that his Mod, thankfully, wasn't fried. He had been the least close to the blast though, and had Dawson covering him, so he wasn't sure about the rest of the people in the hallway.

He moved Martin's body off of his brother and found a large hole in his chest where the EMP must have exploded in Cliff's hand. He was dead. His father was dead. Likely instantly during the explosion.

Daniel stared up at the camera in the hallway and knew he didn't have to say anything to his mother. She saw. He didn't know if he could speak those words anyway.

"I should never have let it get this far..." he heard her say into the intercom, voice breaking. "Now ... now everything has fallen apart. Your father ... He was the only one who could find a cure, Daniel. I'm sorry, but..."

"I know, Mom ... we can try, though..."

"I have to do this…"

"Do what? What are you going to do? Are you coming down here?"

"I can't … it's too late for me anyway. You know what to do, where to go…"

"What do you mean it is too late? Mom? Please, don't leave me!"

"I don't have much longer. And someone has to hit the button, it is the only way."

Daniel's eyes could no longer fill with tears, but his heart was heavy and he had only one thing left to say, "I love you."

"I love you too son," was the last thing he heard his mother say, right before the entire world around him shook.

~ ~ ~

Cliff's face was oddly peaceful behind the glass of the incubation pod. Daniel couldn't help but stare at him and wonder how he could have done this to his family. His parents were dead. They had always seemed invincible to him. Now they were buried in rubble. The whole facility above was rubble. There was no way to reach the outside world without a substantial amount of explosives that could significantly destabilized the mountainside and possibly bury him alive. It was better that he didn't try anyway, he was infected and had no clue how to find a cure.

What was there for him up there anyway? Susan? It was better she thought he was dead. For her sake. For the world's sake.

He thought about ending it all, blasting everything to bits. But … Dawson, Lobbs, Ferris … they were all innocent, and deserved a chance. He walked down the line of pods, checking settings and vitals. They had each survived the blast. He had to go on, for them.

He would find a cure, one day, somehow. Until then, he needed to rest. He slid into one of the pods, closed his eyes and welcomed the deep slumber that ensued.

Thank you for reading.

Please review this book. Reviews help others find Absolutely Amazing eBooks and inspire us to keep providing these marvelous tales.

If you would like to be put on our email list to receive updates on new releases, contests, and promotions, please go to AbsolutelyAmazingEbooks.com and sign up.

ABOUT THE AUTHOR

H.A. Burns lives in a rainy Seattle suburb with her fur babies: a Siberian Husky, an orange tabby cat and an equally scruffy husband. She has been an engineer in the aerospace industry ever since proudly graduating with a degree in Materials Science & Engineering from the University of Washington in Seattle, WA. She has been telling stories to entertain her four siblings her whole life and is constantly coming up with book ideas inspired by dreams, advancements in science and technology, and all the interesting people she meets. Being a busy professional engineer, she would jot down the ideas and say "One Day" to turning them into full novels for many years until a debilitating battle with Ulcerative Colitis stripped her of her ability to do anything else. She realized then that it is amazing what you can do with a laptop on a toilet if you put your mind to it and ignore the smell. Literally making the most of a crappy situation, with literature.

ABSOLUTELY AMA⚡ING eBOOKS

AbsolutelyAmazingEbooks.com
or AA-eBooks.com

www.ingramcontent.com/pod-product-compliance
Lightning Source LLC
Chambersburg PA
CBHW070447030726
47503CB00004B/936